STORIES

FOR

YOUNG HOUSEKEEPERS.

By T. S. ARTHUR.

PHILADELPHIA:
J. B. LIPPINCOTT & CO.
1859.

PREFACE.

There are very few young housekeepers who may not profit, in a degree, by the experience of those who have already met some of the trials to which their new position naturally subjects them. For such, the pictures of domestic life here presented, drawn in the colours of truth by fancy's pencil, may have more than a passing interest. While some of them excite a smile, others will afford subjects for serious thought; and all may be read, the author thinks, without involving a waste of time,—an error into which he would be sorry to lead any one, either young or old.

This makes the sixth volume in our "Library for the Household."

CONTENTS.

STORIES

FOR

YOUNG HOUSEKEEPERS.

WHERE THE MONEY GOES.

There was one thing that Mr. Barnaby could not, as he said, "figure out;" and that was, where all his money went to. He was not extravagant; nor could such a charge be brought against any member of his family. They did not give parties in winter, nor go to the Springs nor the sea-shore during the summer season. They did not keep a carriage, nor buy fine furniture, nor indulge in costly dressing. And yet, though Mr. Barnaby's annual receipts were in the neighbourhood of two thousand dollars a year, the thirty-first of December usually found him with an empty purse. This was the more surprising, as the Malcolms, next door, indulged in many things which the Barnabys would have considered extravagant; though the Malcolms had an income of only fifteen hundred dollars per annum. And, what was more, Malcolm was putting three hundred dollars in the Savings bank every year.

"I can't figure it out," said Mr. Barnaby, one Newyear's eve, as he footed up the cash column of his annual expenses. "Two thousand and sixty odd dollars have gone since last December. But where has it gone? that's the question."

"I'm sure I haven't spent it," meekly replied Mrs. Barnaby, who always felt, when any allusion was made to the amount of money expended, as if her husband designed to charge her with extravagance.

"I know that, Aggy," said Mr. Barnaby, who understood, in a moment, how his wife felt. "I know that you haven't spent any thing more than is necessary. But, for all that, the cost of living has been enormous. We have only two more in family than Malcolm, whose salary is but fifteen hundred dollars; and what is altogether unaccountable, while I haven't ten dollars in my pocket, he has three hundred dollars of his year's salary snugly deposited in the Savings bank."

"I can't understand it," sighed Mrs. Barnaby. "I'm sure we don't indulge in any extravagances. We haven't bought an article of new furniture during the year; while the Malcolms have had a beautiful sofa, a set of candelabras, a large mahogany rocking-chair, and a dressing bureau for which they paid twenty-five dollars."

"I don't know how it is!" said Mr. Barnaby.

"And that isn't all," continued his wife. "Mrs. Malcolm has bought her an elegant muff and boa, a velvet mantilla, and a pin and bracelet worth twenty-five dollars."

"It's unaccountable! We have had none of these things, and yet our expenses outrun theirs some eight hundred dollars! It really makes me unhappy. There is a leak somewhere; but, though I have searched for it long and anxiously, I cannot find it out."

"Still, we must remember," said Mrs. Barnaby, "that we have two more in family, and one of them an extra servant, whose wages and board do not come to less than a hundred and fifty dollars a year; and the additional child will swell the sum, put the expense at the lowest possible point, to two hundred and twenty-five dollars. Then we pay seventy-five dollars more rent than the Malcolms. So, you see, that in these three items, we make up a sum of three hundred dollars."

"Yes, but that isn't eight hundred."

"No, although it is a very important sum for which I have accounted. Half of it I have resolved to save. Mrs. Malcolm does with two girls, and I ought to get along with the same number. I'll send Hannah away next week."

"Indeed, Aggy, you will do no such thing," replied Mr. Barnaby, in a positive voice. "You're worn down with the toil and care of the children, as it is, and must not think of dispensing with Hannah. That would be a poor way to save."

"But I don't see why I can't do with less help as well as other people. There is Mrs. Jones, over the way, with as many children as I have, and she only keeps one servant."

"I am sorry for her; that is all I have to say on the subject. Her husband's income is less than half what I receive. We can afford three domestics as well as they can afford one. No, no, Aggy. If we are to retrench at any point, it must not be in the one you propose."

"I see no other way of reducing our expenses," sighed Mrs. Barnaby.

"Then let them go on as they are going, and we will be thankful for an income sufficient to meet our wants."

"But we ought to be saving something. We ought to be laying up three or four hundred dollars every year."

"I wish we could do so. However, as we cannot, there is no use in making ourselves unhappy in consequence. We shall be as well off fifty years hence as though we laid by a thousand dollars per annum."

Mrs. Barnaby looked serious and unhappy, as she sat, without replying to her husband's last remark; while Mr. Barnaby, regretting now that he had introduced the subject, sought to change it for one that was more agreeable. His efforts to do so were not very successful, and the evening of the New-year was passed in reflections that were far from being pleasant to either party.

Although neither Mr. nor Mrs. Barnaby were able to answer the question, "Where does the money go?" we think the reader will be at no loss to "figure out" the matter, after we enlighten him a little as to the mode in which the financial affairs of the family were conducted.

On the morning that succeeded to the evening on which we have introduced Mr. and Mrs. Barnaby, the former, as was his custom, went to market. As he walked along, he run over in his mind the various articles he must purchase; and being in something of an economical mood, he summed up the amount they would probably cost. When he left the market-house, he had spent three dollars instead of a dollar and three quarters, which latter sum had fully covered, in his previous estimate, all the articles that were really wanted. How the additional dollar and a quarter came to be added, was in this wise. A loin of veal had been determined upon, which was not to cost over sixty-five cents; but a fine fat pair of chickens met his eyes, and the cost was only twenty-two cents more than the veal, which was such a trifle that he decided at once in favour of the chickens. Having bought the chickens, to add a bundle of celery and a quart of cranberries was the most natural thing in the world, and these took twenty cents more, to say nothing of the pound of sugar at eight cents, that would be required to sweeten the cranberries. The man who had the chickens to sell had also some very nice honey, the sight of which created in the mind of Mr. Barnaby the desire to have some. The price was twenty-five cents a pound; though what of that? Mr. Barnaby had no means of taking it home, but Mr. Barnaby was a man of expedients. He never liked to be foiled in any thing, and was, therefore, rarely at a loss for some mode of accomplishing his ends. Just across from the market-house was the shop of a tinman; and, as Mr. Barnaby looked up, he saw the bright tin kettles, of all sizes and shapes, hanging before his door.

"I have it," said he, speaking aloud his thoughts. "Such articles are always useful in a family."

So he walked across to the tinman's, and bought a small kettle, for which he paid thirty-one cents, and then walked back and had a pound of honey placed therein, for which he paid twenty-five cents more. After he had purchased what vegetables he had designed getting, some dried Lima beans presented themselves, and a quart was taken, as the price was but fifteen cents. Some cakes and candies for the children took a shilling more. Thus it was that three dollars were spent, instead of one dollar and three quarters, the sum at first decided upon as sufficient.

When Mr. Barnaby went to market, he put five

dollars in his pocket. On returning home and counting over his change, he could find but two.

"That can't be," he said to himself, searching first in one pocket and then in another. "I haven't spent three dollars."

But nowhere could he turn up another copper.

"Somebody must have given me wrong change." This was the most reasonable conclusion to which he could come, after adding up the cost of the various articles purchased, and forgetting to include the tin kettle, the cakes and candies for the children, and the quart of Lima beans.

"Hadn't you better take your umbrella with you?" said Mrs. Barnaby to her husband, as the latter prepared to leave for his place of business. "It looks very much like a storm."

Mr. Barnaby opened the door and glanced up at the sky.

"I don't think it will rain."

"It will be wisest to take your umbrella. If it don't rain, no harm will be done, and if it should rain, you will save yourself from being wet."

Mr. Barnaby paused a moment to think, and then said, as he stepped out, "I'll risk it."

On his way to his office, Mr. Barnaby passed a window in which were some very handsome bouquets of artificial flowers made from tissue-paper. He paused to admire, and then went in to ask the price.

Once inside of the store in which the bouquets were sold, and in the power of a saleswoman who knew her man the moment he entered, there was no such thing as retiring without becoming the owner of a splendid bunch of flowers, at the moderate cost of fifty cents, which the shop-woman promised to send home immediately.

"Cheap enough," said Barnaby to himself, as he left the shop. "How many dollars have I spent in real flowers that faded, and became worthless in a day; but these will retain their beauty for years. Aggy will be delighted with them!"

During the morning, Mr. Barnaby had occasion to purchase some articles of stationery. While waiting to have them made up into a package, after selecting what he wanted, he commenced looking over the books that were displayed upon the counter.

"Just the thing for Tom," he said aloud, as he opened a book containing a number of gayly-painted pictures. "How much is it?"

"Only thirty-seven and a half cents."

"You may tie it up for me." And he tossed the book to the man who stood behind the counter.

Before twelve o'clock, the rain, which Mr. Barnaby's wife had predicted, began to fall. At one, it was still coming down freely, and at two, Mr. Barnaby's dinner hour, there was no sign of abatement. Mr. Barnaby opened the door of his office and gazed up at the leaden sky; he then looked across the street, and saw, hanging before a door, just the article he wanted—an umbrella. To get possession of this article, he must, of course, purchase it. But he had two umbrellas at home now.

"What if I have?" said he to himself, as the fact was presented to his mind. "It is *here* that I want an umbrella."

Not long was the question of buying another umbrella debated. He couldn't lose his dinner, especially as a fine pair of fat chickens were to be served; and it was raining too hard to think of venturing on the journey home without some protection. He might go home in a cab for fifty cents; but then the half dollar would be gone as certainly as if it were thrown into the street. If, on the contrary, he were to buy an umbrella, even though it cost more, he would be in possession of a useful article, that would have to be bought, as the natural result of the wear and tear of those he now had on hand, before a twelvemonth elapsed. Moreover, he reflected, for as large a family as his, three or four umbrellas were almost indispensable.

Arrived at this conclusion, Mr. Barnaby ran across the street, and supplied himself with a cheap cotton umbrella, at an expense of seventy-five cents.

"Where *does* the money go?" said Mr. Barnaby that evening, as he searched his pockets, and could find but a solitary sixpence remaining of the cash he had taken from his secretary in the morning

"I can't understand it. Certainly I have not spent five dollars." Then he took a piece of paper and his pencil, and tried to "figure it up." But he did not get beyond four dollars; and he would almost have taken his oath that he had not spent a copper more. As for the deficit, that must have occurred through his having received wrong change.

Here the reader has a history of one day's spendings; and he will perceive that from two to three dollars passed from the hands of Mr. Barnaby that had better have remained in his possession. A system like this, pursued every day in the year, would use up from six hundred to nine hundred dollars, and there would be little or nothing to show for it in the end. In the day's expenditure, one dollar had gone, and Mr. Barnaby's memory was entirely at fault in regard to the manner of its disappearance. A dollar, thus wasted each day, would leave, in the annual expense, three hundred dollars unaccounted for. But Mr. Barnaby had never looked at the matter in this light. He did not reflect, that a cent uselessly spent every day is equal to three dollars thrown away in the year.

On the next morning, Mr. Barnaby again went to market, and, as was usual with him, turned over in his mind the various articles he must buy, and fixed upon the sum that would meet all that was really wanted. But, as on the day before, he exceeded this amount. The excess was one dollar, and the articles purchased could all have been left in the market-house, and no member of Mr. Barnaby's family experienced the smallest deprivation in comfort or health.

"What a beautiful bunch of flowers!" said Mrs. Barnaby to her husband, for the tenth time, as they stood together in the parlour after breakfast. "What a pity it is we haven't a glass vase to cover them! They would look so sweet!"

"Wouldn't they?" was all the reply Mr. Barnaby made; but the idea suggested by his wife did not die with the sound of her voice. It entered his mind, and lived there. In imagination he saw that bouquet of flowers—tissue-paper though they were—within a glass vase, their beauty increased twofold.

Mr. Barnaby did not go direct to his office on leaving home that morning, but walked two or three squares out of his way, in order to visit a china-store. Before leaving the store, his purse was lighter by two dollars, that sum having been expended for a glass to cover the bouquet of paper flowers bought for fifty cents.

As Mr. Barnaby walked along, thinking how gratified his wife would be when the vase was brought home, he passed a pickling and preserving establishment, and saw in the window jars of fruit and vegetables of various kinds, preserved in the condition they were in on being taken from the vine or tree. One of these jars was marked "Tomatoes." Mr. Barnaby liked tomatoes very much, and had them on his table from the time they were to be bought four for a shilling until frost withered the vines on which they grew. To have a taste of the delightful vegetable once during the winter could hardly be called extravagance—so thought Mr. Barnaby—even if it did cost something to procure the gratification. So in he went, without debating the matter, and bought a small jar for fifty cents. While the shopkeeper was selecting his change, he took up a small bottle containing less than half a pint, marked "Strawberries."

"Have these the natural flavour?" he inquired.

"O yes," replied the shopkeeper. "They have been hermetically sealed, after exhausting the air, and are in just the state they were when taken from the vines. I opened a bottle yesterday, and found them delicious."

"What is the price of this bottle?"

"Half a dollar."

"How better can I surprise and delight Aggy," said Mr. Barnaby to himself, "than by buying her some of these strawberries?"

That question settled the matter, and Mr. Barnaby's purse was soon lighter by another half dollar. The tomatoes and strawberries were then ordered to be sent home, and Mr. Barnaby, feeling very com fortable in mind, proceeded to his office, and entered upon the business of the day. Between that and nightfall, he gave a shilling to a beggar, who got drunk on the money, bought fifty cents worth of toys for the children, over which they disputed as soon as they received them, and which were all broken up and thrown away in less than twenty-four hours, and ordered home a quarter of a dollar's worth of buns for tea, and found, on sitting down to supper, that his wife had baked enough cake to last the whole family for three or four days.

So passed the second day of the new year; and when, in the evening, reflection came, and Mr. Barnaby found nearly seven dollars less in his purse than when he went out in the morning, he was even more at a loss than on the day before to account for the deficiency. In attempting to sum up the various expenditures into which he had been led, he could not make out over five dollars and a half; and his mind remained totally in the dark as to the balance.

On the third day—but we will not weary the reader by minutely detailing the process by which Mr. Barnaby got rid of his money on the third, fourth, fifth, and sixth days of the new year. What we have given will furnish a clew to unravel the mystery of his heavy expenses, and show, what he was himself unable to find out, where the money went. The amount uselessly spent, or that might have been saved without any abridgment of physical or mental comfort, during those six days, was just fifteen dollars! or at the rate of seven hundred and fifty dollars a year.

The manner of proceeding during this one week shows exactly how Mr. Barnaby conducted his affairs. Not a day passed that he did not waste from one to three dollars in trifles to gratify a bad habit of desiring to have every little thing he saw, instead of waiting until real wants tugged at his purse-strings.

And it was not much better with Mrs. Barnaby. She, too, had acquired the same habit, and sixpences and shillings dropped daily from her fingers, as if they were of but small account.

Thus it went on, as it had been going for years; and when the next thirty-first of December arrived, and Mr. Barnaby examined his expense account, he found that twenty-two hundred dollars had vanished, and that scarcely a vestige of any good it had brought them remained. There had been no additions, except very unimportant ones, to their furniture; no silver plate nor fine jewelry had been purchased; nor had either Mr. or Mrs. Barnaby indulged in any extravagance of dress.

"Where does the money go?" asked again Mr. Barnaby, in a kind of despairing tone.

"I'm sure I cannot tell," sadly replied his wife. "It seems impossible that we could have spent so much. What is there to show for it? Nothing!"

"Nothing at all! That makes the great mystery. Twenty-two hundred dollars!"

While they yet conversed, their neighbours, the Malcolms, dropped in to sit an hour. No very long time passed before the subject uppermost in the minds of the Barnabys showed itself.

"How is it," said Mr. Barnaby, "that you are able to live on so much less in the year than we can, and yet appear to spend more?"

Mrs. Malcolm smiled, and said that she was not aware that such was really the case.

"But I know that it is so," returned Mr. Barnaby. "You do not spend as much as we do by at least seven or eight hundred dollars."

"Probably you put our expenses considerably below what they really are."

"No, I apprehend not. I suppose it costs you from twelve to thirteen hundred dollars a year."

"Yes. That is pretty near the mark."

"I shouldn't like to say how much it really does cost us; but I can assure you it is far beyond that. As to where the money goes, I am entirely in the dark. We have nothing to show for it. I wish you would impart to us your system of economy," said Mr. Barnaby, smiling. "If I could get through the year for fifteen hundred dollars, I would be perfectly satisfied."

"I have no particular system," replied Mr. Malcolm, "unless you call taking care of the little leaks in the cash, a system. When a boy, I lived with a shrewd old farmer in the country, who belonged to the 'save-your-pennies-and-the-pounds-will-take-care-of-themselves' school. One fall, in putting up cider, he trusted to rather a rickety-looking barrel, which showed a disposition to leak. 'I guess it will do,' he said, thoughtfully eyeing the barrel after the cider had been poured into it, and noticing that in two or three places small streams were oozing forth. 'The barrel is a little loose, but it will soon swell.' And so the barrel was placed in the dark cellar with two or three others, for the winter's supply. Two barrels were tapped one after another, and they yielded back the full amount of liquor that had been committed to their charge. But on coming to the third barrel, and taking hold of it to bring it forward to a better position, it was found to be empty. 'Aha!' said the old farmer, 'I see how it is. I thought that leak was of no consequence, but it has wasted the whole barrel of cider. There's a lesson for you, John,' he added, turning to me. 'Take care of the little leaks in your pocket, when you grow up and have money to spend, for they are what run away with most men's property.' I understood him as fully as if he had read me a homily of an hour long. All useless expenditures I now call leaks, and stop them up immediately."

"No doubt we spend a great many dollars that might be saved in the year," said Mr. Barnaby; "but I cannot conceive how all the leaks in our pockets could let out five or six hundred dollars in twelve months."

"It's an easy matter for us to let five or six hundred dollars leak out, and yet scarcely be aware of the daily waste," replied Mr. Malcolm. "Two dollars spent every day, that might be saved, gives six hundred dollars in a year."

"True. But a man could hardly let that much leak away without observing it."

"It is very possible. Suppose you add on, daily, to each of your three meals, a shilling or sixpence more than is necessary; and this may be done so easily as scarcely to be noticed; how much do you think it would be in a year? Why, the important sum of one hundred and thirty-eight dollars!"

"Is it possible?" Mr. Barnaby looked surprised.

"Even so. And if twenty-five cents be added to each meal, a thing easily done, as you very well know, the yearly aggregate is swelled to two hundred and seventy-six dollars."

"In the matter of desserts alone," said Mrs. Malcolm, coming in with a remark, "which rather injures than conduces to health, half a dollar a day, in a family as large as yours, may easily be spent."

"Don't you have a dessert after dinner?" inquired Mrs. Barnaby, in a tone of surprise.

"Not every day," answered Mrs. Malcolm.

"I don't believe Mr. Barnaby would know that he had dined, if he hadn't a dessert on the table."

"Perhaps not," replied Mr. Barnaby; "for then

my first course would digest so easily that it would be hard to imagine that I had eaten any thing. The fact is, now that I reflect upon it, these desserts are to my stomach as the extra pound that broke the camel's back. I don't believe I would have a dyspeptic symptom, if I did not touch puddings, pies, sweetmeats, nuts and raisins, blanc-manges, floating islands, and a hundred and one other things that my good wife prepares for our gratification, and which I eat after my appetite has been satiated on plain and more substantial food."

"Upon my word!" exclaimed Mrs. Barnaby. "And so, after all, these are the thanks I am to receive for my trouble. Dear knows! if it was not for you, I wouldn't worry myself every day about a dessert for dinner."

"And at a cost of over a hundred dollars a year," returned Mr. Barnaby, good-humouredly. "I begin to see a little of the way in which the money goes?"

"There are so many ways in which we are obliged to spend money," said Mr. Malcolm, "that unless we are watchful, a little will leak out at a dozen points every day, and show, in the end, although we remain all unconscious of the waste that is going on, an alarming deficiency. When I first entered upon life, I saw how this was in my own case. Sixpences, shillings, and even dollars did not seem of much importance; though of fives, tens, and twenties, I was very careful. The consequence was, that the small change kept constantly running away; and, in the end, the fives, tens, and twenties had mysteriously disappeared. I saw that this wouldn't do, and reformed the system. I took care of the small sums, and soon found that I always had large sums to spend for things actually needful, and had really more satisfaction in what I obtained with my money than I had before."

"But it is so hard," said Mrs. Barnaby, "to be careful of the sixpences, without growing mean and penurious, and even seeking to save at the expense of others' just rights."

"Perhaps it is," replied Mrs. Malcolm. "But this consequence need not follow. All we have to do is, to deny ourselves the indulgence of a weak desire to spend money for little articles that we could do without and not abridge our comfort in the least, and we will find enough left in our purses to remove us from the temptation to be unjust to others."

"Taking care of the pennies, then, and leaving the pounds to take care of themselves, is your system," remarked Mr. Barnaby.

"Yes," answered Mr. Malcolm. "That is our system, and we have found it to work very well. We not only enjoy every comfort we could reasonably desire, but have nearly two thousand dollars in the Savings bank."

"And yet your salary is only fifteen hundred dollars a year."

"That is all."

"While my income is over two thousand, and I haven't a cent left to bless myself with when the thirty-first of December arrives. But I see where the leak is. I understand, now, clearly, how the money goes; and, by the help of a good resolution, I will stop the leak."

How far Mr. Barnaby was successful in stopping the leak, we do not know. It is hard to reform confirmed habits of any kind, and we are afraid that he found the task assumed a hard one. But if he conquered in the attempt, his reward was ample, compared to the amount of self-denial required for the achievement.

A BAD HABIT CURED.

ONE of the virtues peculiar to society in this country—and, it may be, in other countries, for aught we know—is a tender regard for the consciences of others. People are disposed to interpret St. Paul's injunction to the Philippians, "Look not every man on his own things, but every man, also, on the things of his neighbour," after the most literal fashion. We see this manifested in a great variety of ways, but in none more prominently than in the effort to make people pay due regard to the precept, "*Of him that would borrow of thee, turn not thou away.*"

Mrs. Armand was the very personification of this virtue; and she took good care that none in her neighbourhood suffered condemnation for lack of a living faith in the precept last quoted, as sundry careful housewives could testify.

Mr. Armand differed with his wife in some matters, and particularly in regard to the morality of her borrowing-practices, and often recorded his protest against their continuance; the doing of which satisfied him more and more, each time it was repeated, that "when a woman will, she will, you may depend on't." A fair sample of the discussions held on the subject, may be seen in the following matrimonial passage of small arms, which occurred in consequence of the appearance on the table, one morning, of a strange looking Britannia-ware coffee-pot.

"Where did that come from, Sarah?" was the natural inquiry of Mr. Armand, as his eyes rested upon this handsome addition to the appendages of the tea-tray.

"Kitty melted the bottom off of my coffee-pot yesterday, the careless thing!" replied Mrs. Armand, "and it is not mended yet; so I borrowed Mrs. Lovell's for this morning."

"I wouldn't have done that," said the husband.

"Why wouldn't you?" very pertinently inquired Mrs. Armand.

"Oh! because I wouldn't."

"Give a reason. Men are always fierce enough for reasons!"

"Because I don't think it right to borrow other people's things, when we can do without them."

"We couldn't do without a coffee-pot, could we?"

"Yes; I think so."

"How, pray?"

"Rather than borrow, I would have made tea for breakfast, until our coffee-pot was mended."

"A nice grumbling time there would have been, if I had tried to put you off with a cup of tea!"

"I don't think I am such a grumbler as that, Sarah. I believe I am as easily satisfied as most men. I'm sure I would rather drink tea all my life than take coffee from a borrowed coffee-pot."

"So much for trying to provide for your comfort!" said Mrs. Armand, in a complaining tone of voice.

"I never wish you to do wrong for the sake of securing my comfort," returned her husband.

"Do wrong! Do you mean to say that it is wrong to borrow and lend?"

"It is wrong to borrow on every trifling occasion, for this is to be unjust to others, who are constantly deprived of the use or possession of such things as are their own."

"I wouldn't like to live in a world as selfish as it would be, if made after your model," said Mrs. Armand.

"No doubt it would be bad enough," replied the husband; "but I am sure that borrowers would be scarce."

"But what harm can my using Mrs. Lovell's coffee-pot for a single morning do, I would like to know?"

Mr. Armand answered this interrogatory, not, however, conclusively enough to satisfy his wife. Mrs. Lovell's opinion on the subject being much more to the point, will best enlighten the reader, and so we will give that. Mrs. Lovell was preparing to go down to breakfast, when her cook came to her chamber-door, and said—

"Mrs. Armand, ma'am, wants you to lend her your coffee-pot. She says Kitty melted the bottom off of hers, and it a'n't mended yet. She just wants it for this morning."

"Very well," returned Mrs. Lovell. The tone in which this was said did not express much pleasure. As the girl retired, Mrs. Lovell remarked, in a grumbling way, to her husband,

"And, no doubt, Kitty'll melt the bottom off of mine before night."

"You are not going to let her have that handsome Britannia coffee-pot?" said Mr. Lovell.

"I have no other, and she knows it."

"You might say, that you have only one. She will think that in use."

"No, she won't;" for she is very well aware of the fact, that we don't make coffee, unless when we happen to have company."

"As you had not the resolution to say 'no,' you will have to take your chance."

"And the chances will all be against me. Of that I am certain. I never loaned Mrs. Armand any thing in my life, that it did'nt come home injured in some way."

"Then your coffee-pot will hardly prove an exception."

"I'm afraid not. Oh, dear! I wish that people would let their neighbours possess the little they have, in peace. I've had that set of Britannia-ware for five years, and there is not a bad scratch nor bruise upon any piece of it. If Mrs. Armand lets the coffee-pot get injured, I shall be too angry."

"I almost hope she will," said Mr. Lovell.

"Why, Henry?"

"You will then, in all probability, fall back upon your reserved rights, and throw Mrs. Armand, in future, upon hers."

"What are our reserved rights?"

"In this case, yours will be to refuse lending what your neighbours should buy; and hers will be to buy what she can't conveniently borrow."

"I don't wish to offend her," said Mrs. Lovell, "but, if she does let my coffee-pot get injured, I shall be too much put out."

"In other words, you will say something sharp about it."

"Very likely. I'm apt, you know, to speak out on the spur of the occasion."

"Then I shall be very well content to see the spout knocked off, the handle bent, or a bruise as large as a walnut in the side of your coffee-pot."

"Henry! Why will you say so?"

"Because I happen to feel all I say. This borrowing nuisance is intolerable, and its suppression can hardly be obtained at too dear a cost. How many umbrellas has Mrs. Armand lost or ruined for us in the last two or three years?"

"Don't ask me that question. I've never tried to keep the 'counts."

"Half a dozen, at least."

"You may safely set the number down at that But, if I could get off with umbrellas, I'd buy a case, and let her have one a month, and think the arrangement a bargain. The fact is, I have scarcely an article of movable household goods, or wearing apparel, that doesn't show sad evidences of having been used by some one beside myself. You know that dear little merino cloak of Charley's, in which he looked so sweet?"

"Yes. What of it?"

"Last Sunday, Mrs. Armand had her baby baptized. Of course, she had nothing decent to put on it, and of course sent for Charley's cloak. What could I do?"

"You could have declined letting her have the cloak."

"Not under the circumstances."

"Hasn't her baby a cloak?"

"Yes; but it's full of grease-spots—not fit to be seen."

"It's good enough for her baby, if she don't think proper to provide a better one."

"All very easily said. But I couldn't refuse the

cloak, though I let it go with fear and trembling. Now just look at it!"

Mrs. Lovell opened a drawer, and taking out the dove-coloured cloak, with its white and blue lining, slowly opened it.

"Bless me!" exclaimed her husband, as the back of the collar was displayed, and showed several square inches of discolouration. "What in the world could have done that?"

"Perspiration from the child's head. Charley has worn it twenty times, yet not a spot was to be seen before. But this is not the worst. To keep the baby from crying in church, a piece of red candy was pushed into its mouth."

"Goodness!"

"And as the baby was cutting teeth, the result can hardly be wondered at. Look!"

Mrs. Lovell held up the front of the cloak. From the collar to the skirt were lines, broad irregular patches, and finger-marks, dark, red, and gummy.

"That beats every thing!" exclaimed Mr. Lovell.

"But it isn't all," added his wife," as she turned the cloak around, and showed a grease-spot, half as large as her hand, upon the skirt. "After the child was brought home, nurse took off the cloak and threw it upon a table, where one of the children had just laid a large slice of bread and butter."

"Is that all?" asked Mr. Lovell.

"I haven't looked any further," replied Mrs.

Lovell, tossing the ruined garment from her with an impatient air. "But isn't it too much to bear?"

"What did the lady say, when she brought it home?"

"She sent it in by one of her girls, who said that there were two or three spots on the cloak, for which Mrs. Armand was sorry; but she thought I could easily rub them out."

"Humph!"

"The cloak is totally ruined. I don't know when I had any thing to vex me so much. And it was such a beauty!"

"What will you do?"

"Throw it away. I can't let my baby wear a soiled and greasy cloak. See!" And Mrs. Lovell again went to her drawers. "I've got cashmere for a new one."

"Well, now, this is too bad!" exclaimed Mr. Lovell. "Too bad! If I were you, I'd send her the cloak, with my compliments, and tell her to keep it."

"Oh, I don't wish to make her an enemy."

"Better have such persons enemies than friends."

"Perhaps not."

'What's the use of your making a new cloak for Charley? You'll lend it to Mrs. Armand when she wants to send her baby out, and then"——

"Beg your pardon, husband dear! But I will do no such thing!"

"We'll see."

"And we *will* see."

Mrs. Lovell spoke pretty resolutely, as if her mind were, for once in her life, made up not to be imposed upon.

The breakfast-bell ringing at the moment, Mr. and Mrs. Lovell dropped the subject for the discussion of one rather more agreeable.

The day passed without the return of the coffee-pot, about which Mrs. Lovell could not help feeling some uneasiness. And she had good reason; for nothing came home from the hands of the incorrigible borrower that did not show signs of hard or careless usage.

On the next day, Mrs. Armand called in to pay her neighbours a visit.

"I have'nt sent home your coffee-pot yet," said she, during a pause in the conversation that followed her entrance. "I told Kitty, yesterday, to take ours immediately and get it mended; but I found this morning that she had failed to do so. I never saw such a careless, forgetful creature, in my life."

"It's no matter," Mrs. Lovell forced herself to say, at the cost of a departure from the truth.

"Oh, I knew it was no difference, because you don't make coffee regularly," responded Mrs. Armand; "but, then, I never like to be using other people's things when I can help it. Besides, our Kitty is such a careless creature, that every thing she touches is in danger; and I'm afraid it might get injured. I noticed a little dent in the spout this morning."

"Not a bad one?" said Mrs. Lovell, thrown off of her guard by this admission. The tone in which she spoke expressed some anxiety.

"Oh, no, no!" replied Mrs. Armand quickly. "You would hardly see it unless it were pointed out. But even for so trifling an injury, I can assure you I scolded Kitty well. As soon as I go home, I will start her off with my coffee-pot, if she has not already taken it to the tinner's."

Days passed, but the coffee-pot still remained in the possession of Mrs. Armand. In the mean time, Charley's new cloak of very fine light blue cashmere was finished, and as Mrs. Lovell was a little proud of her baby—what mother is not?—the cloak went out to take an airing, the baby inside of course, every day for a week afterwards.

One afternoon, some friends came in, and Mrs. Lovell persuaded them to stay and spend the evening. Shortly after they arrived, a messenger came from Mrs. Armand, with a request for the loan of Charley's cloak, as the mother wanted to send her baby down to Jones's Hotel, that a friend of her's, who was passing through the city, might see him.

Mrs. Lovell said, "Very well," and took from a drawer the dove-coloured merino cloak that had suffered so severely at the christening, and handed it to the girl who had come from Mrs. Armand.

In a few minutes, the girl returned with the cloak, and said—"It isn't the one that Mrs. Armand wants. She says, please to let her have the blue one. She'll take good care of it."

Mrs. Lovell took the dove-coloured cloak and returned with it to the drawer slowly, debating in her mind what she should do. She must either offend Mrs. Armand, or run the risk of having the new cloak, which cost ten dollars, besides her labour, spoiled as the other had been. She did not wish to do the former; but, how could she submit to the latter? Just as, in her doubt and hesitation, she laid her hand upon the new garment, a thought struck her, and turning to the girl, she said—

"Tell Mrs. Armand that she can have the light cloak in welcome; but Charley is going out, and will wear the blue one."

The girl departed, and Charley got an extra airing that day. Mrs. Armand was exceedingly indignant, and wondered if Mrs. Lovell supposed she was going to send her child out in that "soiled and greasy thing!"

Towards supper-time, Mrs. Lovell's cook asked her if she wished coffee made.

"Oh, certainly," was replied.

"Mrs. Armand has our coffee-pot."

"I know. You must go in for it."

The cook took off her apron, and ran into Mrs. Armand's for the coffee-pot. In a few moments she returned, and said—

"Mrs. Armand can't let you have it before to-morrow. Hers is not mended yet,—and Mr. Armand always drinks coffee for supper."

"But go and tell her that I have company, and cannot do without it," replied Mrs. Lovell, a little impatiently.

The girl went back. When she returned, the coffee-pot was in her possession. As she set it down before Mrs Lovell, she said—

"Mrs. Armand didn't seem to like it much."

"Like what much?"

"Your sending again. She says her husband never drinks tea, and she don't know how she is going to make him coffee."

"But that isn't my coffee-pot!"

"Yes, ma'am."

"Oh, no. Never!" And Mrs. Lovell took up a dingy looking affair that her cook had brought in, and eyed it doubtingly. She remembered her Britannia coffee-pot as a beautiful piece of ware, without a scratch or bruise, and bright as silver. But this was as dull as pewter: a part of the bottom, an eighth of an inch wide and three inches long, had been melted off or turned up; there were several large dents in it; the mouth of the spout had received a disfiguring bruise, and the little jet knob on the lid was entirely broken off! No, no—this was not her coffee-pot. But cook insisted that it was, and soon proved her assertion.

This was too much for Mrs. Lovell, and the forbearance of that long-suffering lady yielded under the too heavy pressure it was called to sustain.

"That my coffee-pot!" she exclaimed, with a most indignant emphasis, and lifting it from the table on which the cook had placed it, she set it down upon a tea-tray, which contained the other pieces belonging to her beautiful set of Britannia. The contrast was lamentable.

"There!" said she, with a glowing cheek, and voice pitched an octave higher than usual. "Take the whole set into Mrs. Armand, with my compliments, and say that I make her a present of it."

The cook didn't need to be told her errand twice. Before Mrs. Lovell had time for reflection and repentance, she was beyond recall.

The dining-room and kitchen of Mrs. Armand's house were in the same story, and separated only by a door. It happened that Mr. Armand was at home when Mrs. Lovell's cook came in and presented the breakfast and tea set, with the compliments of her mistress. The tone in which the message was given, as it reached his ears, satisfied him that something was wrong; and he was put beyond all doubt when he heard his wife say, with unusual excitement in her voice—

"Take them back! Take them back!"

But the girl retreated hastily, and left her in full possession of the tray and its contents.

"What's the matter?" inquired Mr. Armand, as his wife retreated into the dining-room with flushed face and a quivering lip. It was some moments before she could speak, and then she said something in a confused way about an insult. Not being able to understand what it all meant, Mr. Armand sought for information in the kitchen.

"Whose is this?" he said to Kitty, laying his hand upon the Britannia set.

"Mrs. Lovell's," replied Kitty.

"Why is it here?"

"Mrs. Lovell sent it in as a present to Mrs. Armand."

"Indeed!" Mr. Armand looked a little closer.

"Is this the coffee-pot we have been using for a week?"

"Yes, sir."

"Humph!" Light was breaking into his mind.

"Abusing, I should have said," he added. "And because the coffee-pot has been ruined, and the set broken, Mrs. Lovell makes us a present of what remains?"

Kitty held down her head in silence.

After examining the coffee-pot, and contrasting it with other pieces of the set, Mr. Lovell made an angry exclamation, and retired from the kitchen.

He did not re-enter the dining-room, where he had left his wife, but took up his hat, and going out of the front-door, shut it hard after him. In about half an hour he returned.

"Where have you been?" his wife ventured to ask, as he entered the room, where she was sitting in no very enviable mood.

"Trying to repair the wrong you have done."

"How do you mean?" asked Mrs. Armand.

"I've bought a handsome set of Britannia-ware for Mrs. Lovell," replied the husband, "and sent it to her, with a note of apology, and a request from me, as a particular favour, never to lend you any thing again, as you would be sure to injure it."

"Mr. Armand!"

"It's true, every word of it. I never was so mortified by any thing in my life. I don't wonder that Mrs. Lovell sent you the beautiful set you had broken. The fact is, this borrowing system must come to an end. If you want any thing, buy it; and if you are not able, do without it."

Poor Mrs. Armand, whose feelings during the brief absence of her husband were by no means to be envied, now burst into tears and cried bitterly. Mr. Armand made no attempt to soothe the distress of his wife. He felt a little angry; and when one is angry, there is not much room left in the mind for sympathy towards those who have excited the anger.

After supper, while Mrs. Armand sat sewing, her face under a cloud, and Mr. Armand was endeavouring to get over the unpleasant excitement he had experienced, by means of a book, some one rang the bell. In a little while, Mr. Lovell was announced.

"What in the world can he want?" said Mrs. Armand.

"More about the coffee-pot," replied Mr. Armand, as he laid aside his book.

Mrs. Armand made no answer, and her husband left the room where they were sitting, and entered the parlour. Mr. Lovell, who was standing in the floor, extended his hand, and said with a smile—

"I'm afraid my wife's hasty conduct—for which she is extremely sorry—has both hurt and offended you. And as these are matters which, if left to themselves, like hidden fire, increase to a flame, I have thought it best to see you at once, and offer all necessary apologies on her behalf."

"Not hurt in the least!" replied Mr. Armand good-humouredly. "And as for apologies, Mrs. Lovell wants no better one than the wreck of her beautiful coffee-pot, which I have minutely examined. I'm glad she sent it back, just as she did; and for two reasons. It gave me an opportunity to repair the wrong which had been done, and served as a lesson to my wife, such as she needed and will not soon forget. No, no, Mr. Lovell! don't let this make you feel in the least unpleasant."

"But my wife says she cannot think of keeping the beautiful tea and coffee set you sent her."

"Tell her that she will have to keep them. They are hers in simple justice. If she sends them here, they will not be received. So she has no remedy. We want a set, and will keep yours. If a disfigured coffee-pot has to be used, let it be by those who are guilty of the abuse. And now, Mr. Lovell, tell your good lady from me, that if she lends my wife any thing more, I will not be responsible; as I have always disapproved the system, and am now, more than ever, opposed to it."

This last sentence was spoken playfully. After half an hour's good-humoured conversation, the gentlemen parted. It was some days before the ladies met, and then they were a little reserved towards each other. This reserve never entirely wore off. But there was no more borrowing from Mrs. Lovell, nor any one else; for Mrs. Armand was entirely cured of her desire to make others keep the scriptural injunction, to which allusion was made in the opening of our story.

SPOILING A GOOD DINNER.

"COME and dine with me, on Thursday," said my old friend Clayton. "I am to have the company of three or four friends, and wish you to be one of the number."

I accepted the invitation with pleasure, for I liked Clayton. We had been acquaintances from boyhood; and mature years had only tended to strengthen the attachments of youth. I also liked his wife. She, too, had been one of my early friends. Many an agreeable evening had I spent with them since their marriage; and if the story I am about to tell does not give them offence, I hope to spend many more in their pleasant society. As to the telling of the story, that is a part of my vocation; but in matters of this kind, I generally manage to embellish a little here and there, and to change names and vary incidents, in such a way, that the parties who have been made to sit for their pictures are hardly ever willing to see therein any likeness of themselves. And this being the case in the present instance, I hardly think I shall give any offence; although I am not unwilling that my friend's wife should at least have a remote idea that she *might* have been the original of my sketch.

Like all women, and men too, Mrs. Clayton had her faults; and one of these I had frequently had occasion to notice. The fault was this: a habit of making the worst, instead of the best, of a thing. If she took a dress to be made, she always knew it wouldn't fit. If she laid out to start on a journey at a certain time, or to pay a visit, she knew it would rain. If one of her children were attacked with a fever and sore throat—not a very uncommon thing, by the way—she knew it was scarletina.

One evening, I went home with her husband, per invitation, to take tea. Mrs. Clayton expected me, and I was received with the warm welcome that always greeted my appearance. During a pause in the conversation that followed, I heard her say to her husband, in an under tone:

"I've made up some nice cakes for tea, but I'm almost sure, they won't rise, just because I want them to."

"Nonsense!" said he, half aloud, smiling. "You're an old croaker!"

"That's too bad!" she replied, speaking aloud; and then turning towards me—"My husband calls me a croaker, but it is no such thing. I am no more of a croaker than he is."

"Oh yes, Kate, you are a notorious croaker.

You always look at the dark instead of the bright parts in a picture; while I always expect the sunshine; though too often, I must confess, I find the sky overspread with clouds. Still, imaginary sunshine is much better than imaginary clouds—don't you think so?"

I could not but assent to this.

"I am not so sure of that!" replied the wife. "For my part, I would much rather expect clouds and get sunshine, than expect sunshine and get clouds. But I will leave you, gentlemen, to discuss this matter between yourselves, while I go and see that our tea is not spoiled."

In about an hour, during which time we had seen but little of Mrs. Clayton, the tea-bell was rung, and we retired from the parlour into the dining-room. We found her awaiting us at the tea-table, looking the very image of good-humour.

"The cakes are light," I said to myself, scarcely able to repress a smile. I had overheard her remark that she was almost sure they wouldn't rise good.

After we were helped round, my friend said, with a smile—

"All right, I see, Kate, notwith"—

"Come! not one word, Mr. Clayton," quickly spoke up his wife, interrupting him. "It is too bad!" she added, addressing me, "for my husband to do so. I said that I didn't believe the cakes would rise, and I had good reason for saying so.

But it seems I was mistaken, for which I am very thankful, and I think he ought to be the same."

"And so I am," returned the husband, laughing. "The cakes are first-rate. I wouldn't have had them heavy and sour for the world."

My friend put a little too much emphasis on the last part of the sentence, which caused his wife to ask, rather seriously, "Why not for the world, Mr. Clayton?"

"It would have grieved you so," he replied, in an evasive manner, yet meaning just what he said.

"You think I would have taken it very much to heart, do you?"

"All ladies take such matters to heart, and I suppose they can't help it. It is rather a serious affair to have the cakes sour when a friend is invited to tea."

I joined in, pretty much in the strain of the last sentence, in order to make Mrs. Clayton feel less annoyed than she was evidently disposed to be by the first part of her husband's remarks; and, as the latter was as much inclined as myself to restore the disturbed serenity of his wife's temper, slight as that disturbance was, he took good care to say nothing more that was not as soothing as oil. All now was as pleasant, during the tea-hour, as a May morning, with the exception that the lady scolded the servant for neglecting to place a knife and fork at her plate, and during the time seemed to me to be in rather an unamiable mood. Not that I objected to the servant's being scolded for her neglect, for she may have richly deserved it, and of this my fair friend was no doubt well convinced. The error consisted in scolding at the wrong time and place.

But to the dinner. Ten minutes before three o'clock, I rang the bell at the house of my friend, and was shown into the parlour, where I found Clayton and three guests. I made the fourth and tne complement. Three o'clock was the hour for dinner. Just as the clock was striking that hour, our fair hostess entered, looking, I thought, a little flushed and worried. After greeting us with great cordiality, she sat down beside her husband on the sofa, saying, as she did so:

"I'm sorry, gentlemen, but I'm afraid you will have to wait half an hour for your dinner. My cook has been as cross as she could be all the morning, and the fires as little inclined to burn as she to be pleasant."

"No matter," said I, smiling. "We will have the better appetites. Give your cook and the fires their own way, and all will come out right in the end."

All joined in assuring her that it was the same to them whether dinner were ready in ten minutes or an hour; but it did not make her feel in the least more comfortable, or tend to increase our appetites for the coming meal.

"I do think," said she, after a few remarks, pro and con, had been made, all referring to the dinner, "that the ordinary servants we get are the most perverse, self-willed, obstinate creatures in existence! Just the time when you feel most dependent upon them, is the time when they will fail you. Our cook knows her business very well, and I have no trouble at all with her, except when we have company, and then she acts like the very old Scratch! I always dread to see"—

Our hostess checked herself suddenly and looked a little confused, and our friend Clayton gave two or three emphatic "*ahems!*" and struck off at right angles into a new subject. I believe there was not one of us who did not understand the whole sentence as well as if it had been finished; nor one of us who did not more than half regret having accepted the invitation to dine.

Nearly an hour passed, during which time our friend's wife came in and went out of the parlour frequently, the irregular corrugations about her eyebrows growing more and more distinct with the passage of every ten minutes. At length, but not until the cheerful expression of Clayton's face had begun to fade, dinner was announced. We all ascended, chatting freely, to the dining-room, and were in, considering what had passed, a marvellous good humour. Our sharp appetites we considered a compensation for the delay.

We found Mrs. Clayton awaiting us in the dining-room. Her smile was pleasant and cloud-dispersing, but it faded away too soon, and left the whole aspect of her face too much drawn down. There was a bright glow upon her cheeks—unusually bright, and in her eyes an intenseness of expression that took from them their highest charm. I saw that she was over-excited, worried, and unhappy. Things had gone wrong with her, and she had not the philosophy to bear her trials with good-humour, nor the tact to conceal what she felt from the friends whom she had joined her husband in inviting to partake the hospitalities of her table.

"At last!" was the greeting she gave us, to which was replied, in a pleasant tone—

"Better late than never, you know. We shall make up for the delay by doing greater justice to your elegant dinner."

"You'll not find it very elegant, I fear. It's miserably cooked!" she replied, half smiling, half frowning.

"Let us be the judges, madam," returned the one who had replied to her first remark. "I think we shall render a much better account."

"My wife, you know," Clayton said, glancing first at the subject of his remark, and smiling a little sarcastically, "generally looks upon the dark side."

"Yes; I have not forgotten the sour cakes," I replied, laughing.

But somehow or other, the lady did not appear to relish the joke very well. She muttered something in reply that I could not understand, and then commenced doing her part towards helping her guests to the various dishes that were upon the table. She had not proceeded far in this before she discovered that the beef was "burnt to a crisp," the turkey "raw," the potatoes "sobby," and the gravy as "black as a coal."

"Never mind, my dear," said her husband, on her declaring that the beef was burnt to a crisp—"It's only on the outside; all is right within. Here's a slice that would tickle the palate of an alderman, and there are plenty more here just like it. The beef will do very well; don't run it down until we begin, and then speak up for the cook, which you may do with a clear conscience."

"I'm sure the slice you have helped Mr. B. to is not fit to eat. Go, John, and take Mr. B.'s plate up for a better piece."

"Beg pardon, madam," said Mr. B., "I couldn't ask any thing better. I like beef well-done, and always prefer an outside piece."

But nothing would do. Mr. B.'s plate had to go up and an exchange be made for a more juicy slice of beef, which, if what Mr. B. said was strictly true, was not as agreeable to his palate as the other.

"Will you have some of this gravy?" the lady asked, looking at me. "It's as black as a coal," she added, turning it up from the bottom with a spoon.

"I'll take some, if you please," I answered.

The gravy certainly was rather darker than I was in the habit of seeing it, but yet about as near the colour of a coal as the meat was to being burnt to a crisp. There was nothing unpleasant in its taste.

"I don't believe you can eat this turkey, Mr. C.," she said a few minutes afterwards, as she was helping the individual she addressed to a piece of turkey that had been carved at a side-table by the waiter, and placed before her. "It's raw!"

"I like even fowls a little rare," replied Mr. C. "It will just suit me."

"It's well you are all easily suited," returned Mrs. Clayton. "I call the whole dinner about the worst-cooked I have ever seen. I am mortified to death about it."

We assured her, as soon as we had time to test the quality of the good things before us, that all was excellent. And, in saying this, we did not exaggerate in the least. To have a better dinner than that, I would not give the value of a copper. But it availed nothing. Because every thing was not cooked and flavoured just to the point that she approved, it was pronounced unfit to be eaten. Not content with abusing the fare she had placed before us, she scolded the waiter for his omissions in setting the table, a ceremony that both he and the guests would have most cheerfully dispensed with.

At length we were through with the principal course, and then came the dessert. By the way, however, I forgot to mention that, to add zest to our dinner, Mrs. Clayton refused to be helped to any thing, and did so in a way that was especially unpleasant. To see her sitting up straight, with her hands in her lap, and an empty plate before her, while I was feasting on the many delicacies she had provided, affected my appetite considerably. But at length came the dessert.

First some tarts were brought by the waiter and placed on the table before her. The moment the eyes of Mrs. Clayton rested on these, her brows contracted sharply, but she said nothing. I saw that the sides of two or three of them were burnt pretty black; save that defect, their appearance was tempting enough.

"All burnt up! it is too bad!" I could hear her say, in an under tone, speaking to herself, while she was serving them out on plates, and handing them to the waiter to be passed around the table.

The flavour of the tarts was very delicious, and the first few mouthfuls as pleasant to the taste as any thing of the kind I had ever eaten; but, after that, I did not enjoy them much, from thinking about the unhappy temper of our hostess.

Some lemon and cocoa-nut pudding followed.

These were delicacies upon which Mrs. Clayton prided herself, and when they were set before her, her face brightened up. So, I am sure, did mine, for by this time I had begun to feel really unpleasant, and must have shown my feelings in my coun tenance. After these puddings had been served around, Mrs. Clayton asked Mr. B. how he liked them.

"Delicious!" was the reply.

"I believe I will try a piece myself," said the lady.

"Do!" said I, speaking up quickly. "It takes away half the pleasure of the dinner to see you eating nothing, after all your trouble in preparing so many delicacies for us." I felt better at once.

By this time, Mrs. Clayton had lifted a small piece of the lemon pudding to her mouth.

"My gracious!" she exclaimed. "Why, it isn't fit to eat! it's as sour as vinegar! Isn't it too bad? Every thing has gone wrong to-day!"

"It is a little tart, Kate," said her husband; "but I really hadn't noticed it before you spoke. I hope I may never have a worse one."

"Ditto to that!" said Mr. C. And "ditto" went cheerily round the table.

But it did no good. The piece of lemon pudding was pushed aside.

"Try some of the cocoa-nut pudding; I am sure

that is without a fault!" I said, hoping to restore some of her suddenly-lost equanimity.

"I suppose that is no better than the rest," she replied; "it would be strange if it were an exception."

"Only try it!" I urged. In this I was joined by others.

Although I perceived no fault whatever in the pudding, I confess that I saw her make preparations for trying it with some misgivings. If this should prove defective, there was little hope of our getting away from the dinner-table with cheerful spirits.

"It's as dry as a chip!" almost stunned me, even while these thoughts were passing through my mind, though spoken in a low querulous tone.

From that moment I gave up; I spoke not another word. The fruits came on, and we ate them in silence. Poor Clayton looked miserable; he was mortified and worried. We were all relieved when the signal was given for retiring, and gladly escaped from the presence of our hostess, who had the kindness to say to us, that if we ever dined with her again, she hoped she would be able to give us something fit to eat.

"I wouldn't give codfish and potatoes, with a cheerful countenance presiding over them, for a hundred such dinners," said B., as we walked away from the house of my friend Clayton. "It was made up of every delicacy I could desire, but the sauce of cheerfulness and good-humour was not there Bless me! If I had such a wife, I would"—

"What would you do?" said I, laughing, as he paused to think what he would do.

—"Never invite my friends to dine with me," he answered, joining in my laugh. "But isn't it too bad?" he continued, speaking less emphatically, "for a woman of Mrs. Clayton's good sense to spoil a dinner in the way she did ours to-day? If any thing was wrong, why didn't she try to make it up by bright looks instead of dark ones?"

"It's her weakness and want of thought," I replied.

"Her husband ought to teach her better. He ought to *make* her think."

"It isn't always so easy a thing to make a woman do as you please, friend B.," said I. "And the hardest thing of all is to make her give up her peculiar humour and habitudes of mind. If she can be made to see how much she affects the comforts and happiness of others by their indulgence, she may do better, as if of her own accord; but she isn't a person to be driven from her ground by any prompt and bold assault upon, or ridicule of, her foibles and weaknesses. And if ever you get a wife, you will find this out. Mrs. Clayton is a very excellent woman. All her friends like her. But she has the fault of making the worst instead of the best of a thing. This she cannot help. But she can help annoying others with its untimely and unlady-like exhibition; and I am very much in hope that her being led so far astray to-day, will make her as sensible as she ought to be of her defect of character, and prevent an undue exposure of it on another occasion. At least, my charity goes so far."

The next time I took tea with my friend, the biscuits were a little heavy, but not a word was said about it; nor was there a cloud upon Mrs. Clayton's brow! Whether there had been a curtain-lecture or not on the subject of the dinner, I had no means of knowing; nor whether the subject had been alluded to or not between my friend and his wife. Enough that a change had come over her in this particular, and a very agreeable one. For this there was of course, a cause, as there is for all effects. But satisfied with the effect, we shall not waste time in speculating upon, or endeavouring to find out the cause.

OPENING AN ACCOUNT.

The income of Mr. Bradford was not large; and he found it somewhat difficult, as he often said, to get along. The making of "both ends meet" was not the easiest thing in the world, yet he continued to accomplish the feat, year after year, by "pinching and screwing," to use his own language. Mr. Bradford was always looking forward to better times, and confidently believed that, in at least six or twelve months, he would find his affairs in a pleasanter condition. Money with him was always "tight" now; but promised to be easier before long. But this "before long" seemed in no hurry to come. Though it had been on the way a long time, it appeared always to be as far off as ever.

The business of Mr. Bradford was that of a pattern-maker. With plenty of work, he could earn quite a handsome sum weekly. Often he made as much as twenty, and sometimes twenty-five dollars in that time. And again it happened that he would go a whole week without earning any thing at all. These dull weeks were very discouraging times for

Mr. Bradford, seeing that he had a wife and four children to provide for. But taking the good weeks with the bad ones, the year through, all came out right in the end, and the pattern-maker managed to keep out of debt—and this for the reason that he never bought any thing unless he had the money to pay for it. As for credit, he had none, or, at least, he never dreamed of asking for such a thing.

It happened, one day, that he was in the store of a dry-goods dealer with his wife, making some small purchases. Sometimes he dealt at this store, and sometimes at the one over the way. Jones, the keeper of the store in which he now was, knew that the custom was thus divided, and was turning over the matter in his mind as to how he should secure the whole of it to himself, when he heard Mrs. Bradford say to her husband, as she stood examining some cloth,

"This is an excellent piece of goods, and very cheap. Just the thing for the boys; and they both want new suits."

"I can't spare the money now, Jane," replied Mr. Bradford. "You will have to wait a month or six weeks."

"Oh, very well," acquiesced the wife. "It will have to do then."

"That's a first-rate piece of goods," said Jones the storekeeper, coming forward at this moment.

"I bought it at a bargain. Let me sell you half a dozen yards."

"Not now," replied Mrs. Bradford. "In the course of a month or six weeks we may want to purchase."

"You might just as well take it to-day as to wait six weeks," said Jones, "even if you were sure of getting the article then, which you are not. I sold ten yards of it this morning, and don't expect to have any of it left at the end of three days. Mrs. Ellis was looking at it yesterday, and talked of taking seven or eight yards of it for her boys."

"You'll have more when this is gone," remarked Mr. Bradford.

"Not at the price," replied the storekeeper. "We don't pick up bargains like this every day. I've sold hundreds of yards of cloth, inferior to this in quality, for five dollars, and expect to sell hundreds of yards more at the same price."

"What is the price of this?" asked Mr. Bradford.

"Four dollars."

"It's very cheap," remarked the wife.

"Cheap! It's almost thrown away. The price does not pay for the manufacture. You'd better let me cut you off what you want."

"No; not to-day. Haven't got the money to spare," said Mr. Bradford.

"That's of no consequence. I don't want the

money now. I'll charge it, and you can pay the bill when it is most convenient."

"I don't want that," said the pattern-maker, taken by surprise at such a proposition. "In five or six weeks I will have the money, and then we can buy."

"But not at the present advantage. How many yards do you want?"

"Five," replied Mrs. Bradford.

"If you take this now, it will make a difference to you of just five dollars, and that's a matter of some consequence, these times."

"Indeed it is," feelingly replied the pattern-maker.

"I'll cut it off for you," said Jones, beginning to throw open the piece of goods. He read in his customer's face his secret willingness to accept the offer.

"Remember," Mr. Bradford laid his hand on the storekeeper's arm; "I can't pay for it in less than six weeks."

"All the same to me, if it's in six months. I'm in no hurry for the money. You're good enough for it. Glad to book you for five times the amount."

"You're liberal in your credits," remarked the pattern-maker.

"Not to every one. We always know what we are about."

By this time the five yards of cloth were measured

off, and the scissors had commenced the work of separation.

"Isn't there something else you want?" smilingly inquired the storekeeper. "Trimmings, of course."

"Yes, I must have trimmings," replied Mrs. Bradford.

These were furnished.

"Here is some of the cheapest domestic muslin that has been in market for a year," said Jones, at this point, throwing the article mentioned upon the counter. "You'd better take a piece. Always useful in a family. Just look at that goods, madam."

Mrs. Bradford examined it.

"What do you think of that?" said Jones, slapping his hand down upon the piece of muslin, with an air of self-satisfaction. "It's a beautiful piece of goods. And I can sell it for eleven cents and a half."

"That is cheap! I paid twelve and a half for some not near so good."

"I don't doubt it. They sell an article not a hundred miles from here for twelve and a half, not so good as this. I don't know how people have the conscience to ask such prices. I can sell this for eleven and a half, and make a good profit. Shall I send you home a piece?"

"We need a piece of muslin very much," said Mrs. Bradford, turning to her husband. "You want new shirts, and so do the boys."

Mr. Bradford did not reply, for he was not altogether satisfied about the new system of dealing. He was an honest man, and understood that the bills would have to be paid.

"I guess we've trespassed far enough on the kindness of Mr. Jones," said he.

"Feel no hesitation on that score," smilingly answered Mr. Jones. "Buy whatever you want. The higher the bill, the better it will please me."

"Six weeks will not be long in coming."

"I don't want the money in six weeks. If it will suit you as well, I'd as lief have six-month's settlements as any other. I'll open an account with you, and you can get whatever you want in your family without the trouble of hunting up the money just at the time. The bills can be settled in January and July. A good many of my customers deal in this way, and I like it best. If you feel inclined to go upon the list, I shall be satisfied. With some people, the year's income is not evenly distributed, and, as in your case now, the money is a little too late for the season."

"Just so," replied Mr. Bradford, who was really pleased with the storekeeper's offer, as it promised to make things more easy with him than they had been heretofore.

So it was arranged that an account should be opened; and that settlements once in six months should be made. Thus the cunning storekeeper gained two points: he secured the whole custom of the Bradfords, and, by the new system, induced them to buy at least a third more than they would have done if obliged to pay down the cash for every thing.

When Mr. and Mrs. Bradford left Jones's store, the bill against them was fifty dollars. As no cash was to be paid, wants and not means had governed their purchases.

"Jones is a very pleasant, accommodating man," remarked Mrs. Bradford, as she stepped from the store with her husband.

"He is, certainly," was replied. "I hope this new arrangement will make things easier. As he very justly said, the year's income is so unevenly distributed. The money hardly ever comes in just at the right time. There are four months yet to January, and it will be easy enough to pay this bill by that time."

Under this notion, the pattern-maker felt very comfortable, and returned to his shop with lighter feelings than he had known for some time. His wife soon began to appreciate more fully than at first the convenience of the new system. She no longer had to ask her husband for money when any little matter in the dry goods line was wanted, nor to bear the heretofore oft-recurring disappointment on learning that there was no money in the purse not otherwise needed. It was so easy to step over to the store of the smiling, polite Mr. Jones, and say, "Cut me off this," and "Cut me off that."

From that time the wardrobe of the Bradfords was less scantily furnished than heretofore. Real wants, and often imaginary ones, were supplied so easily, that it was a pleasure to buy, instead of a pain, as it had too often been, in consequence of the almost empty purse—for a state of collapse was the usual condition of that important article.

During the four months that intervened, from the time the credit account was opened, until the first of the ensuing January, Mr. Bradford was easier than usual in money matters, though he did not lay by any thing. After the first of December passed, he began to feel uneasy about the bill that would be rendered.

"How much do you think it will be?" he inquired of his wife.

"Not a great deal," she replied. "We haven't bought much since the first purchases that were made. It won't be over sixty dollars, at the extent."

The pattern-maker sighed. Sixty dollars; that was a large sum; and he hadn't five dollars towards it yet.

"Will it be so much?" he asked, in a voice that was by no means cheerful.

"It may not be quite that, but it won't fall very far short."

"Then I must put by at least twelve dollars a week from now until New-year's day. But I'm afraid it can't be done. Every thing is as dull as it can be just now: I didn't get in but seven dollars all last week."

Mrs. Bradford had nothing encouraging to suggest. She could only answer her husband with a sigh.

The weeks passed rapidly away. Christmas came, but it was not the cheerful merry time with the Bradfords it had usually been, for not over twenty dollars were yet laid up for the January bill of the polite and accommodating Mr. Jones. The fine fat turkey that came brown and smoking upon the table, neither looked so inviting to Mr. Bradford, nor tasted as delicious as the turkey that was served one year before; nor had the mince-pies that choice flavour for which the mince-pies of Mrs. Bradford were so distinguished. The thought of Mr. Jones's bill destroyed for the pattern-maker the sweetness of every thing. Nor were the children as happy; for their Christmas presents were few and of trifling value, compared with what they had been in former times. Ah! how sadly does debt interfere with domestic comfort!

During the week that followed, Mr. Bradford was able to add five dollars to the twenty already saved. But he took little comfort in thinking of that sum. Was not the storekeeper's bill sixty? How was he to meet the demand soon to come against him?

At last, New-year's Day arrived. In going to his shop, the pattern-maker had to pass the store of Mr. Jones. He did not even glance in, but he felt as certain that the storekeeper was observing him, and thinking about his large bill, as if he had seen him and looked through a window in his breast.

At dinner-time, when Mr. Bradford came home, he was struck with the sober face of his wife the moment he entered. His first thought, in explanation, was the bill; and he was not wrong in his conclusion. The bill had come in: Mr. Jones always sent round his bills punctually on the first of July and January.

"Has Mr. Jones sent in his bill yet?" he inquired.

"Yes," was replied, in a faint voice; and the eyes of Mrs. Bradford fell to the floor as she spoke.

"How much is it?" The pattern-maker tried to speak steadily while asking this question; but he did not succeed.

There was a pause. It seemed as if the wife could not bring herself to answer. At length, she murmured—

"A hundred and forty dollars; but there must be some mistake."

"A hundred and forty dollars! Impossible!" The countenance of Mr. Bradford fell instantly, and assumed a look of astonishment and distress. He was appalled.

"There is surely some mistake," said Mrs. Bradford. "He has charged somebody else's goods to our account. We don't owe him half that sum."

"Where is the bill?"

Mrs. Bradford drew the paper from her pocket and handed it to her husband, who hurriedly unfolded it, and glanced at the footing-up. It was too true—one hundred and forty dollars was the amount. As soon as the first agitation of the poor man's mind had subsided, he said to his wife—

"If you think there is any thing wrong in this bill, we will examine it, item by item."

"I know it is wrong!" confidently replied the wife. "We never had any thing like that amount of goods."

"Five yards of cloth, at four dollars a yard—twenty dollars. Is that right?" said Mr. Bradford, beginning to read from the bill.

"Yes, that is right, of course."

"One piece of muslin, four dollars and sixty cents."

"Four dollars and sixty cents! It never came to that much." Objected to by Mrs. Bradford.

"Let me see. Forty yards, at eleven and a half. Yes, that is right."

"I didn't think it came to so much. The last piece we had only cost three dollars and a half."

"It was a smaller piece, I suppose."

"Yes, it was; I remember now," said the wife.

Item after item was read off. To almost every one there was some demurrer; but, finally, all but six were fully admitted, and about these Mrs. Bradford would not be positive; still, she could not bring them to mind. However, as this aggregate was only four dollars, they did not materially alter the face of the bill.

Alas for the poor pattern-maker! No appetite for his dinner remained. He sat down in his usual place at the table—it would have been a weakness, producing shame, to have remained away—and took food upon his plate. But he could not eat. It was the same with his unhappy wife. While he was oppressed by a sense of inability to meet the heavy obligation, she was wretched under the consciousness that she was mostly to blame for its existence.

When Mr. Bradford returned to the shop, he went two blocks out of his way to avoid passing the store of Jones, the dry-goods dealer. He did not work any during the afternoon; for to apply himself to his usual occupation was, for the time, out of the question. There was but one idea in his mind, and that—the enormous bill of Mr. Jones. How was it to be settled? He could devise no means. At one time, in the desperation of his feelings, he determined to sell his tools, and thus cancel the obligation. But a little reflection showed him the folly of this. Evening found him in no way relieved of the burden under which he was suffering. What was he to do? How was the bill to be paid? These were questions to which had come no satisfactory answers. Half the night he lay awake, pondering over the matter. On the next day, in going to his shop, Mr. Bradford again avoided passing the store of Mr. Jones. How could he meet him?

At dinner-time, the first question asked by Bradford was, if the storekeeper had sent about the bill?

"No," faintly replied his wife; to which a deep sigh was the only response.

On the third day, Mr. Bradford's mind, though still greatly distressed, began to rally. He was not a man to walk round an obligation, if a path that way could be found. It was this very honesty of character that made his pain so acute. It was time to see Mr. Jones, and come to some understanding with him. But what should he say to him? What could he say to him? His money was what the storekeeper wanted; yet to pay the bill was impossible. He had, now, just thirty dollars. This he was ready to pay over; but how little would that satisfy Mr. Jones? Moreover, the pattern-maker was proud and sensitive, if he was poor; and the idea of going to the storekeeper, and admitting that he had run up a large bill with him at the same time that he had not the ability to settle it, made him faint at heart. At last, however, he saw only one right way to act, and that was, to go to Mr. Jones and confess the truth.

The storekeeper was younger than Mr. Bradford, by at least fifteen years; and this disparity of age, with some other circumstances, had heretofore given the pattern-maker a certain feeling of superiority when in his company. But this feeling had all departed, and he approached him as one approaches another who has power over him.

It cost Mr. Bradford, it may well be imagined, a hard struggle to enter the store of his creditor. When Mr. Jones smiled blandly and reached out his hand, he could not return the smile or the warm pressure.

"I—I—Mr. Jones," he stammered, "I received y-your bill."

"We always send in our bills on the first of the year," replied Mr. Jones, his smile partly fading away, for he understood perfectly the meaning of his customer's manner.

"Yes, so I am aware; but I find your bill much beyond what I anticipated," said Mr. Bradford, who was regaining his steadiness of tone.

"I believe it is all right." This was said with some gravity of manner.

"Oh, yes," was quickly responded. "I don't question its correctness at all. I only alluded to the amount; sixty dollars was at the outside of my anticipations."

"Bills amount up, Mr. Bradford."

"So I perceive; and it's a lesson I shall not soon forget. It is the first account I ever let run up at a store, and it's the last one. Heretofore my money measured my wants, and hereafter I mean to let the same rule govern in all my purchases."

"As you like about that," said the storekeeper, who did not particularly fancy the tone in which this was spoken.

This restored to the mind of Bradford its sense of humiliation. He felt that he was the weaker and the humbled party in the transaction, and must assume the air of one who sued for favour.

"I am not a man with a large income, Mr. Jones," said he, speaking in a subdued voice, "and to me a bill of a hundred and forty dollars is no light matter. I never had such a bill against me before, and I never mean to have one like it against me again. Nothing could have been farther from my imagination than that it was accumulating at such a rate. But what is now to be considered, is the settlement. That, let me frankly tell you, cannot be done at once; I have been able to save but thirty dollars towards it. If you will take that on account, I will pay it, and agree to give you ten dollars a month until the balance is paid off."

Mr. Jones was silent for some time after this proposition was made; he did not like it at all. His bill was due, and he wanted the money. Mr. Bradford he had considered a first-rate customer, and in looking over his accounts, had set him down as one who would cash up at a moment's warning. But he understood the position of his debtor, now that an explanation had been made, perfectly, and knew that, let him do as he would, the money would not come a day sooner; and he was also aware that it was in his power to lose or retain his customer, according as he treated him in the present difficulty. So, overcoming his feelings of disappointment as rapidly as possible, and endeavouring to hide what was not suppressed, in an assumed tone of voice, he at length replied—

"I'm sorry, of course, Mr. Bradford, not to get the money at this time; but, as you haven't got it to pay, I can't expect to receive it, and there's no use in crying over what can't be helped. I'll take the thirty dollars you have with you—it will be so much in hand—and the other you can pay as soon as convenient."

"I'll agree to pay you ten dollars on the first of every month, punctually," said Bradford, with a long-drawn respiration. He felt a sense of relief, yet the pressure of shame was still heavy.

"Very well; that will do."

Jones tried to affect an indifference that he did not feel. He was laying out a line for the future custom of the pattern-maker, at the same time that he was drawing on the old debt as hard as he thought prudent.

Bradford paid over the thirty dollars, and got a receipt.

"When you want any thing more in my line, you won't forget me, of course," said the storekeeper.

"No, certainly not," answered Bradford. "I shall feel under obligation to spend my money with you; but we shall not spend much until this bill is settled."

"Don't let that trouble you; it will be all wiped out in a few months."

"I hope so," replied Mr. Bradford, as he left the store. A sense of relief followed this arrangement; a difficulty had been met and overcome; a mortifying ordeal had been passed, but a sting remained behind.

Slowly the months passed away, and regularly the ten-dollar instalments were made. But the pattern-maker never met the storekeeper without feeling humbled, while a portion of the debt stood against him; and even after the obligation was entirely cancelled, a sense of humiliation remained. While the debt was unpaid, Bradford required his family to make all their purchases at the store of Jones; but since the bill has been settled, not a dollar of the pattern-maker's money has entered the till of the latter. The credit system did not turn out a matter of much gain or pleasure to either party.

MR. AND MRS. SUNDERLAND'S EXPERIENCES.

AGREEABLE NEIGHBOURS.

"You don't know what a beautiful new parlour-carpet the Henleys have just bought," said Mrs. Sunderland to me, as I came in to dinner; "and it was only a dollar and a quarter a yard. It's worth almost as much again as ours was when new, and we paid a dollar thirty-seven and a half."

"Carpets are cheaper now than they were when we bought," I returned, a little coldly.

"True. That was a long time ago. I have just been looking at ours. They are really very much defaced. Don't you think we can afford to buy new ones? I feel quite ashamed of them; they are so worn and faded."

"You did not think so indifferently of them until you saw Mrs. Henley's new one."

"Oh, yes, I did. But, I thought, may-be you

might think we couldn't afford others, and so I didn't say any thing about it. But now that the Henleys, who are really no better off than we are, have put down a beautiful new carpet on their parlour, I feel as if we ought to do the same. Ours look awfully shabby."

"To carpet our parlours will cost at least fifty dollars, Jane."

"Oh, no, it won't, nothing like it."

"It is easy to make the calculation. Figures never lie. It will take twenty yards for each parlour."

"Not more than eighteen," replied my wife.

"It takes five breadths, and each room is four yards long."

As I said this, I took a rule from my pocket, and, in a few moments, proved the assertion I had made as to the length of the room.

"Four fives make twenty," said I, as I arose from my bent position, "and twice twenty make forty. Forty yards of carpeting, at a dollar and a quarter a yard, will cost just fifty dollars."

"A'n't you mistaken?" returned my wife, who is not overly smart at figures. "Forty yards, at a dollar a yard, is only forty dollars. The forty quarters won't make ten, certainly."

"Divide four into forty, and you have ten. Or, multiply ten by four, and you have forty. Forty yards of carpeting at a quarter of a dollar a yard will, therefore, make ten dollars; and ten dollars added to forty dollars will make just fifty."

"True enough! But I wouldn't have thought it. Fifty dollars is a good big sum; but then, you know, we don't want parlour-carpets every year. It is six or seven years since these were bought. We shall have to get new ones very soon at any rate, and we might as well buy them now as at any other time; and better too, for I don't believe they will be as cheap in six months from this."

My wife was fairly set out for new parlour-carpets, and meant to carry her point. This I understood very well, and not caring to fight a battle in which the odds were all against me, abandoned the contest, and gave her fifty dollars to buy the carpets, inwardly anathematizing Mrs. Henley, and wishing her a thousand miles away.

I had a very comfortable income of a thousand dollars a year, out of which I laid it down as a rule that I ought to save at least two hundred dollars. This I had been able to do for a couple of years, until, unfortunately, the Henleys moved next door, and my wife made the acquaintance of the very agreeable Mrs. Henley, whose husband received a salary of twelve hundred dollars per annum, all of which was regularly spent by the year's end. I had nearly four hundred dollars snugly laid away in the Savings bank when the Henleys became our neighbours. The amount had already dwindled away until only two hundred remained, when the parlour-carpets were to be replaced by new ones. These new neighbours and acquaintances were very agreeable people, certainly. I liked Henley very well, and my wife was perfectly fascinated with Mrs. Henley, who was a woman of some taste, but had rather extravagant notions for one in her circumstances.

Our style of living had been plain from the beginning, and with this style we were both very well satisfied. At the time of our marriage I had about a thousand dollars laid by, and this sum we expended in furniture, keeping in view comfort and convenience rather than show. For two or three years, we found it necessary to expend all that could be saved out of my salary, which, during that time, was only eight hundred dollars, in completing the comforts of our little household. After that, my salary was increased, and I was able to save something. With the pleasant prospect, if health continued, of being able to save enough to purchase, in time, a comfortable dwelling, I was going on in a very self-satisfied state of mind, when the Henleys moved next door. Three weeks were allowed to go by, and then my wife suggested that it was no more than right for her to call upon our new neighbours, who were, she had ascertained, very respectable people. I had no objections to offer; and, therefore, made none; and she, accordingly, one day made the proposed complimentary visit.

"I called to see Mrs. Henley this morning," she said to me when I came home to dinner.

"Well—how did you like her?" I returned, half indifferently.

"Very much, indeed," replied my wife, expressing herself warmly. "She is one of the most agreeable women I ever met—a perfect lady in her manners. She says that I am the first one who has yet called upon her. She appeared pleased; and said that she should put me down at once in the number of her friends. They have every thing very nice about them. Mahogany chairs in the parlour, which is one long room, and a beautiful marble-top centre-table. On the mantle they have a vase of flowers in the centre, and candelabras at each end."

As my wife said this, she glanced toward the mantels in our plainly-furnished parlours. On one of them was a pair of cut-glass lamps, and on the other nothing.

"I really think, Mr. Sunderland, we might afford a pair of candelabras," she digressed to say. "They furnish a room so well, and only cost twelve or fifteen dollars."

I said nothing in reply; but thought our glass lamps looked very well, and that, for the mere appearance of the thing, twelve or fifteen dollars was too much for persons in our circumstances to spend for candelabras.

For some time my wife continued to run on about

her agreeable neighbour. She had noticed every thing in the parlour arrangement of her house, and the minutest particular of her dress, all of which she described.

Two days only elapsed before Mrs. Henley returned the call, and asked my wife if she wouldn't go shopping with her on the next day. This she promised to do, and as she had several articles to purchase herself, asked me for ten dollars with which to buy them.

"I declare!" said she to me, when I met her at dinner-time, after the shopping expedition with Mrs. Henley, "I've been out the whole morning and spent all my money, without buying an article I intended to get. I was going to buy you half a dozen pocket-handkerchiefs, a piece of muslin to make up, and some canton-flannel for you, not one of which articles have I got."

"What have you bought?" I asked.

"I will show you," she replied, and brought out a bundle from one of her drawers. As she unrolled it, she said—"We met with some of the cheapest collars I ever saw in my life. Real French lace, and only two dollars a piece. There, just look at that!"

And my wife displayed before my eyes a worked collar that was no doubt all she alleged in regard to it, but as I was no judge, I could not be qualified to the fact.

"Isn't it sweet?" she said.

Of course I could do no less than assent.

"And it was only two dollars and a half. Mrs. Henley bought one without a word, and I couldn't resist the temptation to do the same. I hadn't a single handsome collar to my name, and felt really ashamed when I went out with Mrs. Henley, who had on one that didn't cost less than five dollars, and mine was a mean, common-looking thing, that I had before we were married."

I hadn't a word to say.

"Wasn't I right to get it, Mr. Sunderland?" my wife asked, looking me intently in the face.

"Certainly, my dear. You needed a fine collar, and you did right to buy one."

"Now look at this."

A rich, showy dress-pattern met my eyes.

"Isn't that lovely?" said my wife.

"It is," I returned.

"Now, how much do you think it was a yard?"

"Indeed I don't know."

"Only forty cents," said my wife with an air of triumph. "Last season, nothing like it could be had for less than fifty cents. Mrs. Henley said she had not seen any thing so cheap or handsome this season, and she has been about a good deal. She took a pattern at once, and as I am in want of a good dress, I did the same. It will make up beautifully. Don't you think so?"

"Yes, I think it will." What else could I say? My wife needed a dress, and this she considered both pretty and cheap. If it pleased her, I was satisfied.

Half a dozen little matters, of which I did not clearly understand the use, completed the list of purchases—things my wife would not have dreamed of wanting had she not been out shopping with her agreeable neighbour. On the next day I furnished ten dollars more to get the muslin, canton-flannel and pocket-handkerchiefs, which my wife said must be had immediately. As she had been so kind as to go shopping with Mrs. Henley, that lady very kindly consented to go out with my wife. The piece of muslin was bought, but the handkerchiefs and canton-flannel were omitted. The ladies saw a couple of silk bonnets, the price of which was only six dollars each, which so struck their fancies that they forthwith concluded to buy them.

"It is just the thing!" said my wife to me, drawing the really handsome and becoming bonnet upon her head, and looking twenty per cent. younger and prettier. "Now don't you think so?"

"I do indeed," I could not help saying, and with a warmth of manner that greatly pleased my good wife.

"I should have had to get a winter bonnet in a few weeks, and pay at least six dollars for one neither so good nor handsome as this. They were selling off, and I could not let the opportunity for securing a bargain like this pass."

I had nothing to advance by way of objection. Ten dollars more were supplied for shopping purposes, and the canton-flannel and pocket-handkerchiefs secured this time.

Thus began my wife's acquaintance with her agreeable neighbour, Mrs. Henley. From that period money went more rapidly. It cost, for shopping purposes alone, just double what it had done before. My wife's appearance and that of our two little ones was very much improved, and this was agreeable enough, but I could not help feeling that it was all costing too much. I found that, instead of having fifty dollars at the end of the quarter, to lay up, I hadn't a dollar. All was not spent in shopping, of course; but what was true in the clothing department was true in every other department also.

Before the Henleys had been our neighbours three months, the glass lamps had disappeared from the mantle of our front-parlour, and a set of candelabras were to be seen in their place.

Mr. Henley, upon whom my wife insisted I should call, I found an intelligent, agreeable man, and frequently spent a pleasant evening with him. As for the ladies, they were soon as thick as pickpockets, and saw each other every day. From the first week of their acquaintance, the ideas of my wife began gradually to enlarge, and her taste to become refined.

The thought of economy gradually faded from her mind. Mrs. Henley became her model, and Mrs. Henley's ideas of things her ideas. She used, every fall, to put up a few jars of preserves—and these were generally confined to peaches and plums, the cost of which did not exceed five dollars. But this, the first season of her acquaintance with Mrs. Henley, she was visited with a regular preserving mania. Quinces, peaches, pears, plums, pine-apples, water-melon-rinds, and the dear knows what all! were boiled down in the best double-refined loaf-sugar, and sealed up in glass jars, the number of which I will not pretend to give. Brandied peaches, too, had to be put up in the best white brandy, for which I paid somewhere between three and four dollars a gallon. Altogether, I am sure the brandy, fruit, sugar, and jars did not cost a fraction less than thirty dollars. I said so to my wife, but she scouted the idea as preposterous.

And so the thing went on for more than a year, before the new carpets were bought, my deposits in the Savings bank steadily decreasing, until I had not over two hundred dollars left. I really began to feel serious, and to wish that Mrs. Henley had been married to the man in the moon.

The new carpets looked very fine. I had to acknowledge that. But the chairs and the card-table appeared rather ashamed of themselves in such genteel company.

"Mrs. Henley says our chairs will never do."

I had been looking for this. "Confound Mrs. Henley!"

Don't suppose, reader, that I uttered this aloud. I was not quite so rude. I only thought it.

"We were looking at some excellent mahogany chairs, when we were in Walnut street this morning, at four dollars a piece. That would only be forty-eight dollars a dozen, and we paid twenty-five for these cane-seats. It's a pity we hadn't bought mahogany chairs when we were about it. But these will do very well for the chamber."

When Mrs. Sunderland gets a thing into her head, there is no getting it out. After she had said this, I saw the new chairs already in our parlours. This was in imagination; but the real vision came soon. A draft upon my deposits in the Savings bank for fifty dollars, furnished my wife with the means of gratifying her desire to have a set of cushioned chairs. Mrs. Henley pronounced them beautiful, but suggested that there was still something wanting to complete the effect. There must either be a sofa-table, or a centre-table with a marble top.

"Mrs. Henley is very kind in her suggestions," I could not help saying, a little sarcastically. My wife did not like this at all, and met it with a warm defence of her agreeable neighbour. I was silenced. No more was said about a centre or sofa-table for a week or two. Then my wife, with the aid of her friend, discovered the very thing that was wanted, in a handsome sofa-table, with a black Italian marble slab, the price of which, exceedingly moderate, was only twenty-two dollars. As there was a pair of them, and the Henleys bought one, although they had a handsome centre-table already, I couldn't object very strongly, and I did not.

Carpets, chairs and sofa-table were costly articles, and their purchase made quite a distinct impression upon the little fund I had saved. But, besides these marked impressions, there was a gradual wasting away of my cherished deposit. Mrs. Henley was a woman who always wanted something, and never was satisfied unless she were spending money. In the course of a year and a half, she had so filled my wife with her spirit, that our current expenses, instead of coming within eight hundred dollars, exceeded a thousand per annum, and my four hundred dollars were all drawn out of the Savings bank. I had cause to feel sober.

"This will never do," I would say to my wife. "We are living beyond our income."

"I am sure I try to be economical," she would answer. "I don't see how I could spend less. We live no better than other persons in our circumstances live. I am sure Mrs. Henley spends two dollars on herself where I spend one."

"We used to get along very comfortably on eight hundred dollars a year. But we have not only spent a thousand dollars a year for the last two years, but have drawn every thing out of the Savings bank we had laid up."

"Yes, dear, but look how much furniture we have bought. These carpets, those chairs and tables, and that elegant rocking-chair; besides the dressing-bureau, wash-stand, and mahogany bedstead."

"True. But are we any happier than we were?" I replied. "To speak for myself, I can say that I am not."

"We shall not have them to buy again. They will last us our lifetime," suggested my wife, by way of consolation.

"Yes, but my dear, we are living at an expense of at least eleven hundred dollars, and my salary, you are aware, is but a thousand."

My wife looked very serious.

"I don't know what we shall do," said she, in a desponding tone.

"If you don't, I must find out," was my mental reply.

When I left home, I took the way direct to the store of my landlord.

"Mr. L——," said I, "have you another house a mile or two away from the one I now occupy?"

"Vacant, you mean?"

"Of course."

"Yes. I received the key this morning of a very

excellent house up in Spring Garden District. But the rent is two hundred and fifty."

"Fifty dollars more than I now pay. No matter. That will do. Now, Mr. L——, I want you to write me a formal notification to leave your house within three days."

"Why so? That is a strange proceeding."

I gave him a history of the effect produced upon my finances by our very agreeable neighbours, and declared that if he did not do as I wished, I would be ruined.

My landlord laughed at me, but promised to do as I desired. You may judge of my wife's surprise when a peremptory notice to quit was received.

"He can't get you out until the end of the quarter," suggested Mr. Henley.

"I wouldn't go for him!" said Mrs. Henley, with strongly marked emphasis.

But I affected to be greatly indignant at the landlord's note, and said I wouldn't live in his house another week if he gave it to me rent free for a year. On the next day I took my wife out to see the new house in Spring Garden. She strongly objected to going so far away.

"So far away from where?" I asked.

This she was not able to answer very satisfactorily. When, however, she saw the house, and found it to be so much larger, handsomer, and more convenient than the one we had left, she waived all objections, and we were snugly settled in it before a week had elapsed. The only thing that my wife regretted in the change, was the loss of her agreeable neighbour, Mrs. Henley. I need not express my feelings on that subject.

Soon we had matters and things going on in the old way, and I am now laying up from one to two hundred dollars a year, and shall continue to do so I hope, unless the Henleys take a fancy to move into our neighbourhood, which heaven forbid!

So much for our very agreeable neighbours. They were pleasant people certainly, but their acquaintance cost too much.

SAVING AT THE SPIGOT.

SINCE our removal into Spring Garden, Mrs. Sunderland's old and very agreeable neighbour, Mrs. Henley, has only paid her one or two formal visits. Withdrawn from her sphere and influence, the mania for spending money which raged for a couple of years has subsided, and my wife sees her error quite as clearly as I do, and laments it even more bitterly. She is exceedingly anxious to save at every point, in order to make up what has been lost, and in attempting to do so has, in several instances, demonstrated with great clearness the folly of the man who was charged with saving at the spigot while he was letting out at the bunghole.

We have usually employed one domestic to cook and do general housework, and hired a washerwoman and ironer every week. Our washings are pretty large—at least so my wife says, and she ought to know. After we moved into Spring Garden, my wife concluded to dispense with the ironer, and this saved sixty-two and a half cents a week. Of course she had to take her place; so our one servant had just about as much to do as she could get through with.

I expressed my objection to this, but my wife said that she would rather do it.

"But you are not strong, Anna," I urged, "and will find standing all day at the ironing-table much too fatiguing."

"I suppose I will be a little tired, but that is no matter. Getting tired won't hurt me."

"*Over* fatigue might, though," I returned.

"I will guard against that," she made answer.

"Still, Anna, I would rather pay the woman. You have enough to do in the family."

"A half dollar and eleven pence is a good deal to pay out every week, besides giving a woman a day's boarding, and might just as well be saved as not. So, Harry, you needn't say a word about it. I've made my mind up to do a share of the ironing, and you know very well, by this time, that if I will, I will, you may depend on't."

"And if you won't, you won't, so there's an end on't," I returned, good-humouredly. "Well, I suppose for me to object is useless; but I doubt if you save any thing in the long run."

"Very well, doubt away, but *I* know, that if I save sixty or seventy cents a week, I will save thirty or thirty-five dollars a year. If I am not very smart at figures, I can at least calculate that."

Of course my wife had her way, and the very next week undertook to do half the ironing. When she got up on Tuesday morning, the ironing day, I saw by the expression of her face that she was not well.

"Does your head ache?" I asked.

"Yes, a little."

"More than a little, I apprehend, Anna. You do not look at all well. Of course you will not attempt ironing to-day."

"Certainly I will," she replied.

"You are very wrong, Anna. You might make yourself sick," I urged.

"Oh, no. I shall feel better after a while. I told Hannah last week that I shouldn't want her any more. So I must do it, sick or well."

It was in July, and the day had opened breezeless and sultry. Even while sitting quite still at my desk, the perspiration was starting from every pore. About eleven o'clock, however, there was a change. The air began to move gently from the east, and by twelve was blowing freshly. The thermometer had already fallen several degrees. The change was delightful. New life seemed to rush through every vein.

At two o'clock, I went home to dinner. By this time, the difference in the temperature since morning was at least twenty degrees. The sky was obscured by clouds, and the wind that was blowing steadily from the north-east, penetrated my thin summer-clothing, and actually produced a sensation of chilliness.

On arriving at home, I found my wife with flushed cheeks and a look of extreme fatigue, standing at the ironing-table, which was placed across the kitchen-door, into which the cool wind was passing, and of course, striking full against her. She was dressed in a thin, loose wrapper, and her neck and a part of her bosom exposed to the cool air.

"Anna, you are very imprudent to stand in that draft, overheated as you are," I said, the moment I saw her.

"The air is delightful," she merely returned.

"But you will take cold," I urged.

"No danger. I'm not afraid."

"It might be the death of you. Not afraid to stand, in the overheated state in which you are, in a chilly east wind?"

"There—there, Harry?" my wife said a little impatiently. "Don't come here to worry me now

I'm so tired, that if it wasn't for this cool, bracing air, I could'nt stand."

"Are you almost done?" I asked.

"Yes, very nearly. It took that Hannah about all day to do what I have done this morning. I can iron two pieces to her one. I wouldn't have her again in the house."

I couldn't help thinking of the story I had heard about two labouring-men, one an old hand at the business, and the other green. They were set to work at some kind of excavation, and the new hand threw two shovelfuls of earth to the old one's one; but in the long run, the old hand, who worked up to his strength, but without exhausting it, did twice the labour of the other. My inference, which proved to be correct, was, that Hannah did a fair and reasonable day's work, while my wife, working on the high-pressure principle, did a great deal too much—double what she could have done working day after day.

"A'n't you going to eat any thing?" I asked, at dinner-time, finding my wife declined being helped to any dish on the table.

"I don't feel the slightest appetite," she returned.

"Try a piece of this lamb," I urged. "It is very nice."

But she shook her head, saying, "I couldn't swallow a morsel of it."

Of course I did not eat with much appetite. In fact, I hardly tasted the food I put into my mouth.

"It's the last time *she* does the ironing," I said to myself, as I walked slowly back to the office where I was engaged in writing. "I call this poor economy. Ten chances to one if she don't make herself sick; and there won't be much saving in that."

As evening approached, and my thoughts began to turn toward home, I felt uneasy. I expected to find my wife suffering from entire physical prostration. My fears were not idle. The reality, indeed, was worse than my fears. She was in bed, and suffering from a severe pain in her side, that was so much increased by breathing that she could hardly help crying out at every inspiration. Coughing or pressure caused intolerable pain.

Once before, my wife had been attacked with pleurisy, and I knew too well the alarming symptoms. In her overheated state, the cold air had caused a sudden check of perspiration, and inflammation of the pleura was the consequence.

I started immediately for our family physician, and was fortunate enough to find him in. He accompanied me home. On arriving, we found that all the smyptoms had become much worse since I left. My poor wife screamed with nearly every breath.

Bleeding was instantly resorted to, which gave temporary relief. But, before ten o'clock, the pain returned with great violence. I again went for the doctor, who repeated the bleeding, and then ordered leeches, fifty of which were applied. But the pain only abated in a partial degree. All night she suffered most cruelly, and was so bad in the morning that I had to go for the doctor again soon after daylight.

More blood was then taken by the lancet, and fifty more leeches applied to the chest before relief was obtained. Then I had the satisfaction to see her sink away into sleep, the first time she had closed her eyes since the attack.

She slept for a couple of hours, and then awoke with a return of the pain in her side, to allay which leeching was again resorted to.

For five days this bleeding and leeching was kept up, before the inflammation was sufficiently subdued to allow of revulsive treatment. Three large blisters were applied to her chest and arms.

It need hardly be said, that with such a disease and such treatment, my wife was reduced so low that a nurse had to be obtained for her. She was weak as an infant; for, added to the pain and the severe mode of attacking the disease resorted to by the physician, she took but little nourishment for many days. Nearly three weeks elapsed, from the time she was taken before she was well enough to come down-stairs and take her usual place at the head of the table, and then she had so little strength left, that she could not do the most simple needle work. Months elapsed before her health was fairly restored—I will not say "fairly restored," either, for she has never been as she was.

And now let me calculate the amount of saving made by my wife in dispensing with a woman once a week to help do the ironing. The saving was exactly sixty-two and a half cents to a fraction. That was the creditor side of the account. The debtor side outbalanced it seriously, as far as the account was entered up, which never could be accurately done. Indeed no attempt to strike a clear balance was ever made.

The first and most imposing item was the doctor's bill, which was exactly twenty dollars. Then, five dollars were paid for leeching, and nine dollars to a nurse for three weeks' service. Here was thirty-four dollars of unmistakeable expense. Beyond this was the loss of nearly two months' time by my wife, to make up for which a seamstress had to be employed for several weeks at half a dollar a day. Instead of being able to get along with one domestic and a washerwoman and ironer, two girls have had to be hired ever since. Taken all in all, it may be fairly concluded that for sixty-two and a half cents that my wife saved at the spigot on the occasion referred to, she let seventy or eighty dollars escape from the bunghole.

As in duty bound, I made the circumstance the occasion of sundry appropriate hints. My wife saw her error plainly enough, and acknowledged it with expressions of regret for her folly; but many weeks did not elapse after she considered herself well enough to go about the house, before she suggested that one domestic would be enough in the family. But I vetoed the proposed reduction of help in such a determined manner, that I carried my point. Still the propensity to save a present half-dollar at the risk of losing ten, is so strong, that if I did not constantly interfere, and almost command things to be done or left undone, we would suffer almost as much from my good wife's efforts to save as we did from her mania to spend, as related under the head of "Agreeable Neighbours."

MY WIFE'S PARTY.

A BETTER woman than Mrs. Sunderland does not exist anywhere, though I, her husband, do say it myself. I consider her one of the "salt of the earth," and I think I ought to know. Still Mrs. Sunderland has her weaknesses, and one of these is a disposition to think well of everybody. On this head, I believe, no one can accuse me of weakness. I am not aware that, as a general thing, I think any better of people than I ought to think. No—I am not blind to anybody's faults, though I can see and appreciate excellences as well as any one. But to my story.

After we had risen a little in the world, and could afford not only to live in our own house, but to enjoy our share of the elegances and luxuries of this life, we found ourselves surrounded by a good many who, before, were not over-liberal in their attentions. Mrs. Sunderland believed their friendship sincere; but I reserved to myself the right to doubt the genuineness of some of the professions that were made. I didn't like the "My dear Mrs. Sunderland!" nor the particular solicitude expressed by not a few in every thing that concerned my wife's welfare; and when she talked about Mrs. Jones being such a kind, good soul, and Miss Peters being so disinterested in every thing, I shrugged my shoulders, and reserved the privilege of a doubt in regard to all being gold that glittered.

Not having been raised in fashionable life, we had no taste for display, and, although we had our share of company, whether we cared about it or not, we had never ventured so far to sea as to give a party, although we had accepted several invitations to assemblages of this kind. But some of Mrs. Sunderland's good friends and acquaintances insisted upon it, last winter, that she must give an entertainment, and they used such cogent arguments that she, good soul! was won over. I remained for a long time incorrigible; but, as nothing could put it out of Mrs. Sunderland's head that it was due to her position and relations to give a party, I, with much reluctance, withdrew my opposition, and forthwith the note of preparation was sounded.

"Who shall we invite?" was the first question.

Our circle of acquaintance had considerably increased within two or three years, and when we went over the list, it was found to be rather large.

"You will have to cut down considerably," said I.

"To do so without giving offence will be difficult," replied my wife.

"Better cut all off, then," was on my tongue, but I repressed the words, feeling that it would be unkind to throw cold water upon the affair at this stage of its progress.

"You havn't got Fanny and Ellen on your list," I remarked, after a good number of erasures had been made. They were two of my nieces; good girls, but poor. Both were dressmaker's apprentices. They were learning a trade in order to relieve their father, an industrious, but not very thrifty man, from the burden of their support. I liked them very much for their good sense, agreeable manners, and strong affection for their parents.

"Shall we invite them?" inquired my wife.

"Certainly!" I replied. "Why not?"

"Will they be able to make a good appearance? You know that a number of fashionable people will be here."

"If you doubt it, we will send them each a handsome dress-pattern with the invitation."

"Perhaps we had better do so," was Mrs. Sunderland's approving remark, and the thing was done as I had suggested.

The pruning down of the invitation-list was no easy matter, and it was not without many fears of giving offence that my wife at last fixed upon the precise number of persons who were to honour us with their company.

The exact character of the entertainment was next to be considered, and an estimate of cost made. Several ladies, *au fait* in such matters, were consulted; and their opinions compared, digested, and adopted or rejected as they agreed with, or differed from, what we thought right.

"It will cost at least a hundred dollars," said Mrs. Sunderland, after we had come to some understanding as to what we would have. The sum seemed large in her mind.

"If we get off with two hundred, we may be thankful," I replied.

"Oh, no. It can't go above a hundred dollars."

"We shall see."

"If I thought it would cost so much, I would"—

"There is no retreat now, Mrs. Sunderland. We have taken the step initiative, and have nothing to do but go through with the matter as best we can.

My word for it, we shall not be very eager to give another party."

This threw a damper upon my wife's feelings that I was sorry to perceive, for now that the party must be given, I wanted to see it done in as good a spirit as possible. From that time, therefore, I was careful not to say any thing likely to awaken a doubt as to the satisfactory result of the coming entertainment.

The evening came in due time, and we had all things ready. I must own that I felt a little excited, for the giving of a fashionable party was something new in the history of my life, and I did not feel altogether at home in the matter. Unaccustomed to the entertainment of company, especially where ceremony and the observance of a certain etiquette were involved, I was conscious of an awkward feeling, and would have given double the cost of the party for the privilege of an escape from the trials and mortifications it promised to involve.

In order to give additional beauty and attractiveness to our parlours, we had purchased sundry articles of ornamental furniture, which cost over a hundred dollars, and which were of no manner of use but to look at.

It was so late before the élite of our company began to arrive, that we were in some doubt whether they were going to come at all. But, towards nine o'clock, they came along, and by ten we were in the full tide of successful experiment. My nieces, Fanny and Ellen, were among the first to appear, and they looked pretty and interesting.

As soon as the first embarrassment consequent on the appearance of the extra-fashionables had worn off, and I felt at home once more in my own house, I began to look around me with an observant eye. About the first thing that attracted my attention was the sober aspect of a certain lady, whose husband, by a few fortunate adventures, had acquired some money, and lifted her into "good society," as it is called. She was talking to another lady, and I saw that their eyes were directed towards my nieces, of whom I felt a little proud; they looked and behaved so well.

"What's all this about?" said I to myself, and I kept my eyes upon the ladies as intently as they did upon Ellen and Fanny. Presently I saw one of them toss her head with an air of dignified contempt, and, rising up, make her way across the room to where her husband stood. She spoke to him in evident excitement, and directed his attention to my nieces. The sight of them did not seem to produce any unpleasant effect upon him, for he merely shrugged his shoulders, smiled, and answered in a few words that I could see were indifferent. But his wife was in earnest, and, placing her arm within his, drew him away toward the door. He remonstrated, but she was not in a humour to listen to any thing, and, with surprise, I saw them retire from the parlours. My first impression was to follow them, but the truth flashing across my mind, I felt indignant at such conduct, and resolved to let them do as they pleased. In a little while, the offended lady, bonneted, cloaked, and boaed, came sweeping past the parlour-doors, with her husband in her train, attracting the attention of a third part of the company. A moment after, and she had passed into the street.

"Who is that? What's the matter?" went whispering about the rooms.

"It is Mrs. L——."

"Mrs. L——! Is she sick?"

"Why has she gone?"

But no one seemed at first to know. Soon, however, the lady to whom she had communicated the fact that we had insulted our company by inviting "mantua-maker girls," whispered to another the secret, and away it went buzzing through the rooms, finding its way as well to the ears of Fanny and Ellen as to those of the rest of the company. About one-half of the ladies present did not exactly seem to know whether they ought to follow the example of Mrs. L—— or not; and there was a portentous moment, when almost the waving of a finger would have caused our party to break up in disorder.

The moment my nieces understood the feeling that had prompted the lady to withdraw indignantly, they arose, and were retiring from the room, when I intercepted and detained them with as little ceremony as possible. They begged hard to be permitted to retire, but I said no! for my blood was "up," as the saying is.

"Ellen and Fanny are worth as many Mrs. L——'s," said I to myself, "as you can find from here to Jericho."

The disaffected ones noticed, I suppose, my decision in the matter, and thought it prudent not to break with Mr. and Mrs. Sunderland, who could afford to be independent. Money is a great thing! Humph; there was a time in our history—but, no matter. We are people of character and standing now.

We had rather a dull time after the withdrawal of Mrs. L——. For a little while the spirits of the company rallied, under the effects of wine and a good supper, but they soon flagged again, and a sober cast of thought settled upon almost every countenance. My poor wife found it impossible to retain a cheerful exterior; and my nieces looked as if almost any other place in the world would have been a paradise in comparison.

At least an hour earlier than we had anticipated, our rooms were deserted, and we left alone with our thoughts, which, upon the whole, were not very agreeable. Mrs. Sunderland, the moment the last guest retired, went back into the brilliantly-lighted parlours, and, sitting down upon a sofa, burst into tears. She had promised herself much pleasure, but, alas! how bitterly had she been disappointed! I was excited and indignant enough to say almost any thing, and a dozen times, as I paced the rooms backward and forward, did I check myself when about uttering words that would only have made poor Mrs. Sunderland feel ten times worse than she did.

"The next time we give a party"—

"We won't!" said I, taking the words out of my wife's mouth. She was recovering from her state of mortification, and beginning to feel indignant.

"You've said it exactly," responded Mrs. Sunderland. "I call this throwing away a couple of hundred dollars in a very bad cause."

"So it strikes me. When fifty or sixty people eat an elegant supper, and drink costly wine at my expense again, they will behave themselves better than some of our high-bred ladies did to-night. As for Mrs. L——, Fanny and Ellen are worth a hundred of her. It's my opinion that if she knew every thing she would curtail her dignity a little. If I'm not very much mistaken, her husband will go to the wall before a twelvemonth passes."

On the next day we settled all accounts with confectioner, wine-merchant, china-dealers, and waiters. The bills were over a hundred and fifty dollars, exclusive of a hundred dollars paid, as before intimated, for parlour-ornaments to grace the occasion.

"So much paid for worldly wisdom," said I, after all was over. "I don't think we need to give another party."

Mrs. Sunderland sighed and shook her head. Poor soul! her kind and generous nature was hurt. She had looked upon a new phase of character, and the discovery had wounded her deeply.

A few months after this unfortunate party, from which so little pleasure and so much pain had sprung, I said to my wife, on coming home one day:

"It's as I expected. Pride must have a fall."

"Why do you say that? What has happened?" inquired Mrs. Sunderland.

"L—— has failed, as I predicted, and his lady wife, who turned up her aristocratic nose at our excellent nieces, is likely to see the day when she will stand far below them in society."

I spoke in an exulting voice. But my wife instantly reproved my levity. She cherished no animosities, and had long since forgiven the offence.

So much for MY WIFE'S PARTY.

THE HOUSE-CLEANING.

TALK of a washing-day! What is that to a whole week of washing-days? No, even this gives no true idea of that worst of domestic afflictions a poor man can suffer—house-cleaning. The washing is confined to the kitchen or wash-house, and the effect visible in the dining-room is in cold or badly-cooked meals; with a few other matters not necessary to mention here. But in the house-cleaning—oh, dear! Like the dove from the ark, a man finds no place where he can rest the sole of his foot. Twice a year, regularly, have I to pass through this trying ordeal, *willy-nilly*, as it is said, in some strange language. To rebel is useless. To grumble of no avail. Up come the carpets, topsyturvy goes the furniture, and *swash!* goes the water from garret to cellar. I don't know how other men act on these occasions, but I find discretion the better part of valour, and submission the wisest expedient.

Usually it happens that my good wife works herself half to death—loses the even balance of her mind—and, in consequence, makes herself and all around her unhappy. To indulge in an unamiable temper is by no means a common thing for Mrs. Sunderland, and this makes its occurrence on these occasions so much the harder to bear. Our last house-cleaning took place in the fall. I have been going to write a faithful history of what was said, done, and suffered on the occasion ever since, and now put my design into execution, even at the risk of having my head combed with a three-legged stool by my excellent wife, who, when she sees this in print, will be taken, in nautical phrase, all aback. But, when a history of our own shortcomings, mishaps, mistakes and misadventures will do others good, I am for giving the history and pocketing the odium, if there be such a thing as odium attached to revelations of human weakness and error.

"We must clean house this week," said my good wife, one morning as we sat at the breakfast-table—"every thing is in a dreadful condition. I can't look at nor touch any thing without feeling my flesh creep."

I turned my eyes, involuntarily, around the room. I was not, before, aware of the filthy state in which we were living. But not having so good "an eye for dirt" as Mrs. Sunderland, I was not able, even after having my attention called to the fact, to see "the dreadful condition" of things. I said nothing, however, for I never like to interfere in my wife's department. I assume it as a fact that she knows her own business better than I do.

Our domestic establishment consisted at this time of a cook, chambermaid and waiter. This was an ample force, my wife considered, for all purposes of house-cleaning, and had so announced to the individuals concerned some days before she mentioned the matter incidentally to me. We had experience, in common with others, on our troubles with servants, but were now excellently well off in this respect. Things had gone on for months with scarcely a jar. This was a pleasant feature in affairs, and one upon which we often congratulated ourselves.

When I came home at dinner-time, on the day the anticipated house-cleaning had been mentioned to me, I found my wife with a long face.

"Are you not well?" I asked.

"I'm well enough," Mrs. Sunderland answered, "but I'm out of all patience with Ann and Hannah."

"What is the matter with them?" I asked, in surprise.

"They are both going at the end of this week."

"Indeed! How comes that? I thought they were very well satisfied."

"So they were, all along, until the time for house-cleaning approached. It is too bad!"

"That's it—is it?"

"Yes. And I feel out of all patience about it. It shows such a want of principle."

"Is John going too?" I asked.

"Dear knows! I expect so. He's been as sulky as he could be all the morning—in fact, ever since I told him that he must begin taking up the carpets to-morrow and shake them."

"Do you think Ann and Hannah will really go?" I asked.

"Of course they will. I have received formal notice to supply their places by the end of this week, which I must do, somehow or other."

The next day was Thursday, and, notwithstanding both cook and chambermaid had given notice that they were going on Saturday, my wife had the whole house knocked into *pi*, as the printers say, determined to get all she could out of them.

When I made my appearance at dinner-time, I found all in precious confusion, and my wife heated and worried excessively. Nothing was going on right. She had undertaken to get the dinner, in order that Ann and Hannah might proceed uninterruptedly in the work of house-cleaning; but as Ann and Hannah had given notice to quit in order to escape this very house-cleaning, they were in no humour to put things ahead. In consequence, they had "poked about and done nothing," to use Mrs. Sunderland's own language; at which she was no little incensed.

When evening came, I found things worse. My wife had set her whole force to work upon our chamber, early in the day, in order to have it finished as quickly as possible, that it might be in a sleeping condition by night—dry and well aired. But, instead of this, Ann and Hannah had "dilly-dallied" the whole day over cleaning the paint, and now the floor was not even washed up. My poor wife was in a sad way about it; and I am sure that I felt uncomfortable enough. Afraid to sleep in a damp chamber, we put two sofas together in the parlour, and passed the night there.

The morning rose cloudily enough. I understood matters clearly. If Mrs. Sunderland had hired a couple of women for two or three days to do the cleaning, and got a man to shake the carpets, nothing would have been heard about the sulkiness of John or the notice to quit of cook and chambermaid. Putting upon them the task of house-cleaning was considered an imposition, and they were not disposed to stand it.

"I shall not be home to dinner to-day," I said, as I rose from the breakfast-table. "As you are all in so much confusion, and you have to do the cooking, I prefer getting something to eat down town."

"Very well," said Mrs. Sunderland—"so much the better."

I left the house a few minutes afterwards, glad to get away. Every thing was confusion, and every face under a cloud.

"How are you getting along?" I asked, on coming home at night.

"Humph! Not getting along at all!" replied Mrs. Sunderland, in a fretful tone. "In two days, the girls might have thoroughly cleaned the house from top to bottom, and what do you think they have done? Nothing at all!"

"Nothing at all! They must have done something."

"Well, next to nothing, then. They haven't finished the front and back chambers. And what is worse, Ann has gone away sick, and Hannah is in bed with a real or pretended sick-headache."

"Oh, dear!" I ejaculated, involuntarily.

"Now a'n't things in a pretty way?"

"I think they are," I replied, and then asked, "what are you going to do?"

"I have sent John for old Jane, who helped us clean house last spring. But, as likely as not, she's at work somewhere."

Such was in fact the case, for John came in a moment after with that consoling report.

"Go and see Nancy, then," my wife said, sharply, to John, as if he were to blame for Jane's being at work.

John turned away slowly and went on his errand, evidently in not the most amiable mood in the world. It was soon ascertained that Nancy couldn't come.

"Why can't she come?" inquired my wife.

"She say's she's doing some sewing for herself, and can't go out this week," replied John.

"Go and tell her that she must come. That my house is upside down, and both the girls are sick."

But Nancy was in no mood to comply. John brought back another negative.

"Go and say to her, John, that I will not take no for an answer: that she must come. I will give her a dollar a day."

This liberal offer of a dollar a day was effective. Nancy came and went to work on the next morning Of course, Ann did not come back; and as it was Hannah's last day, she felt privileged to have more headache than was consistent with cleaning paint or scrubbing floors. The work went on, therefore, very slowly.

Saturday night found us without cook or chambermaid, and with only two rooms in order in the whole house, viz. one chamber on the second story. By great persuasion, Nancy was induced to stay during Sunday and cook for us.

An advertisement in the newspaper on Monday morning, brought us a couple of raw Irish girls, who were taken as better than nobody at all. With these new recruits, Mrs. Sunderland set about getting "things to right." Nancy plodded on, so well pleased with her wages, that she continued to get the work of one day lengthened out into two, and so managed to get a week's job.

For the whole of another precious week we were in confusion.

"How do your new girls get along?" I asked of my wife, upon whose face I had not seen a smile for ten days.

"Don't name them, Mr. Sunderland! They're not worth the powder it would take to shoot them. Lazy, ignorant, dirty, good-for-nothing creatures. I wouldn't give them house-room."

"I'm sorry to learn that. What will you do?" I said.

"Dear knows! I was so well suited in Ann and Hannah, and, to think that they should have served me so! I wouldn't have believed it of them. But they are all as destitute of feeling and principle as they can be. And John continues as sulky as a bear. He pretended to shake the carpets, but you might get a wheelbarrow-load of dirt out of them. I told him so, and the impudent fellow replied that he didn't know any thing about shaking carpets; and that it wasn't the waiter's place, any how."

"He did?"

"Yes, he did. I was on the eve of ordering him to leave the house."

"I'll save you that trouble," I said, a little warmly.

"Don't say any thing to him, if you please, Mr. Sunderland," returned my wife. "There couldn't be a better man about the house than he is, for all ordinary purposes. If we should lose him, we shall never get another half so good. I wish I'd hired a man to shake the carpets at once; they would have been much better done, and I should have had John's cheerful assistance about the house, which would have been a great deal."

That evening I overheard, accidentally, a conversation between John and the new girls, which threw some light upon the whole matter.

"John," said one of them, "what made Mrs. Sunderland's cook and chambermaid go aff and lave her right in the middle of house-clainin'?"

"Because Mrs. Sunderland, instead of hiring a woman, as every lady does, tried to put it all off upon them."

"Indade! and was that it?"

"Yes, it was. They never thought of leaving until they found they were to be imposed upon; and, to save fifty cents or a dollar, she made me shake the carpets. I never did such a thing in my life before. I think I managed to leave about as much dirt in as I shook out. But I'll leave the house before I do it again."

"So would I, John. It was a downright mane imposition, so it was. Set a waiter to shaking carpets!"

"I don't think much has been saved," remarked the waiter, "for Nancy has had a dollar a day ever since she has been here."

"Indade!"

"Yes; and besides that, Mrs. Sunderland has had to work like a dog herself. All this might have been saved, if she had hired a couple of women at sixty-two and a half cents a day for two or three days, and paid for having the carpets shaken; that's the way other people do. The house would have been set to rights in three or four days, and every thing going on like clockwork."

I heard no more. I wanted to hear no more; it was all as clear as day to me. When I related to Mrs. Sunderland what John had said, she was, at first, quite indignant. But the reasonableness of the thing soon became so apparent that she could not but acknowledge that she had acted very unwisely.

"This is another specimen of your saving at the spigot," I said, playfully.

"There, Mr. Sunderland! not a word more, if you please, of that," she returned, her cheek more flushed than usual. "It is my duty, as your wife, to dispense with prudence in your household; and if, in seeking to do so, I have run a little into extremes, I think it ill becomes you to ridicule or censure me. Dear knows! I have not sought my own ease or comfort in the matter."

"My dear, good wife," I quickly said, in a soothing voice, "I have neither meant to ridicule nor censure you; nothing was farther from my thoughts."

"You shall certainly have no cause to complain of me on this score again," she said, still a little warmly. "When next we clean house, I will take care that it shall be done by extra help altogether."

"Do so by all means, Mrs. Sunderland. Let there be, if possible, two paint-cleaners and scrubbers in every room, that the work may all be done in a day instead of a week. Take my word for it, the cost will be less; or, if double, I will cheerfully pay it for the sake of seeing 'order from chaos rise' more quickly than is wont under the ordinary system of doing things."

My wife did not just like this speech, I could see, but she bit her lips and kept silent.

In a week we were without a cook again; and months passed before we were in any thing like domestic comfort. At last my wife was fortunate enough to get Ann and Hannah back again, and then the old pleasant order of things was restored. I rather think that we shall have a different state of things at next house-cleaning time. I certainly hope so.

DOING AS OTHER PEOPLE.

"DID you notice that beautiful sofa which Mr. Hamilton has bought?" said Mrs. Foster to her husband, as they gained the street on leaving the house of a friend.

"Yes, I noticed that they had a sofa."

"It was a beauty. Oh, I wish I had one, Henry! Our parlours look so naked with nothing in them hardly, but a dozen common chairs."

"I am sure, Hannah, they are neatly carpeted, and have a pair of good tables and a looking-glass."

"But that's no kind of furniture. Everybody has a sofa now, and I'm sure we might."

"But I am not able to buy a sofa, Hannah."

"I am sure you earn as much as Mr. Hamilton does, and our family is no larger."

"I don't know how it is, then," Mr. Foster replied, thoughtfully. "We cannot afford to live in the same style that Mr. Hamilton does."

"Oh, you only think so. Certainly there can be no good reason why we may not. Nearly all of our acquaintances have handsomer things about them than we have, and I am sure that we ought to do as other people do who are no better off."

"I don't know about that, Hannah. I should not like to do altogether as some 'other people' do, of whom I could tell."

"Yes, but this is another matter."

"Well, perhaps it is. But, really, I don't think we can afford to buy a sofa."

"Oh, yes, we can. You earn twelve dollars a week, and I am sure that is good wages. We can live on eight dollars easily, and with the other four we might buy a great many nice things for our parlour during the course of the year."

"But don't you think it would be much better for us, Hannah, if we can really save four dollars a week, to put into the Savings bank, instead of spending it for what we don't want?"

"Oh, but we can put money into the Savings bank after we get a sofa. Four dollars a week comes to over two hundred dollars a year; but a beautiful sofa will not cost over forty or fifty dollars. Mrs. Hamilton says that they paid forty-five dollars for theirs, and that the cabinet-maker does not want his money for six months. We could get one like it, and save more than enough to pay for it long before the six months are out."

"Still, Hannah, we haven't saved half that sum in the past six months, or, indeed, in the whole time that has elapsed since our marriage."

"No, but we can do it easily enough if we try; eight dollars a week is plenty for us to live on. I will be as saving as I can in every thing. The children will want but very few clothes for some time to come, and you have several pairs of old pantaloons and one or two old coats that I can cut up and make for them when those they have are worn out."

"Who made Mr. Hamilton's sofa?" Mr. Foster asked, evidently moved by his wife's arguments.

"Mr. Bruce, around in Thompson street; and Mrs. Hamilton says that he had another just like hers."

"How much did you say?"

"Forty-five dollars."

"Forty-five dollars," (musingly.) "Eleven fours make forty-four. If we could save four dollars a week for a little over eleven weeks, we could pay for it."

"Yes, indeed! and we can easily save that much," Mrs. Foster said, in a very lively tone.

"You think so."

"I *know so.*"

A sigh followed this positive assertion of his wife, for Mr. Foster felt by no means so certain. But as his better half seemed confident, his own mind gradually became assured, and finally it was agreed that he should go the next day and buy a sofa on a credit of six months, if that time could be obtained on the purchase. In due time the sofa was obtained, for Mr. Foster was known to the cabinet-maker as an honest and industrious mechanic.

"Oh, is it not beautiful?" Mrs. Foster exclaimed, as the highly-polished piece of furniture was brought in, and placed in a small parlour.

"It is certainly a comfortable affair," the husband said, seating himself, and rising and falling with the spring of the seat.

For some time, Mrs. Foster enjoyed her new sofa, with a feeling of lively pleasure. About four weeks after, she called in again with her husband to spend an evening with Mr. and Mrs. Hamilton.

"How neat and even elegant they have every thing?" said Mrs. Foster, as she proceeded homeward, after their visit had been completed.

"Yes, they certainly have every thing around them very comfortable."

"And Mr. Hamilton earns no more than you do."

"No."

"How beautiful their set of cane-seat chairs looked! And how much more beautiful they are than common wooden ones like ours."

"And yet, Hannah, the latter are just as comfortable."

"Oh, no, indeed! Why, how you talk! There is no chair so pleasant as the cane-seat chair."

"But they cost a good deal."

"Only twenty-five dollars a dozen. And you

know we can save that much in about six or seven weeks."

"So then you are bent on having a set of these chairs?"

"Oh, no—not bent on it. But then I think we ought to have a set. Other people can have them, who are no better off; and I don't see any reason why we can't do as other people do."

"I don't myself see exactly how we are going to do as other people in the matter of buying a set of cane-seat chairs. One thing is certain, we have not yet saved a cent towards paying for our new sofa, and it is four weeks since it was sent home."

"Oh, but, Henry, you know that we have had to pay George's quarter-bill in that time, which was four dollars. And then we have bought a barrel of flour."

"Very true. But will there not be, every week or two, something or other to take one, or two or three, or even five dollars more than what is required for all current expenses?"

"Oh, no. Why should there be? Eight dollars a week will meet every thing."

"I could hope so, Hannah."

"I *know so,* Henry. Other people can get along on this sum, and I am sure that we can."

The husband did not feel so confident; still, he allowed his better judgment to come under her influence, and his true perceptions as to the consequences were obscured. On entering their own neat and comfortable home, for Mrs. Foster was quite a tidy housewife, they seated themselves upon the sofa, now the pet article in their house.

"How mean those chairs do look!" Mrs. Foster said, with a toss of the head and slight curl of the lip.

"They don't look so handsome, certainly, as Mr. Hamilton's; but, then, they are very good chairs of their kind."

"Of their kind! Oh, yes, of their kind; but they are not the kind that other people have."

"Yes, but who wants to live as some people live? Some have no parlour at all; not a spare-room, nor a spare-bed in the house."

"But that wouldn't suit me at all. I like to live as other people in similar circumstances live; as, for instance, the Hamiltons, who are not a bit better off than we are."

"I am sure, Hannah, that it puzzles me to tell how they live in the style that they do, on twelve dollars a week."

"It's plain enough, I think; they save three or four dollars out of their ordinary expenses, and spend that in getting comfortable things around them."

"Then, if they save money, certainly we should."

"Of course, and we can save just as they can. You will get a set of cane-seat chairs, won't you?"

"We cannot buy them now, for I have not a single dollar ahead."

"That needn't matter, you know, for you can buy just as many as you want on credit. You know half a dozen chair-makers who would be glad to sell them to you on credit."

"Don't you think it would be better for us to wait until we have saved enough to buy them with? Then there would be no danger of our not being able to pay for them."

"Oh, but we can pay for them easily enough."

"Well, if you think so," the husband said, yielding his better convictions to the persuasions of his wife.

On the next day, Mrs. Foster, by permission of her husband, went to a chair-maker with whom he was acquainted, and bought a dozen cane-seat chairs, which were to be paid for in six months. The bill amounted to twenty-four dollars. It was with no ordinary degree of pride and pleasure that she surveyed her new chairs after they had been sent home; but all at once she perceived that her parlour-carpet, which was of cotton, had become much faded, and really disgraced her new sofa and chairs.

"A'n't they beautiful!" she remarked to her husband when he came home in the evening from the shop.

"They are certainly very beautiful chairs, Hannah."

"But,"— hesitating.

"But what, Hannah?"

"But, indeed, this carpet really looks too bad."

"How looks bad, Hannah?"

"It is all worn and faded, and is nothing but a common piece of cotton carpeting at best."

"It cost me sixty cents a yard though, Hannah."

"But that is no price to pay for a good carpet. Mrs. Hamilton gave a dollar and a quarter; and I am sure that we can afford to have as good things as she can. You earn as much."

"If I do, somehow or other it does not seem to go as far," the husband replied, in a half-desponding tone.

"There is no reason why it should not. And then, not only Mr. and Mrs. Hamilton, but half a dozen others that I know of, who have elegant ingrain carpets, sofas, and cane-seat chairs, and I don't know what all, have no larger income than we have."

"I am sure I don't know how they manage—I can't get any ahead. It takes all that I can earn to buy something to eat and wear, and have enough left to pay the house-rent."

"Why, I am sure, Henry, we can live on eight dollars a week, and you can earn twelve."

"I am afraid not."

"Oh, yes, we can. I'll guaranty that our expenses shall not exceed eight dollars."

"They have exceeded it, you know."

"That was only because we did not economize properly. And the last four weeks, you know, we have had some extra expenses that do not occur more than once in three months."

Thus Mrs. Foster urged, and her husband soon yielded. The desire to do as other people did—to have things about her as other people had them, was too strong to be resisted, and obscured all ideas of prudence. Thirty yards of ingrain carpeting were bought on trust, at one dollar and twenty-five cents per yard, amounting to thirty-seven and a half dollars.

For the first time in his life, Mr. Foster found himself burdened with debt—a debt of more than one hundred dollars. This was a sum of no mean importance for a man of family, the extent of whose earnings was but twelve dollars a week, and especially for one who had a nervous shrinking from the thought of being in debt.

Various efforts were now made to reduce their weekly expenses down to the minimum standard of eight dollars. Sometimes it would seem to fall below that, but again it would swell beyond it in spite of every effort. At the expiration of the fourth month from the time the sofa was bought, they had managed, by the closest economy, to lay up twenty dollars. About this time, on returning from a visit to a friend, Mrs. Foster, who was too fond of contrasting her own condition with that of other people, said—"I am really almost ashamed to go out, sometimes, Henry. I've never had a silk dress since we were married; but other women can have them. Mrs. Jones, who called to-night where we were visiting, had a beautiful black silk, and so had Mrs. Maxwell, and their husbands are only mechanics, and earn no more than you do. Mrs. Hamilton has two silk dresses, a light one and a dark one, and has besides a beautiful Cashmere shawl and lace collars, and I don't know what all; and I haven't got any thing. I think you might get me one silk dress in your life."

"But how in the world am I to get it for you, Hannah, without the money?"

"We've got twenty dollars laid up, you know."

"Yes, I know; but I need not tell you that it is to go towards paying for the sofa, and the money will be due in two months."

"In two months! Oh, we can easily save enough in that time to pay for the sofa. Four dollars a week will be thirty-two dollars. I only want twelve for the dress, and that will leave eight out of the twenty we have now, and eight added to thirty-two will make forty. If you pay him forty, punctually, you needn't fear but that he will wait willingly enough for the other five a week or two."

"But we haven't saved four dollars a week, Hannah."

"Yes, but we can do it, and *must* do it."

"Can't you wait a little while longer, Hannah? You have done without a silk dress for a good many years, and surely you might get along still, until our things are all paid for."

But Mrs. Foster could not listen to the voice of reason. Other people had silk dresses, and she felt "mean," as she expressed it, whenever she went out anywhere. Twelve dollars were therefore expended for a black silk dress, and two more to get it made. This reduced the reserved fund of twenty dollars down to six dollars.

Week after week now passed rapidly, and in spite of every effort to save money, the wages of Mr. Foster melted away like snow in the warm sunlight. Finally, the time came when the sofa must be paid for, and there were only thirty dollars made up. But ten of this sum had to go for a month's rent, which fell due at the same time. Twenty, then, were all that Mr. Foster could raise, and the price of the sofa was forty-five dollars.

"Really, Hannah, I don't know what I shall do about this! I cannot bear the thought of not paying Mr. Bruce for his sofa on the day that the money falls due."

"But I wouldn't trouble myself about it, Henry. If you can't, you can't; and Mr. Bruce will have to do as other people do."

"How is that?"

"Wait for his money until you can give it to him He'll no doubt be glad to get twenty down and trust you for the balance."

"He has trusted already six months, and now his money is due according to contract."

"Well, it's no use to trouble yourself about it. Pay him twenty dollars and give him the four dollars a week that we save. That will soon pay him off."

"But we don't save four dollars a week."

"Yes, but we can, though, and we must."

"I am not so sure, Hannah."

"But I am. Other people, who get no more than we do, can live comfortably and buy a great many nice things; and there is no reason why we may not do the same."

This was a silencing argument. Still it was to Henry Foster a profound mystery how Mr. Hamilton and others could make an appearance so far beyond his own, and yet receive no higher wages. With a keen sensation of shame and reluctance, he proceeded to the shop of Mr. Bruce, on the day the money for the sofa was due, and thus accosted the cabinet maker:

"I regret exceedingly, Mr. Bruce, that I cannot pay you all the money that is due for the sofa that I bought from you six months ago. I have only twenty dollars now, but you shall have the rest in a few weeks."

"I regret it also, Mr. Foster," the cabinet-maker

replied, "for I have a note to pay to-morrow, and calculated on you as certainly as if I had the money in my own hands. But, we must only do the best we can. You will give me your note at thirty days for the balance, upon which I have no doubt that I can raise the money."

This was so reasonable a proposition, that Mr. Foster could not object to it, and accordingly gave his note for twenty-five dollars at the time proposed. This arrangement brought a temporary relief of mind. Four weeks, however, soon rolled round, and notwithstanding the proposed economy, ten dollars only had been saved, and that sum would be due for rent in a few days. The landlord was punctual, and Foster had not the heart to tell him that he must wait. Three days afterwards the note fell due, and there was not a dollar to meet it. The amount was only twenty-five dollars, but that was an important sum when demanded and the debtor not able to produce it. With the bank notice in his hand, Mr. Foster was driven at last to call upon the cabinet-maker.

"I am sorry, Mr. Bruce," said he, "but really, I cannot pay this note to-day."

Mr. Bruce smiled and replied—

"I have no control over it, Mr. Foster; I passed it away to Mr. Strong, the broker."

"Do you think he will give me a little more time on it?" asked the debtor.

"I am sure I do not know, Mr. Foster. Perhaps he will. You had better go and see him, any how."

Acting upon his advice, Henry Foster went, though with great reluctance, to the office of Mr. Strong.

"You have a small note of mine," said he, in a hesitating tone.

"Well?" was the quick and somewhat harsh interrogatory.

"I am not able to pay it to-day, sir."

"Then why did you give it? No man ought to give his note without a certainty of paying it when it falls due."

"I thought I would be able, and intended paying it, but I have been disappointed."

"Well. What do you want?"

"I want you to let me have a little more time."

"How much?"

"A month."

"If you will pay me three dollars, I will extend the time one month."

"Oh yes, I will do that!" said Foster, instantly, relieved by the idea of getting a whole month's respite on twenty-five dollars, for the small sum of three dollars.

"I will come in and arrange it in the course of an hour," said he, and then returned to his shop and obtained an advance on that week's wages of the amount needed. This was paid to the broker and the note renewed.

But trouble was only beginning. Twenty-four dollars, for the cane-seat chairs, became due in three days after, and the chair-maker's bill came in promptly.

"I cannot really pay this for a week or two," said Foster.

"I want money very badly, and the time upon which you bought them is up," was the reply.

"I know it is. And I regret very much that I cannot pay you, but so it is."

A pause ensued, in which the chair-maker had hard thoughts about Mr. Foster, and Mr. Foster had mortifying thoughts in relation to himself.

"Well, what is to be done?" at length asked the chair-maker, in a tone that touched acutely the feelings of Mr. Foster.

"Really I do not know. I hope that I shall be able to give it to you soon."

"How soon? Name a time."

"That is hard to do." And Foster looked thoughtful and troubled.

"Can you pay me in a month?"

"I will try."

"Will you give me your note at thirty days?"

"Certainly."

And the note was given A temporary relief of

mind followed this arrangement,—soon, however, to be succeeded by gloom and despondency.

As was to have been expected, both of the notes fell due at a time when there was no money to pay them. Here, then, was more trouble. It so happened that the last note, like the first, had been sold to Mr. Strong, the broker. The second due-day of the note given for the balance of the sofa came round first. After a good deal of apparent reluctance, the broker agreed to renew for thirty days longer, for four dollars, which sum was paid. On the second note, he seemed less willing to give an extension; but finally agreed to do so for four dollars more. To pay these two sums, and the rent which had again fallen due, Foster had to take the small amount that he had been able to save, and also get an advance of a week's wages.

Little real pleasure did he derive from his sofa, chairs, and carpet. A few months before, all had been contentment. He then owed nothing, and had no real want unsupplied. Now he knew not a moment's true enjoyment. The most he could possibly save out of his wages were two dollars a week; and at the rate he was now paying interest on his two notes, even if he should be permitted to renew them, all of that amount would be regularly consumed. The prospect was gloomy; more especially, as the carpet was soon to be paid for.

About two weeks before the time when the next

ordeal had to be passed through, Foster came home from his work one evening with a sadder face than usual.

"What do you think, Hannah?" said he. "All of poor Hamilton's things have been taken and sold for debt."

"Oh!" ejaculated Mrs. Foster, her face growing pale with instinctive fear.

"It is too true, Hannah. I am told that he is behindhand three or four hundred dollars."

"It isn't possible!"

"I have always wondered how he and several others whom we know, could afford to live as they did, and their wages no more than mine. In his case, at least, I now understand it perfectly. He has lived beyond his means."

Mrs. Foster was silent—for she felt that, through her persuasion, her husband had been induced to imitate their example and go beyond his means. For some time past, she had ceased to take the delight in her new furniture that she at first experienced. The consciousness of being in debt, and in debt with little hope of paying, preyed upon her husband's mind, and his uncomfortable state was very naturally superinduced upon her. More than once had she regretted the influence exercised by her in reference to the sofa, chairs, etc., but it was too late for regrets to be of any avail.

Time passed on, and brought the whole amount

due by Foster within the compass of three days. That amount was nearly one hundred dollars. He felt that it was utterly impossible to pay it, and even if he were to get the debt regularly renewed, the enormous interest charged by the broker would more than equal the principal within a year.

The trial at last came upon him. The rent fell due first. He had just ten dollars, and that was paid. Next came the note of twenty-five dollars. After some debate in his mind, he determined not to call upon the broker, but to let the note be protested. That consequence of course resulted. He was served with a protest—and three days after, with another. Then came the bill for carpets, and as it became known that he had suffered two notes to be protested, the demand was urgent.

The broker, however, generally did his business in a summary manner. Warrants were issued against Foster, which had to be answered.

"What shall I do now?" he asked himself. "Give security? No—that will never do. What have other people to do with my debts? I will not ask any one to go my security. I will stand or fall alone."

"Hannah, I have been warranted to-day for that sofa, and them chairs," said he.

"Warranted, Henry?" ejaculated Mrs. Foster, turning pale.

"Yes, I have been warranted! and he clenched

his teeth hard together, for it was a severe trial to his natural feelings.

Mrs. Foster gave way to tears and self-reproaches. "It is all my fault. But what shall we do, Henry?"

"*We must do as other people do,*" replied Henry.

"And how is that?"

"Sell off our things and pay our debts! You were anxious to do as other people, and this is what other people do, who, like us, have been so foolish as to live beyond their means."

Mrs. Foster did not reply, but she felt keenly the rebuke. In the course of the next week, under an execution which followed a confession of the judgment rendered against him, Henry Foster's sofa, chairs, and carpets, with his pair of tables and looking-glasses, were sold at public auction. Happily for him, they brought just enough to pay off the claims against him, and make him a free man once more.

The old carpets were put down, and the old chairs replaced; but the tables and looking-glasses were gone. Still, Mrs. Foster's heart was lighter than it had been for some time.

"I am tired of doing as other people do," said she, with a subdued, half-sad smile, to her husband, when quiet was again restored.

"And so am I, Hannah, heartily tired. Getting fine furniture on trust, *like other people,* may be pleasant enough—but having it sold for debt, *like other people*, is not so pleasant a part of the affair."

"Not quite," was Mrs. Foster's simple response. From that time she has been a wiser woman.

WILL PEOPLE SAY?

CHAPTER I.

"But what will people say?" Mrs. Ashton asked, looking into her husband's face with a concerned expression.

"I don't know that we ought to think about what others may say," replied Mr. Ashton, thoughtfully.

"Why, how you talk, husband! I am sure it is of the first importance to avoid singularity!"

"So you always say, and yet I never can see the force of your position. People will talk about each other; and even make censorious and disparaging remarks of those who are most perfect."

"I am not so sure of that, husband. *I* never hear others remarked upon, that they do not deserve all that is said of them."

"So you think, Sarah. But they would have quite a different idea of themselves."

"They would, like hundreds of others, over-estimate themselves, that is all."

"True, Sarah. And those who talk about us might say the same thing, if we found fault with what we considered the false position in which they placed us."

"I should like to know who says any harm of us," Mrs. Ashton quickly remarked, with indignant surprise.

"Some of your best and dearest friends," her husband replied, quietly.

"Who?"

"Oh, as to that, I am as wise as you."

"Then why do you speak as you do?"

"Because I am not disposed to think we are an exception to the general rule. When I hear every one else remarked upon, I can hardly suppose we are going to escape."

"But it is the follies and foibles of others that are remarked upon."

"Of course. And our follies and foibles are thrown in with the rest."

"How you do talk! But, seriously, you are not going to leave this beautiful house, for a mean, little two-story affair?"

"I should think it would be the most prudent thing we could do to get a smaller house. My business is falling off, and I shall have as much as I can do to make both ends meet this year."

"But you can easily make up the next season. Besides, if we should come down in our style of living, people would say that you were going behind-hand, and had been forced to adopt a system of retrenchment."

"Well, suppose they did! What harm would that do?"

"Do! Why, harm enough! Besides subjecting your family to unpleasant remarks and slights, you would lose your business standing, and without a fair credit, a merchant, you know, has up-hill work."

"Your last remark is far the most sensible one you have made, Sarah, and has in it much weight. I see its force plainly, and am resolved to keep a good face upon things for a while longer."

"I knew you would come into my way of thinking," said Mrs. Ashton, smiling triumphantly.

CHAPTER II.

"MR. PUNCTUAL says be kind enough to send him a check for that," remarked a lad, as he came up to the desk where Mr. Ashton sat musing, presenting, at the same time, a bill for a quarter's rent of his dwelling, amounting to two hundred and fifty dollars.

"Tell Mr. Punctual that I am a little short to-day, but will send him the check to-morrow."

"Yes, sir," replied the lad, and withdrew.

Mr. Ashton then resumed his employment of ascertaining how near his resources for the day would come to meeting the several notes and balances of borrowed money that were due.

"Five thousand dollars to pay," said he to himself, musingly, "and but five hundred in bank."

"Mr. Elder says, please send him the three hundred dollars you borrowed of him last week," said a porter from a large house up town, who had entered the counting-room unperceived.

Mr. Ashton started, as if a blow had suddenly been struck upon the desk by his side. But he recovered himself in a moment, and said with a smile,

"Very well, tell Mr. Elder that he shall have it by twelve."

The porter withdrew, and the merchant resumed his calculations.

"I am hard up at almost every place where I am in the habit of borrowing," said he. "Let me see. I wonder if I can't venture on old Humphreys for five hundred dollars. Yes, I *will* try him. I know he has it, and he won't refuse me. Well, that sum, with five hundred dollars in bank, make a thousand. Now, who shall I try next? There is Martin & Co., Jones & Milford, Todd & Kimber, and Mallonee. I must raise the balance among them somehow."

This matter settled, Mr. Ashton started out on his

money-hunting expedition. His first effort was with old Humphreys, as he called him.

"Well, Mr. Ashton, how are you this morning?" said that individual, with a pleased smile, as the other entered his counting-room. Humphreys was a merchant of the old school. Into the dashing "go-ahead" schemes of the times, he never entered. He had gotten rich in the old, cautious, straightforward way; and, in still pursuing his long adopted business policy, was adding dollar to dollar, slowly and surely.

"A pleasant day, this, Mr. Humphreys," said Ashton, in an assumed, lively, unconcerned tone.

"Pleasant indeed, Mr. Ashton! Is there any news stirring?"

"Nothing strange, I believe. How is business?"

"Oh, about as usual with me. How is it with you?"

"Rather dull. Money comes in slow these times. And, by the way, have you five hundred or a thousand dollars that you can spare for a few days?"

"I have a good deal more than that, Mr. Ashton, for which I have no present use. But whether I can loan it to you is another question."

Humphreys was a plain-spoken, or rather an eccentric man, as it was called, and Ashton knew this. He was not, therefore, at all surprised at the plain straight-forwardness of the answer.

"Yes, that is the question, Mr. Humphreys. I

am short to-day, and you would be doing me a favour by making up the amount. I can easily hand it back in a day or two."

"You own a carriage and a span of horses, do you not?" inquired old Humphreys.

"Yes," the merchant replied, a little annoyed at the question.

"How much did they cost you?"

"I paid a thousand for the carriage, and eight hundred for the horses."

"And you live in one of Millington's beautiful houses, at a thousand dollars a year, I believe?"

"Yes."

"Mr. Ashton; I don't want to offend you. But I must speak plain. A man who keeps a carriage and horses worth eighteen hundred dollars, and pays a thousand a year for rent, never ought to borrow money to pay his notes. If your ready money is short, go home and sell your carriage and horses, and supply the deficiency. And if that won't do, move into a house at three hundred dollars rent, and save seven hundred. That is sensible advice, and if you take it, it will do you more good than if I were to lend you five thousand dollars. I am a plain-spoken old man, Mr. Ashton, and you must not be offended."

If not seriously offended, certainly the money-hunter was pained and confused. He did not linger to reply, but, bowing low, hastily withdrew.

"They're hard run when they come to me, ha! ha!" said the old fellow, laughing to himself, as Ashton withdrew. "They may ruin each other if they choose, but old Humphreys stands or falls by himself."

Mr. Ashton returned to the counting-room, and took a brief pause to recover his spirits and self-possession. He then sallied out again. But by this time it was eleven o'clock, and at twelve he had promised to return Mr. Elder three hundred dollars.

"Any thing over to-day, Martin?" said he, in a lively tone, as he entered the store of Martin & Co.

"Well, I don't know, Ashton. Perhaps we can spare a little. Step back a moment, and I will see."

Mr. Ashton's heart felt lighter. After looking over his bank account, Mr. Martin said—

"I'm really very sorry, Ashton, but we have only about fifty dollars in bank. I thought we had more. But here are four hundred in uncurrent funds, averaging about two per cent. discount. You can have that sum for a couple of weeks. Perhaps you can turn it to advantage."

"That is pretty tough, but, if you can't do any better for me, I suppose I must try it."

The four hundred dollars were counted out to him, and he passed his check for the amount, dated two weeks ahead.

"Plenty of money to-day, Milford?" asked Mr. Ashton, entering the counting-room of Jones & Milford.

"Plenty as blackberries in December," was the reply.

"I want five or six hundred to-day. Can't you squeeze me out a part of it?"

"Not a dollar. We are, ourselves, short."

"Then I need not tarry here long," our borrower said, and hurried away.

"Ashton is confoundedly hard run, I'm thinking," remarked Milford to his partner.

"Yes. And I'm not at all sure that he is going to stand it long. The fact is, he is not a prudent business-man, and, besides that, makes almost too great a dash. Isn't that his carriage passing?"

"Yes. And Mrs. Ashton is in it, dressed like a queen, while her husband is running about hunting up money to pay his notes."

"Poor man! His weak desire for an establishment and vain show will, I fear, ruin him at last."

In the mean time, the subject of these remarks had turned towards his own counting-room. Arrived there, he drew a check for three hundred dollars, ante-dated one day, and then proceeded with it to the store of Mr. Elder, who had sent for his account of borrowed money.

"Here's a check dated to-morrow," said he. "You can deposit it to-day."

"Very well," replied Mr. Elder, "that will answer."

"I'm glad of it, for I am short to-day. Good morning." And Ashton hurried away to try some more of his business friends. By one o'clock, he had raised three thousand dollars. But half of it was in uncurrent funds. During the process, he had met with more than one rebuff, that touched him to the quick.

"And now what is to be done?" he asked himself despondingly. For about the space of five minutes he sat musing in silence. At length he got up slowly and deliberately, and went to his desk. From this he took a large pocket-book, and selected business notes, having over four months to run, and less than six, to the amount of two thousand five hundred dollars. With these he again sallied out, and soon found himself at the premises of an individual known as a shaver.

"I want some money to-day, Keener?" he said abruptly, as he entered. "There is the collateral," throwing down a package of notes of hand. "And let me have it quickly, for I have some borrowed money, besides notes, to pay, and must not keep my friends waiting."

"How much do you want?" inquired the broker, slowly and carefully going over the notes, and examining the endorsements.

"Two thousand dollars."

"For how long?"

"Thirty days."

"I hardly think I can spare it. And, anyhow, this security is not all of it first-rate."

"You know that it is perfectly good, Keener; and you know that you can get the money if you haven't it by you. I am hard run to-day, and must have the amount named."

"You are hard run, then?" the broker remarked, looking Ashton keenly in the face.

"Yes, I am, Keener. You have stood by me in several tight places, and you must not forsake me now."

"Well, I don't know," resumed the broker, in a deliberate tone. "I can't say that I am satisfied with some of these notes."

"They are all as good as the bank, Keener."

"If not better than most of the banks, I wouldn't give much for them."

"But I know them to be perfectly good. However, if you can't accommodate me, say so, and let me be moving."

"Well, let me see. You want it very much?"

"Indeed I do."

"To accommodate you, then, I will let you have the two thousand dollars for sixty."

"That is three per cent. a month!"

"I know it is. But consider that I am risking a good deal. The security is not all strong."

"It is perfectly good, Keener."

"I can't do better for you, Ashton. And I don't care about the operation, anyhow?"

"Hand it over then," said the merchant. The intimation ingeniously thrown in by the broker, that he was indifferent about the matter, decided him to accept the offer without further parley.

All the preliminaries settled, Mr. Ashton pocketed his two thousand dollars, less sixty, and went back to his counting-room. He then assorted his uncurrent funds, amounting to about fifteen hundred dollars, on which he had to pay a discount of forty dollars, making his loss, on that day, in discounts, one hundred dollars. His borrowed money returned, and his notes lifted, the merchant turned homeward, as his dinner-hour had arrived.

CHAPTER III.

"The fact is, Sarah, we must sell our carriage, and try to curtail a little," said Mr. Ashton, after dinner.

"Sell our carriage? Impossible!"

"We could get along once very well without a carriage, and I think we must do so again."

"But what will people say to see us coming down? If we had never owned a carriage, I would not advise you to get one, seeing business is so dull, as you say; but it will never do to give it up now. People would say that we were going to the wall, and there would be enough to try and push us there, if that were once said. Oh, no, don't think of it!"

Silenced, but not convinced that it was right to continue his present style of living, Mr. Ashton returned to his store, and sat conning over plans and projects for raising money on the next day, when the entrance of some one disturbed his train of thought.

"Good-day, Mr. Ashton," said the individual, who proved to be his landlord.

"Good-day! how do you do, Mr. Punctual?" replied the merchant, with a feeling of uneasiness.

"You have put my bill off again," said that personage, coming abruptly to the point, "and now I have come for it myself. I like promptness in dealing, and am never satisfied with any thing else. When you have lived in my house for three months, my part of the contract is fulfilled; then I look for you to fulfil yours. Do you understand?"

"Perfectly," said Mr. Ashton, turning to his desk, and filling up a check for two hundred and fifty dollars. It is true that he had no money in bank, but then the check could not be presented until the next day, and that would give him a little time.

The landlord received the check in silence, and, bowing low, departed.

took up the last note I had out in the world. No man can now say that I owe him a dollar."

"You feel very comfortable then, of course," his wife replied, smilingly.

"I do feel very comfortable; much more than I did when I sported an elegant carriage, and lived in a style of splendour beyond my ability to support."

"People can't say that we make too great a show to be honest," Mrs. Ashton remarked, good-humouredly.

"That they cannot; and, if they did, it would make but little difference, for there would be no truth in the allegation. It is the truth that people say about us, that is of most importance."

"So I felt when you explained to me your real condition, and I saw, too plainly, that there was room for the remark made."

"I certainly was in a bad way, then. Every day I had to rack my brains for the means of lifting my notes and paying my borrowed money; and when night came, I was sick and dispirited, and unfit to enjoy an hour's pleasant social intercourse. If I dreamed, it was of money, and notes, and ruin. Fifty times it has occurred that there has been but twenty minutes, or ten dollars, between me and bankruptcy; and yet I was doing a very fair business. The fortunate sale which I made of the carriage gave me fifteen hundred dollars in cash, which helped me a good deal; *it was so much money that did not have to be returned.* In a short time, we got into this little snug affair of a house, at one-fourth the rent we had been paying, and I found quarter-bills of sixty-two and a half dollars much more easily paid than those of two hundred and fifty dollars; and, besides this, our family expenses have been, quarterly, five hundred dollars less."

"Impossible, Mr. Ashton!"

"It is a fact, for I have kept, regularly, an account in my business, of all moneys paid out for other than business purposes. Our carriage-driver was a tax of three hundred dollars a year. Feed for two and sometimes three horses, extra servant-hire about a large house, and extra waste for extra servants, and the thousand expenses which such an establishment involves, swell up into no unimportant sum."

"And all this was not so much for the comfort it gave as to provide for the question—*What will people say?*" remarked Mrs. Ashton, smiling. "How vain and foolish I was!" she added, more gravely.

"All these things," resumed Mr. Ashton, "made a heavy aggregate. Over three thousand dollars, in the last year, saved from expenses, and obtained in the sale of horses and carriage, helped my business wonderfully. And besides that, when I had once commenced, from a full conviction of its necessity, a system of reform and economy, I carried it out in my store. I was more prudent and cautious in buying and selling, reduced my business more to a system, and made my calculations to rely less upon borrowing and more upon business returns. Gradually, I succeeded in reducing all my transactions to a safe and legitimate line, and now I feel the happy result of good resolutions, followed by a rigid determination to carry them out. People may talk as much as they please now; I know that no one can say I owe him a dollar."

"And you are so much happier than you were, dear husband! and I am so much happier. To do right and then rest satisfied, I feel is much better than to be anxious that others may admire or speak well of us. A single year's experience has taught me a great deal."

"We are both gainers, then," Mr. Ashton replied; "that is, we are better and wiser. May we never forget the lesson we have learned, that the true sources of happiness lie within ourselves."

IT'S ONLY A DOLLAR.

"IT'S only a dollar," said Mr. Jones, drawing the coin from his pocket, and throwing it upon the counter before which he was standing.

"And cheap enough at that," remarked the florist, sliding the dollar into his drawer. "It's one of the finest roses we have."

"It certainly is very beautiful," said Mr. Jones, as he lifted the flower and departed.

"Oh, what a beautiful rose!" exclaimed Mrs. Jones, as her husband came in. "Where did you get it!"

"I bought it from ——," was the reply.

"For how much?"

"Only a dollar."

"That was cheap."

"Yes, indeed. Cheap enough."

The rose, after receiving its meed of admiration, was placed among a collection of choice plants, and then, tea being announced, the young couple, for they had only been married about six months, sat down to partake of their quiet evening repast.

Mr. Jones was clerk in a banking institution in the city of ——, with a comfortable salary of twelve hundred dollars a year. He possessed the confidence of the officers of the bank as well as of the board of directors, and was generally esteemed by all who knew him. But he had a too common defect of character—his desires were not only in advance of his income, but he too frequently thought of little beyond their gratification. True, these desires were not of a kind usually denominated extravagant. He did not think of buying a carriage, nor even a fast-trotting horse, nor of filling his house with costly and elegant furniture. Such acts of imprudence were too palpably wrong to tempt him to their indulgence. His restless desires were like the "continual dropping" which wears away even the hardest substances. Small in their single demands, but important in the aggregate of their effects. The same disposition was manifested by his wife. Thus there was no check to the evil.

While they sat at the tea-table, on the evening just alluded to, Mrs. Jones said—

"How I should like to go to the concert to-night!"

"Would you, Julia?"

"Indeed I would. I am so fond of music."

"So am I. But can we afford to go?"

"Oh, yes," said Mrs. Jones. "The tickets are only a dollar apiece!"

"True. And it would be strange if we could not afford a couple of dollars now and then! Well, suppose you get ready as soon as tea is over, and we will go."

"I shall be so delighted!" the young wife remarked, as she took the arm of her husband, on leaving their neat and comfortable dwelling, to proceed to the concert room.

And she was delighted, for there was a rare combination of musical talent, and she had a taste that could appreciate the excellences of the different performers.

On the next morning, as they sat at breakfast, Mr. Jones said—

"And so you were very much pleased last night, Julia?"

"Pleased is too tame a word, Henry. I was delighted! It was a rich performance throughout."

"So was I. A cheap gratification at two dollars."

"Don't speak of the money, Henry. Money should not be thought of in connection with it. What are two paltry dollars, in comparison with such a feast of the soul? Can the most exquisite tones of music be estimated by the dollar's worth? No—no."

"I must confess that I feel as you do, Julia," the husband replied; and then each sat silent for a few moments, busy with newly arising thoughts.

"I saw a pair of most beautiful vases in ——'s window, yesterday, as I was passing his store," said Mrs. Jones, looking into her husband's face. "Oh, they were really exquisite!"

"Did you ask the price?"

"No. But I wish, as you pass this morning, that you would step in and see what they will cost. I should like to have them very much."

"Certainly, and if the price is not too high, I will purchase them for you."

"Oh, I should be so delighted to have them!"

Mr. Jones, on his way to the banking-house, stepped into the china-store to look at the vases. He knew them by a description which his wife had given him. They were gilt and painted china, and were really beautiful, as she had said.

"What do you ask for these vases?" he inquired, after looking at them for a few moments.

"Only five dollars," was the reply.

"Five dollars—five dollars. That is not dear."

"Dear? no indeed! It is scarcely half what they are really worth."

"But I hardly think that I can afford to give so much for a pair of vases that are of no real use," said Mr. Jones, musingly.

"The price is only five dollars, Mr. Jones, which is not going to make or break any man."

"No, that is very true. It's only five dollars

Well, you might as well send them home, for my wife has set her heart on them."

And so saying, Mr. Jones took out his pocket-book, and selected a five-dollar bill, which was paid over for the vases.

"How kind you are," said his wife, as he came in to dinner, "to buy me those beautiful vases! How rich, and, at the same time, how neat they are!"

"They are indeed beautiful. When I saw them, I could not resist the temptation."

"What did they cost?"

"Only five dollars."

"That was cheap."

"Cheap enough. They could not have been bought a year ago for less than ten dollars."

"I have been making some purchases, also," Mrs. Jones remarked, after they had admired the vases for a few minutes.

"Ah, indeed! Well—what have you bought?"

"Some woman's finery of course. I have been out shopping, and could not resist the temptation to buy several articles that I did not expect to purchase. See here."

And Mrs. Jones referred to a small pile of dry-goods that was lying on one of the pier-tables.

"Is not that a beautiful piece of linen cambric? I did not just want it now, but it was a remnant, and the storekeeper asked only a dollar for it. I shall want it. And then see this elegant little handkerchief. A'n't it a beauty? It was only a dollar."

"It is certainly very pretty."

"And I have bought you, besides," continued the happy wife, "three of the finest bandannas I have ever seen. A'n't they lovely?" displaying her purchases.

"They are, indeed, Julia. Though I am not exactly in want of them, for I have about a dozen or so now."

"Yes, but you will want them."

"So I will."

"And then they were so cheap. Only a dollar and a quarter apiece. Why, I paid for those last ones of yours, a dollar and a half, and they were not near so good."

Several other articles were displayed; this costing only half a dollar, that only a dollar, and the other only two dollars—amounting in all to ten or twelve dollars. And yet there was not one of them that was really needed. But then they cost but little, and were cheap at the prices paid.

"Oh, Harry! That is kind of you," said Mrs. Jones, on the evening of the next day, as her husband presented her with an elegant gold-mounted card-case. "I just wanted one like this. It is handsomer a great deal than Mrs. Perry's, and she thought her's a beauty."

"You think it very pretty, do you?"

"Oh, yes. How kind you are, to think of me so often. How much did you pay for it?"

"Only five dollars."

"That was cheap. Mrs. Perry's cost, she told me, seven, and I would much rather have mine."

"Yes, I think it cheap enough."

"There is another thing that I want, dear, and I wish you would get it for me."

"What is that, Julia?"

"A gold pencil-case. Will you buy me one?"

"Certainly."

Five dollars were spent on the next day for a gold pencil-case. But it was only five dollars, and not of much consideration.

"I saw one of the most beautiful japonicas to-day, that I ever laid my eyes on," said Mrs. Jones, on the same evening, after her husband had come home.

"Ah, where did you see it?"

"In the florist's window, in —— street."

"Did you ask the price?"

"No. But I wish you would go to-morrow, and if the price is not too extravagant, buy it for me."

"Certainly. We shall soon have a rare collection."

"That we will. And I am so fond of flowers!"

On the next day, Mr. Jones called to see about the japonica.

"What is the price?" he asked.

"Three dollars."

"Isn't that high?"

"Oh, no. They bring four and five sometimes. Indeed, I ought to have four for this one."

Mr. Jones paused for a moment or two, and then said mentally,

"It's beautiful; and it's only three dollars—that can't break me."

"You may send it home, Mr. ——," speaking aloud.

"Very well, Mr. Jones; it shall be sent home immediately."

The three dollars were paid, and Mr. Jones proceeded to the bank.

The aggregate of their expenditures for articles not really needed, on that and the four preceding days, was thirty-six dollars! Is it any wonder, then, that under such a system, they found themselves, at the end of the first year of their marriage, over three hundred dollars in debt? The only wonder is that they were not still further involved. And they would have been, had not Mr. Jones possessed about two hundred dollars above what was necessary to furnish their house, when they were married.

"Really," said Mr. Jones, when he became fully convinced of the fact that he owed the sum above indicated, "I cannot understand this."

"There must be some mistake, certainly," his wife replied.

"So it would seem. But I cannot discover where it lies. Our income is twelve hundred dollars a year, and I had two hundred dollars over, when we were married. Surely, we cannot have spent seventeen hundred dollars in twelve months."

"Impossible!" responded Mrs. Jones.

"It does seem impossible, Julia. But where is it gone?—for it has certainly gone somewhere."

"I am sure *I* cannot tell. We have not lived extravagantly, that is certain. Our rent is only two hundred dollars. We keep but one servant. It is all a mystery to me."

"And one just as profound to me," replied Mr. Jones.

"Is there no way by which we can reduce our expenses?" Mr. Jones remarked, after a silence of some minutes, which was to both a troubled silence.

"If there is, I for one, wish to adopt it; for, of all things, I have a horror of being in debt."

"Really, Julia, I don't see where this reduction is going to take place. We pay less for our house than is paid by two clerks in bank, that I know, who get but one thousand dollars a year. We keep but one servant, and they keep two, and each has, besides, three children to provide for, and we have none."

In vain did Mr. and Mrs. Jones search for the

cause of this strange condition of things. But an event occurred that relieved their minds from the trouble that disturbed them. One of the tellers died, and Mr. Jones was advanced to his place, and his salary increased to fifteen hundred dollars.

"I have good news to tell you, Julia," said he, with a brighter countenance than he had worn for several weeks.

"Indeed! What is it?"

"I have been promoted to the place held by Mr. Spencer."

"Oh, I am glad of that! And your salary"—

"Is fifteen hundred dollars."

"How providential this increase is!" said the wife. "I have been so troubled about being in debt, but now we will soon find all straight again."

"Yes. All will be well now."

But not having discovered the true cause of embarrassment, which remained still operative, the effect followed as a matter of course.

On the evening of the day after, while walking out with his wife, Mr. Jones stepped into a jeweller's shop, actuated by no other motive than an idle curiosity to look over the elegant and tasteful articles there displayed.

"Ah, Mr. Jones! how do you do? Good evening, Mrs. Jones! Pleasant evening, ma'am! Really, Mr. Jones, I must congratulate you! I see that you have been appointed to fill Mr. Spencer's place."

Thus ran on the jeweller, thinking meantime of his goods, and wondering if he should make a sale to the new bank-teller.

"You have some fine goods here, Mr. Darling." And Mr. Jones took a survey of the cases and shelves, all arrayed in jewels, plate, and articles of rich and costly workmanship.

"Yes, we have some very beautiful goods."

"Have you any of the new style of cameos?" Mrs. Jones asked.

"Oh, yes, ma'am. We received some to-day that really surpass any thing I have before seen."

And as Mr. Darling said this, he took from his case, one after the other, some dozen cameos of the latest styles and laid them before the delighted eyes of Mrs. Jones.

"They are very beautiful indeed! What is the price of this one?"

"Ten dollars, ma'am."

"I really should like to have one," said Mrs. Jones.

"Well, suppose you suit yourself," was the prompt reply of the husband.

"The price is only ten dollars," remarked the jeweller, in a tone half expressing contempt at the idea of so small a sum.

"Select one, Julia, if you can please yourself."

Mrs. Jones did not require a second invitation. The breastpin was chosen, and ten dollars transferred from the pocket-book of her husband to the drawer of Mr. Darling.

"Don't you want something in this line?" the jeweller now said—presenting a very pretty ladies' watch.

"Isn't that a dear little watch!" ejaculated Mrs. Jones, her eyes sparkling with delight, as she took the article named in her hand, and examined it carefully. "I must really have one, Henry, as soon as you can afford it."

"Oh, he can afford it well enough," replied Mr. Darling, with a winning smile.

"I am not so certain," the husband said musingly. "How much do you ask for it?"

"Only a hundred dollars."

"I cannot spare a hundred dollars now."

"Oh, never mind that. If you want the watch, I shall not ask for the money for the next five or six months."

"Then you must buy it for me, Henry."

"Well, if I must, I suppose I must."

"Of course you will want a handsome gold chain and swivel," the jeweller now said.

"Why, yes. I suppose I ought to have a chain," was the reply of Mrs. Jones, taking in her hand a gold chain which Mr. Darling had already produced

"This is very fine," she remarked, on examining it

"Yes, it is an elegant piece of chain."

"How much will one cost?"

"Only forty dollars. I can add that to the bill. The money is of no consequence to me now."

Of course the gold chain accompanied the watch. Before the young couple left the store of Mr. Dar ling, their bill was over two hundred dollars. A pair of fruit-baskets, with several other articles, were added to their purchases, and then they returned home, quite delighted with themselves and all the world.

On the next day, three bills were presented to Mr Jones, amounting, in all, to two hundred dollars, and the payment asked as an especial favour.

"You shall have the amount of your bill in three or four days," was the reply of Jones to each, without there being in his mind any distinct idea as to the manner in which payment was to be made. Three or four days rolled round very quickly, and the creditors came with the usual promptness of such individuals, and again asked for their money. The amounts were promptly paid. Having now charge of the money-drawer, it was the easiest thing in the world—so it occurred to him, after considering the difficulty in which he was placed—to use two hundred dollars, and put in its place a ticket with the words, "*Due cash*, $200," to be withdrawn and the money replaced when his quarter's salary should fall due. This operation once begun, it came very natural to continue it, to meet other demands for money.

The periodical time for counting the cash by the proper officers came on the very day that Jones's quarter's salary fell due. He owed the drawer three hundred and seventy-three dollars; or, within two dollars of the amount due him for the previous quarter. The ticket was taken from the drawer and the money restored. All came out right when the cash was counted, and then another quarter was commenced. But sundry unnecessary purchases, on the "It's only a dollar" principle, made during the previous three months, added to the ordinary household expenses, had caused a number of little bills to accumulate, to pay which a resort was again made to the money-drawer. Another three months rolled quickly around, and the cash was again to be counted. On referring to his memorandum of money used, he found that it bore this disturbing evidence—"*Due cash,* $500." There would be a deficiency of more than one hundred dollars, after the amount of his salary had been replaced in the drawer—and should this appear, on counting the cash, the consequence would be the inevitable loss of his situation; besides, the disgrace that would attach to his character.

Henry Jones slept but little during the night previous to the day on which the cash was to be counted. He was in a dangerous position, and he felt it most sensibly. There was but one way to save himself that he could think of, and that was to borrow one hundred and twenty-five dollars, with which to make the cash balance, and return it again after the counting process should have been gone through. But he felt a great reluctance to ask any one to loan him money. He was not in business, and received a salary all-sufficient to support his family. There was, therefore, no good reason why he should want to borrow money, and he felt that for him to ask the favour would be a ground of suspicion against him that all was not fair. Still, no other plan suggested itself, except one immediately dismissed from his mind—which was to pledge his wife's gold watch and his own for a few days. Julia knew nothing of his difficulty, and he shrank from the thought of making her acquainted with it.

On the next morning, after breakfast, Jones called upon a friend in business, and said—

"Martin, I want a hundred and twenty-five dollars until to-morrow. I have a bill to pay, and my quarter's salary is not due until then—and the person to whom I owe has a note to pay and wants the money badly. Can you do me the favour I need?"

"Certainly—certainly," responded Mr. Martin, turning to his desk and filling up a check for the desired amount.

Jones felt as if a mountain had been removed from his shoulder, as he left his friend's store with the check in his hand. The falsehood he had uttered so deliberately did not cost him a thought. The regular periodical business of counting the cash took place, and all was found to be right.

On the next day, a small slip of paper was laid in his drawer, bearing the memorandum—"*Due cash, $500.*" With this sum, he paid his jeweller's bill, which had accumulated during the six months to the round sum of three hundred dollars. One hundred and twenty-five were paid to Mr. Martin, which left him but seventy-five dollars out of the five hundred. This was, of course, soon frittered away.

"You look a little pale, Mr. Jones," said a horse-dealer to him one day, about a month after this second ordeal. "I am afraid you confine yourself too much."

"Perhaps I do."

"You should take a good deal of exercise, Mr. Jones."

"I know that. And I do walk for an hour every morning."

"That is no kind of exercise! You ought to ride on horseback, Mr. Jones. There is nothing like it for you men who are so closely confined in banks and stores."

"I have no doubt but that I should feel greatly the benefit of riding for an hour or two each day."

"That you would, Mr. Jones! It would make

you feel like a new man; and would certainly add ten years to your life."

"I believe I must try it, at least," said Mr. Jones, musingly. "I feel that I need healthful exercise in the open air very much."

"I have a very spirited animal, that I think would just suit you," remarked the horse-dealer. "Suppose you come round in the morning and give him a trial. I am sure you will be delighted with him."

"Perhaps I will," said Mr. Jones.

In the morning, before breakfast, sure enough, he was at the stables of the horse-dealer, and was soon mounted upon a really noble animal. He was so delighted with his ride, and so pleased with the horse, that a desire to possess him at once sprang up in his mind.

"What do you ask for this horse?" he inquired, on dismounting at the stables.

"Only a hundred and fifty dollars."

"He is certainly worth that sum."

"That he is. Why it's almost giving him away."

"If I felt able, I should really be tempted to buy him."

"Able! I know fifty men, who, if they were as able as you, would each own his horse before night. There is Gardner, whose salary is only one thousand dollars a year. He keeps a horse, and a beautiful creature it is, too. Don't talk about being able, Mr. Jones! And then just think what a benefit it would be to your health."

The tempter prevailed, and the weak young man resorted to the bank funds again. His memorandum was changed from "five hundred dollars due cash"—to six hundred and fifty dollars.

"I have bought me a horse, Julia," said he, after he had completed the purchase.

"Have you? Well, do you know what must come next?"

"No."

"I can tell you then."

"Speak out."

"You will have to buy me a horse, too. I have no idea of your riding out alone every morning, and, perhaps, every evening."

"I am sure I should like your company very much, Julia. I didn't know that you were fond of riding."

"But I am—passionately fond of it."

Seventy-five dollars were paid for a horse for Mrs. Jones. And now, every morning, and almost every evening, this thoughtless and imprudent couple might be seen dashing out into the country on their own horses.

But time passed steadily onward, and soon brought around the next examination-day. As it drew near, Mr. Jones began to feel a nervous dread of its approach, for the ticket in the drawer bore the ominous words—"*Due drawer*, $1000."

It now became necessary to enter upon some regular system of borrowing, and to have it so arranged as to prevent the possibility of a failure.

"Will you have two hundred dollars to spare day after to-morrow?" he asked of his friend Martin.

"Yes, and double the amount, if you want it."

"Thank you; but I don't care about more than two hundred; and you can have it again in a day or two."

Two other friends were called upon, in like manner, and from each a like amount was promised, all of which he received in due time and placed among the funds of the bank, to make his account good.

But it is needless to trace the course of Henry Jones step by step. For full five years he continued this system, unsuspected by any one. At the end of this time, the memorandum, which, to prevent accident, was carried in his pocket-book, read thus: "*Due cash*, $5650." And yet, during all this time, the cash of the institution was regularly counted every three months; and on each occasion the deficiency was borrowed from at least twenty different persons, not one of whom harboured the least suspicion of the affable and seemingly light-hearted teller.

But Henry Jones was far from being happy; he felt that the sword hung over his head, suspended by a single hair, and liable to fall by the agitation of a breath. Yet, so strange was the infatuation into which he had suffered himself to fall, that, instead of endeavouring to come back and live below his income, he was increasing his expenses every year. From the "It's only a dollar" principle of action, both he and his wife, now the mother of two sweet babes, had risen into the "It's only a hundred dollars" principle, and were speeding onward to their ruin with daily-increasing velocity. But nothing of the true condition of affairs did Mrs. Jones know. She vainly imagined that fifteen hundred dollars a year were sufficient to supply all the extravagances, for persons of their station in life, into which they entered so thoughtlessly. Among other acts of folly, they had given up the neat and comfortable dwelling at two hundred dollars a year, and now occupied an elegant house at five hundred dollars, attached to which was a small hot-house filled with a most choice collection of plants, many of which were rare and costly exotics. They alsc had a carriage of their own, and a boy, of course, to attend to the horses.

But with all these appendages of happiness, as was before said, Mr. Jones was far from being happy. How could he be? He was in the charmed circle of the serpent's eye, and possessed no internal power of breaking the spell and rushing away from the threatened danger; but still, over all the anxiety and fear within, he drew a veil, and assumed, as far as possible, both at home and abroad, an exterior of apparent cheerfulness.

About this time began the commercial embarrassments that were prolonged for so many years. Money became scarcer and scarcer, and it was with the utmost difficulty that Mr. Jones could obtain the required sum, even for a single day, to make good his account.

"I must have four hundred dollars to-morrow," said he, on one of these periodical occasions, stepping into the store of a friend.

"Most gladly would I accommodate you, Mr. Jones, but to-morrow I have two thousand dollars to pay, and I have not yet received the first dollar. How I am to get through, Heaven only knows."

There was that in the earnest, even anxious tone of the merchant, that left no room for Mr. Jones to urge his suit. He turned away from the store with a feeling of faintness.

"How much can you spare me to-morrow?" he asked of another business-man, who had always, heretofore, accommodated him with the utmost cheerfulness.

"Not one dollar, Jones, and I am sorry for it. I am in the tightest place that I have known for the last ten years. I have heavy payments to make to-morrow, and no resources."

"I am really sorry for it," Mr. Jones replied;

and in spite of his effort to seem in some degree unconcerned about not receiving the money for which he had asked, the merchant could not help perceiving that his countenance fell and assumed a very troubled aspect.

"So am I; but I must meet the difficulty like a man, and do my best to overcome it."

"Can you let me have a few hundred dollars to-morrow?" Mr. Jones next asked of a friend who had never hesitated to loan him any sum that he wanted.

"Indeed, Mr. Jones, I cannot. These are dreadful hard times. And I am sure that I cannot tell how I shall get through to-morrow. But, in a few days, you can have as much as you want."

Thus, wherever the teller went, he found the same complaint of scarcity and want of money. Not over one thousand dollars were tendered him, and that sum would be of no use, for it would require nearly six thousand to make good his account.

"What must I do?" was a question more easily asked than answered. And it was asked over and over again, with a vain looking for some glimmering of light in the distance. But all was darkness and uncertainty, with a distinct knowledge that destruction lurked in his path.

The morrow at length came, after a night such as no honest, or even dishonest man, could wish to pass—a night of wakefulness and fearful forebodings

Sweetly by his side slept his unconscious wife, and his still happier and innocent children. How his heart ached for them as he thought of the disgrace that would attach to his name, if a discovery of his error were made; of the change in all of his external circumstances that must be the inevitable consequence.

The hour for opening the bank at length came; and Mr. Jones was at his post, with the same cheerful air and kind manner that had gained for him the respect and regard of both the officers and customers of the institution. And yet, with all this assumed exterior, there was a terrible feeling within, for there had occurred to his mind no device by which he could put off the evil day. Once the thought occurred to him to state openly and fully his case to the committee of examination, before the process of counting the cash should be entered upon. But this was instantly rejected, with the mental ejaculation—

"It cannot—it must not be known!"

All through the day, while his hands were busy in receiving and paying out money, his mind was intent on devising some plan of relief from the dreadful dilemma into which he had fallen. Once a gleam of hope shot suddenly across his mind, but it quickly faded away, and left the darkness still more gloomy and intense. Like the darkness of Egypt—it could be felt. That hope came thus. A check for six thousand dollars was presented, and he paid out, in mistake, six hundred. The lad who offered the check, rolled up the money without counting it, and glided quickly from the bank. As the teller was dropping the check into one of the compartments of his money-drawer, his eye detected the error. His recollection of paying but six hundred dollars was clear and distinct.

"Now I am safe!" was the sudden inward exclamation, while a thrill of joy ran through every nerve and fibre of his body.

"That would be wilful and premeditated dishonesty," a voice seemed to whisper in his ear.

"But I can make it good hereafter, in a way that need involve no disclosure. And the firm is rich and will not be put to inconvenience in consequence."

"Don't do it," urged the opposing, and better spirit within him.

"But I shall be ruined if I do not."

"And ruined tenfold if you do," was the internal earnest objection.

"What *shall* I do!" the poor man uttered almost audibly. And then started, lest his words had passed to the ear of some one standing by.

"Act honestly as far as you can, and await the result of your culpable folly," said the inward whisper.

"You have made a mistake, sir," said the principal of the firm whose check of six thousand dollars had been paid with six hundred, coming up to the counter, while the struggle in the young man's mind was undecided. That was the trying moment, and the decision had to be made instantly. The struggle was, as it had of necessity to be, brief.

"I discovered the mistake, sir, as soon as your lad left," the teller replied with a smile, as he counted out the balance of the check.

"I am greatly obliged to you, sir," said the merchant, as he received the money. "Some tellers correct no mistakes."

"Right is right," responded Mr. Jones mechanically, while his own voice sounded to his ear hollow and despairing.

The merchant bowed and left the counter, and hope, that had glimmered for a moment with a lurid light, faded away into darkness.

Steadily the hours rolled away, and at last the clock struck three, and the doors of the bank were closed. The committee were already in waiting to make their periodical examination. All that remained was for Mr. Jones to enter up his checks and notes, strike his balance, and present his account. As he proceeded to do this, he seemed to be reeling about instead of standing still, and had it not been for the mechanical habit that he had acquired, it would have been impossible for him to have proceeded with any degree of correctness.

He had not proceeded far in the labour before his eye rested upon the six thousand dollar check.

"This might have saved me," he murmured, pausing in his work.

"And it *shall* save me!" he added with inward vehemence. "It *shall* save me!"

His balance was at length struck, and the periodical counting took place. All appeared right, and the committee separated.

"Mr. Jones," said the cashier to the teller, after the president and the two directors, who had formed, with the cashier, the committee, had withdrawn. "There seems to be a little error here," laying his hand upon the entries of the day.

The heart of Mr. Jones gave a strong bound, and then its motion sank into low and tremulous pulsations, while his face grew instantly pale.

"Where, sir?" he asked, in a low tone, scarcely above a whisper.

"Here," said the cashier, laying his finger first upon the charge of a check for $6000—and then upon a similar charge, in another part of the day's operations—"Melwyn's check appears to be charged twice, for I only observed, in running my eye over the checks, but one drawn by them." And the cashier looked Jones steadily in the face. The eyes of the latter fell under the searching expression; and as they did so, his face grew deadly pale, for he felt conscious that his defalcation would now come to light. A brief pause followed, when the cashier said, in a tone that had something of kindness in it—

"Come into my room, in a few minutes, Mr. Jones," and then, himself retired to the place he had indicated.

Thither he was soon followed by the teller.

"Sit down, Mr. Jones," the cashier said.

And the teller sat down. But the very chair in which he seated himself seemed as if on fire.

"I am afraid, Mr. Jones, that all is not right," the cashier began, "and I am exceedingly pained to find myself obliged to express such a thought."

There was something of kindness and concern in the tones of the cashier's voice, and as the heart of the latter melted down, a gleam of hope seemed to glance before him.

"All is not right, sir!" he said, with one appealing glance, and covering his face with his hands, gave way to tears.

To this succeeded a full confession, by the teller, of his difficulties, and the nature and extent of his defalcation.

"But how is it possible, Mr. Jones, that you could become so embarrassed?" the cashier asked.

"I can hardly answer that question to myself," the teller replied—"I have not gambled, nor bought lottery tickets. All has gone in the maintenance of my family."

"Then you must have lived very extravagantly, Mr. Jones; for, with a larger family than yours, my expenses are not over eighteen hundred dollars a year."

"I believe I have, sir—and there, no doubt, is the secret of my embarrassment. I never intended to wrong the bank. But I was thoughtless and extravagant. But, do not expose me! I was not dishonest in my intentions—and will not abuse your confidence, if you will again favour me with it."

"But how can I help exposing you, Mr. Jones. Are you not a defaulter to the amount of six thousand dollars?"

"True, sir! But I will repay that, gradually. I will live on half of my salary, until the other half makes good the loss. Oh, sir! think of my wife and children, and spare us the disgrace and ruin!" And the teller clasped his hands, and looked up, imploringly, into the cashier's face.

The latter was moved. But his position involved duties that could not be sacrificed to feelings.

"How can I depend upon you, Mr. Jones?" said he, after a long silence. "Once you have deceived me—how can I trust you again? What security have I that you will not again be led astray?"

"Oh, sir, the reflections of this dreadful hour will be your security—this dreadful hour, in which I stand trembling on the brink of infamy and utter ruin!"

"Go home, Mr. Jones," said the cashier, after a silence of full five minutes, in which he strove in vain to decide his course of action. "Go home, and give me time to think. By to-morrow morning I will decide what it is right for me to do."

"Oh, sir, do not keep me so long in suspense! It will kill me."

"I cannot decide before," the cashier said gravely. "And now, go home, sir, and be prepared for the worst, for I cannot tell what will be the result of my deliberations."

We will not attempt to portray the feelings of Mr. Jones during the dreadful night that followed—nor those of his wife, to whom he told all as soon as he returned home.

On the next morning he went early to the bank, in a state of intense anxiety. The cashier met him as soon as he entered, and then the two retired to the cashier's private room. Poor Jones felt like a criminal on his way to the gallows, with one faint hope in his mind of a reprieve—a hope more truly painful than the certainty that there was no escape.

"Sit down, Mr. Jones," said the cashier, solemnly, and Mr. Jones sat down.

A silence of many moments ensued. The cashier's brow was clouded, and it was evident that he was undetermined how to act. His duty as a public officer prompted one course, and humanity another. At last he said, in an earnest voice—

"Mr. Jones!—can I, *dare* I trust you?"

"Oh, sir, do not hesitate! This hour of intense, almost hopeless agony, is the guarantee for my future faithfulness. Trust me, sir, and I will be true to your confidence."

"But how will you make good the deficiency in your account?"

"It will require time, sir; but I believe I can do it. My true deficiency is $5,650. There was due yesterday, and yet undrawn, a quarter's salary. I have a carriage and a pair of horses, which will bring not less than seven hundred dollars—they cost a thousand. My wife's jewellery, and my own, including watches and gold chains, we estimated last night at not less than six hundred dollars. We have been thoughtlessly extravagant in these matters. How we ever accumulated so much really worthless stuff, I can hardly tell. But we were always buying something. And then our plants and flowers would certainly bring a hundred dollars. There are among them many that are very rare and beautiful. Besides these things, we have a great deal of costly furniture, and ornaments, which we will let go. In all, I feel sanguine that I can reduce the debt I owe the bank to three thousand dollars. I have told my wife all about my present dreadful condition, and she says—'Let all go.' She is willing to come down to the poorest condition, so that I may not be exposed and ruined. Six hundred dollars a year, she is confident, will be enough for us, and she proposes that we move into the suburbs of the city, where rent will be low, and the change in our appearance not be so much noticed. In four years, at the longest, I will be able to make all straight again."

For more than a minute, the cashier mused in silence—then extending his hand, he said—

"Mr. Jones, I will trust you."

The teller burst into tears and sank upon a chair.

"What a gulf of ruin I have escaped!" he said, at length rising, and again grasping the cashier's hand.

It was on a calm summer evening, about four years after, that Mr. and Mrs. Jones sat near a window of their neat little dwelling, far in the suburbs of the large city of which they were residents. Every thing around them was neat, plain, and comfortable.

"This day I am a free man!" Mr. Jones said, after a brief pause in their conversation. "I drew my quarter's salary this morning, and after paying off the balance of my debt to the bank, have just one hundred dollars left. How narrow an escape I have made! It makes me tremble whenever I think of it."

"Oh Henry,"—and his wife leaned upon his arm and looked him tenderly in the face, while the moisture dimmed her eyes—"how glad am I to see this hour!—this hour, that I have scarcely dared hope for. We have had a hard lesson to learn, but I feel that it has been a salutary one. We shall again be happy."

"Yes, far happier than, with our former views and feelings, we could even have been under circumstances the most prosperous. I could not have believed, once, in the possibility of our being contented with every thing around us so plain as we now have it. But I find that it is not so much the external circumstances that make happiness, as the internal condition of the mind. If we look out of ourselves for happiness, as sad experience has proved, we meet only disappointment, and are in danger of becoming in circumstances that may sadden every moment of our after lives. Let us, then, never forget the past four years. They are full of lessons of wisdom."

Nor were those troubled years ever forgotten. Their lessons of prudence and economy—their thought-exciting incidents—their seasons of sad reflection, made an impression that never wore off. Mr. Jones occupied a high position of trust in the community, and none suspect that once his feet well-nigh slipped, while he tottered on the brink of ruin and infamy.

HIRING A SERVANT.

"WELL, I'll just give up at once; so there, now! It's no use to tıy any longer!" said Mrs. Parry, passionately, as she came into the parlour, where her husband sat reading, and threw herself upon the sofa.

"Why, what is the matter now, Cara?" inquired Mr. Parry in a quiet tone, for he had seen like states of excitement so often that they had ceased to disturb him.

"The matter? Why, a good deal! Sally is going away day after to-morrow, and I shall be left without a cook again. And what shall I do then? Can you tell me that?"

"Hire another," was the unmoved reply of Mr. Parry.

"Yes, it's easy enough to say 'hire another,' but saying and doing are two things. I never expect to get another as good as Sally, and *she* has been troublesome enough, dear knows!"

Mr. Parry laid aside his newspaper, folded his hands together, and assuming a resigned attitude, looked his wife in the face, with an air of composure that annoyed her exceedingly.

"You seem always to think this trouble about servants a very little matter," said she, somewhat pettishly; "I only wish you had the trial of it for awhile!"

"I have no desire, I can assure you, Cara," he replied, in a soothing voice. "I never envied you, or any other woman, the pleasures appertaining to household duties. But you must allow me to think that much of the difficulty and annoyance which is too frequently experienced, might be avoided."

"No doubt you think so. All men do. I verily believe there never was a man yet who possessed true sympathy for the peculiar trials incident to housekeeping."

"Come, come, Cara! that is a sweeping declaration," Mr. Parry replied, smiling. "I, for one, think that I feel for you in all your various and conflicting duties; and, were it in my power, would lighten every one of them. But, as I cannot do this, I cannot of course think that, in entering into them, you do right to allow them to make you unhappy."

"It is easy enough to talk, Mr. Parry; but how do you think that I or any other woman can look on unmoved and see every thing in disorder? If dinner is late, or badly cooked, you are very sure to speak about it; and how do you think I can feel easy when I see that, through the inattention of the servant, such a thing is going to happen, or feel at all pleasant after it has happened?"

This was carrying the truth right home; and Mr. Parry remembered, all at once, that at sundry times he had grumbled because dinner was not on the table promptly; and, on various occasions, because the meat was overdone or underdone, or the vegetables cold or badly cooked. He therefore sat very still, and did not reply. Mrs. Parry perceived the impression she had made, and continued:—

"Or, how do you think that I can feel otherwise than I do in prospect of just such things again, and a dozen others more annoying still? I've had trouble enough with Sally, to get her to understand how things ought to be done, and it disheartens me outright now that she is determined to go away. I don't care so much about myself, but I know how these household irregularities annoy you, and that you blame me for them, even though you don't say any thing."

Mr. Parry was silenced for the time. He saw that he was thrown completely "in the wrong," and that it would be useless to attempt then to argue himself out of his unenviable position. His wife, thus victorious, had the uninterrupted privilege, for that day, at least, of being just as unhappy as she wished, in prospect of Sally's departure and the annoyances that were to follow this event.

During that day and the next, a gloom pervaded

the household of Mrs. Parry. Sally felt more than ever anxious to be away. Once or twice the idea of remaining passed through her mind; but a sight of Mrs. Parry's overcast countenance instantly dispelled it.

On the morning of the day on which Sally was to leave, an Irish girl, who had learned, through the chambermaid, that the cook was going away, applied for the situation.

"Are you a good cook?" inquired Mrs. Parry.

"Oh, yes, ma'am; I can cook any thing."

"Where did you live last?"

"I am living in a tavern, ma'am."

"Why do you wish to leave there?"

"I don't like the place. You are so much exposed in a tavern."

"What is your name?"

"Margaret."

"Well, Margaret, you can come on trial to-morrow morning. Sally is going to stay to-night."

And so Margaret went away, promising to come back in the morning. At dinner-time, Mrs. Parry seemed a little more cheerful.

"I've engaged a cook," she said, after the meal was nearly over.

"Have you, indeed! Well, I'm glad of that, Cara. You see you've had all your trouble for nothing."

"I'm not sure of that," she replied. "It's one thing to hire a cook, and another thing to be pleased with her. She's an Irish girl, and you know that they are never very tidy about their work."

"But they are, usually, willing and teachable. Are they not?"

"Some of them are. But, then, who wants the trouble of teaching every new servant her duty? It's enough to pay them their wages."

"Still, in thus teaching them, we are doing good. And we should always be willing to take upon ourselves a little trouble, if, in doing so, we can benefit another."

"That would be too generous! I might, on your principle, be willing to do nothing else but teach ignorant servants their duty, and thus fit them to make other houses pleasant, instead of my own. For, it generally happens, when you have made one of them worth having, she knows some one with whom she would rather live than with you. There was Nancy, that didn't know how to wash a dish or cook a potato when I took her. She lived with us a year, until she could turn her hand to every thing, and then went to Mrs. Clayton's, where she has been for six years. Mrs. Clayton told me, day before yesterday, that she was the best woman she had ever had in the house, and that she would not part with her upon any consideration. And here is Sally, with whom I have had my own time. She's getting to be good for something, and now she's contented here no longer."

"That does seem a little hard, Cara. But, then, don't you feel a gratification in reflecting that, through your means, Mrs. Clayton has obtained a servant who fills her place so well as to give satisfaction to the family?"

"I can't say that I do," Mrs. Parry replied in a half positive, half hesitating tone.

"Then, if you do not," her husband said, seriously, "it is time that you began, at least, to make the effort to feel thus. The reason that we are so often made unhappy by the actions of those around us, is, because we regard our own good and our own comfort of primary importance. Any thing that disturbs these, disturbs us. But, if we desired to impart benefits as well as to receive them, we should come, as a necessary consequence, into a state of mind that could not be easily agitated. We would see, in the wrong actions and in the short-comings of others, that which affected them injuriously, as well as ourselves, and in trying to modify or correct them, we would have a reference to their good as well as to our own."

"That may all be true enough; but I am sure that I could never act from such disinterested motives. It is not in me."

"It is not in any one, naturally, to act thus, Cara But that is no reason why good principles may not be formed in us. You can at least see, I suppose, that, if all acted thus with reference to the good of others, every thing in society would move on much more pleasantly than it does."

"Oh, yes, of course. But if only a few, why, they might work their lives through for the good of others, and be no better off by it."

"A selfish idea, I see, is uppermost in your mind, Cara," her husband said kindly, and with an encouraging smile, for it was not often that he could get her to consent to talk rationally on such subjects. "The few who thus acted would not have in their minds the idea of a reward. The delight which naturally springs up in the mind from the performance of good actions to others, would be to them a much higher gratification than any thing that could be given to them as an external reward for what they had done. Let me see if I cannot make this plain to your mind. Suppose Mrs. Clayton had so thoroughly educated an ignorant servant as to make her fully acquainted with all the household duties that might be required of her; and that, after she was thus fitted for the performance of these duties, this servant left her, and finally came into your family. Do you not think that Mrs. Clayton might feel delight in the thought, that through her efforts to instruct that servant, she had acquired the ability of obtaining a comfortable home at any time, and you had the pleasure of having one in your family who lightened you of many a care, and caused your household arrangements to move on harmoniously?"

OBEDIENCE IN CHILDREN.

I WAS visiting a lady, not long since, for whom I have a particular regard. She is intelligent, vivacious, and exhibits none of those little faults that spring from inordinate self-love, and which are always so destructive of pleasant social intercourse. But she has two marked defects of character—want of order and firmness. These were seen particularly in the habits of her children. She has two little girls and a boy, children of fine dispositions, and who have a full share of their mother's spirits. As their government was not orderly, there was nothing orderly about them; and as my friend was not firm and consistent in her management, they were by no means obedient.

I was sitting in the parlour with Mrs. Carver, (that is my friend's name,) on the occasion referred to, when Johnny, a bright little fellow, who had seen some four or five summers, came rushing in quite rudely, and crying at the top of his voice,

"Mother! mother! I want some of the peaches I saw Jane put in the closet just now.'

"Why, Johnny! Is that the way for you to come into the parlour when I have company?" said Mrs. Carver, in a rebuking tone, while the colour rose to her face. "I am ashamed of you. Go and speak to Mrs. Elmwood."

But Johnny thrust both thumbs into his mouth, cast his eyes to the floor, and leaned back heavily against his mother.

"Come, sir! Go and speak to the lady, this minute. I won't have such silly actions in any little boy of mine. There, now! Go at once and speak to Mrs. Elmwood."

The mother pushed the child towards me as she said this, while he held heavily back. I reached out my hand and took his, drawing him, as I did so, towards me, and saying in an encouraging voice,

"Oh, yes; Johnny will come and speak to me, and kiss me, too."

I attempted to kiss him as I said this, but the urchin shrank back, and drew his head down upon his breast in such a way that I could not succeed in accomplishing my design.

"I declare!" exclaimed Mrs. Carver, in an impatient half-mortified voice, "if ever I saw such a set of children as mine are! They have no more breeding than if they were so many heathens. I try to teach them manners, but it's of no use."

Then speaking to the little boy, she added—

"Go out of the parlour this minute, you unman

nerly creature, you, and don't show your face here again this afternoon!"

Johnny went slowly towards the door, where he stopped, and leaning against it, with one finger in his mouth, and his head still crouched upon his breast, rolled his eyes upwards in order to see across the room, and said, sulkily—

"I want some of them peaches."

"Well, you can't have any, for being such an unmannerly boy. Peaches are for well-behaved, good children."

Johnny lingered a few minutes, swinging himself around one side of the door-frame, and then disappeared.

"The fact is, my children mortify me to death, sometimes. I can't beat good manners into them," remarked Mrs. Carver. "I see children who can behave like little men and women; but it isn't the case with mine. And I don't think it's my fault, either. I try my best to teach them to be polite and act as they ought to do. But it's no use. It seems in them to be rude and uncouth. I wash the pig, but it is a pig still. Oh, dear! I get discouraged sometimes."

"You, Johnny! Bring back them peaches!" was heard cried, at this moment, from the dining-room, by a domestic, simultaneously with which came the rapid pattering of Johnny's feet, as he descended the stairs, laughing loudly and triumphantly, while,

"Didn't I get them? Ha! ha! Didn't I get them? ha ha!" echoed through the house.

"Now isn't it too much!" ejaculated my friend. "That Johnny is the most persevering little rebel I ever saw. Nothing will prevent him from accomplishing his end. If he is of the same disposition when he gets to be a man, he'll get along in the the world, and no mistake."

"Didn't you tell him that he couldn't have any peaches?" I made free to ask, for my friend was some twenty years my junior, and permitted me to speak quite plainly to her.

"No, I don't think I did."

"Oh, yes, you said that he could not have any for being so unmannerly."

"So I did. Well, never mind. He's got them now, and I don't wish to set the house in a roar, which will be the case if I were to take them from him."

"But think, my dear Mrs. Carver," said I, "of the effect upon him of this act of disobedience."

"I hardly know which would be worse; spoiling his temper, or permitting him to be disobedient sometimes. If I were to take the peaches from him now, he wouldn't get done crying for these three hours. The fact is, I don't believe in being too strict with children, and seeing every little thing they do. I am satisfied that it has a bad effect."

"We should always see direct acts of disobedience, and never pass them over."

"If I were to do that, I would be constantly punishing my children. They never mind, unless forced to do so."

Just then, Johnny came to the parlour-door, with a peach in his hand, and exclaimed, in an exulting voice,

"Aha! I would have them! Aha!"

"You—!" and the mother started forward with a threatening look. Johnny scampered off, laughing as loud as he could.

"The saucy dog!" said Mrs. Carver, smiling. "How can I punish him? He is such an impudent rogue."

I did not like to say much to her, as I was a visitor. But I could not smile in return. To see such bad treatment of a child made me feel serious. Johnny was a fine boy; bright, playful, and generous; but his mother's want of order and consistent firmness were ruining him.

My friend talked much of her children, and I endeavoured to throw in occasionally a word of good advice, but it didn't do much good. The error in the mode of governing her children was radical. She had not laid down certain primary principles as true, and certainly to be carried out. Impulse ruled her more than reason. There were times when she did see in clear light a better course than the one she was pursuing; and then she would act upon truer principles. But these were evanescent states. They quickly passed away and gave place to old habits.

Towards evening her husband came in. He is an excellent man, but deeply immersed in business. The cares of his household he gives up entirely to his wife. He has no time to attend to the children, and does not attempt to govern them at all. How far I think him in error here, I need not say. He is accountable for his wife's bad management, almost as much as if it were his own. I do not see how any father can think more of his business than of his children, and be blameless; or how any father can, with a clear conscience, leave the sole care of rightly training up his little ones to a wife who is not qualified to give their young minds that bent which will fix them in true and orderly habits.

Mr. Carver came in towards evening, and, until tea was announced, I passed the time with him in very pleasant conversation. He found leisure to read a good deal, even of the lighter works of the day; but had not time rightly to direct the habits of his children.

When the tea-bell rang, there was the sound of scampering feet from three different parts of the house, and loud cries of delight from as many children. When we entered the tea-room, Johnny and his two sisters were already seated at the table, and one of the girls had a piece of bread on her plate, and was helping herself to butter.

"Jane!" exclaimed Mrs. Carver, in a reproving tone.

Jane finished helping herself to the butter, and then sat back in her chair, without showing any consciousness of having acted wrong.

"Give me some cake," cried Johnny, reaching his hand over the table, as we all sat down.

Mrs. Carver gave him a piece of cake, and then commenced pouring out the tea.

"I want my tea before Jane," said the spoiled urchin, in a loud voice. "Sha'n't I have mine first?"

"Oh, yes. Any thing, if you will only be quiet," returned the mother.

This I thought a fair beginning, and composed myself to look on and observe, expecting, certainly, that I should have a rare specimen of table etiquette among children. And I was not disappointed.

"Then give me some of that preserved ginger," responded Johnny.

"Come, sir, be quiet!" said the father, but he did not seem to be much in earnest. At least, the child did not regard his words as of any consequence. He certainly did not obey them.

"I want some ginger."

"Do, father, give that child some of the ginger, if it's only for peace' sake."

The ginger was accordingly supplied.

"There, now, you didn't give me my tea first," cried Johnny, as his mother handed me a cup of tea; "and you said you would."

"Johnny! If you don't take care, I will send you from the table," replied Mrs. Carver. "Now, don't let me hear another word from your head."

While his mother was saying this, Johnny was rising upon his feet, and, with his hands upon the table, leaning over, and about to reach for something that had attracted his eyes.

"Sit down, sir!" The mother spoke with some decision, but more impatience.

Johnny slowly sank back in his chair, whimpering,

"You said you'd give me my tea first, and you didn't."

"Do, Jane," remarked Mr. Carver, "give the child his tea, or we shall have no peace with him."

"Poor fellow! he's sleepy and fretful. The days are too long for him to keep up without a nap," said the mother apologetically, as she poured out a cup of milk and water, which was served to Johnny next.

"You didn't give it to me first," was the child's response to this accommodating act, drawing himself back, and pouting out his lips.

"Well, never mind, Johnny. I forgot. Drink it, that's a good child, and then this lady will tell her little boy what a fine fellow you are. You are a man. Sit up, now, like a man."

But Johnny kept his pouting look and position. Mrs. Carver proceeded to wait upon the rest of the table.

"You didn't put any sugar in my tea," said Helen, the oldest, about seven years old, in a fretful tone. "You never make my tea sweet enough."

"Helen!" and her mother looked reprovingly at her.

"You don't never do it, mother," continued the child.

Mrs. Carver added another lump of sugar to Helen's cup.

"Give me another lump," cried little Jane.

It was tossed into her cup of tea.

"There, now! I didn't want it in my tea." This was said with a snarling look and tone.

"Where did you want it, pray?"

"Why, I wanted it in my hand."

"Here, take this, then." A lump of sugar was given to Jane.

"I want a lump of sugar to eat, too," now cried out Helen. "Give me one, mother."

The request was granted. By this time, Johnny had began to recover a little from his sulky humour. He bent forward to the table, and, after putting his spoon in his tea, and before tasting it, cried out,

"You haven't sweetened my tea."

"Yes, I did, Johnny. I put a large lump into it."

"No, you didn't." He began to cry.

"I tell you I did, Johnny. Taste it."

"No, you didn't."

"Well, there! Take that." Another piece of sugar was thrown across the table. "I hope you will be quiet now."

But that was a vain expectation. Johnny put the lump of sugar into his cup, and then, in a crying voice, said,

"You gave Helen and Jane a lump of sugar to eat."

"Dear bless the children! They really seem bewitched," exclaimed Mr. Carver, in despair. "Here's a piece for you to eat, also. Now, don't let me hear another word out of your head."

In the hope of settling the impatient, exacting, fretful child for the rest of the meal, the father helped him to every thing upon the table that he said he wanted, filling his plate with double the quantity that it was possible for him to eat. This was no sooner done, and the child forced to be satisfied, than Helen broke forth, with—

"I wish, mother you would make Jane push her chair away from mine. She always crowds right up against me at the table."

"Jane, do push your chair farther off from Helen's. There is room enough." Mrs. Carver spoke fretfully.

"There, will that do!" said Jane, angrily, drawing her chair far away from that upon which Helen was seated, and getting on to the very corner of the table.

Then came importunities from the two little girls for various things. They would eat neither bread, biscuit, nor rusk, but must be helped first to the richest cake, and also to the sweetmeats. In this they were indulged, evidently for peace' sake. In about five minutes, tolerable quiet was gained, but not sufficient for pleasant conversation. There were constant interruptions and annoyances, especially from Johnny, who was in a most captious humour. Both Mr. and Mrs. Carver were worried and mortified by the conduct of their children.

"If you speak again, Helen, I will send you from the table!" the mother at length said, in a calm, determined voice.

In less than a minute, Helen's voice drowned every other one at the table.

"Helen!" said Mrs. Carver, looking steadily into the child's face, "do you remember what I said just now?"

Thus actually calling the attention of Helen to the fact that she was about breaking her word.

Helen was silent again; but only long enough for her mother to half finish a remark she had commenced making to me.

"Will you be silent, as I tell you?" stormed the mother.

There was a calm; soon, however, interrupted by a loud bawl from Johnny.

"What is the matter with you?" asked Mrs. Carver.

"Jane went and took a piece of my cake," cried the child, with open mouth, stuffed so full that the crumbs dropped out into his plate.

"Jane, give him back his cake."

"I didn't take it, mother."

"Yes, you did take it," cried Johnny, louder than before.

"I only took a teenty tawnty little piece."

"Why did you touch it at all? Go away from the table."

Jane hesitated.

"Do you hear? Go down stairs, this moment!"

Jane descended from her chair slowly, began to cry, and left the room bawling at the top of her voice. In a little while, her cry ceased, and in two minutes from the time she left, she was back again, uninvited, and in her place at the table. The only notice of this act of disobedience was—

"Don't let me see you touch any thing in Johnny's plate again! You know that he won't bear it."

Thus the meal progressed, and finally came to a conclusion. To me it was a most unpleasant scene. I think I never saw children act so rudely in my life, or appear less under parental control.

I returned to the parlour with Mr. Carver, after tea was over, leaving the mother to contend with the children until she could induce them to go away from the table. Although they had been eating steadily on from the time the tea-bell rang, they seemed, when we had concluded our meal, as little disposed as ever to quit.

"I'm afraid my wife hasn't the best government in the world," remarked the husband to me, as we reached the parlour. "I am sure, children might be taught to behave more orderly. I tell her so, sometimes; but she says, very justly, perhaps, that if I had the care of them, I would not find the task so easy a one as I imagined."

I did not like to speak in very broad terms of disapprobation of a young wife to her husband, and so I only replied in some generalities respecting the management of children. From this the subject took a turn into a more pleasant theme, which continued for about ten minutes. Then we were forced to pause from hearing a storm among the children overhead. All three were crying as loud as they could scream, and Mrs. Carver was scolding at the top of her voice. As a *finale* to the whole, Helen, Jane, and Johnny were severely spanked all round and sent to bed. This produced the desired effect—it put a quietus on them for that day.

"Well, I declare!" exclaimed Mrs. Carver, entering the parlour with a glowing face a few minutes afterwards, "if I don't have a time of it! Every night I have to go over just this scene. The children get tired out, and fretful, and then nothing can please them. I try my best to have patience, but they worry me out. They distress me to death with their contentions. There seems not to exist a particle of love between them. Each looks upon the other as a rival. It may be all my fault, but certainly I don't see it, if it is. I think of them all the time, and do my best to make them happy."

"Perhaps you do not prescribe just laws, and compel an implicit obedience to them?" I ventured to suggest.

"I hardly think it right to govern children by fixed laws. There should be exercised towards them great forbearance, and they should often be excused for faults," was my friend's reply.

"As to laws," I returned, "they should be few and plain, and founded upon right principles. To these, absolute obedience should be exacted."

"Name a law such as you approve," said Mrs. Carver.

This was putting me in rather a delicate position. But my young friends knew me well, and I could make free with them. So I replied,

"The first and most important law should be this:—prompt and unmurmuring obedience to every parental command. When the father or mother gives a direction, the child should be required unhesitatingly to obey it. On no account should he be permitted to think that there is the least possibility of disobedience without punishment."

"I hardly think there is such a law in operation here," remarked Mr. Carver, smiling, and looking at his wife.

"No, that there certainly is not. And I should like very much to see the one who could carry it out. I must confess that it is not in my power. Were I to punish for every act of disobedience, I should be at it every hour in the day."

"Perhaps," I suggested, "after a few times, they would think obedience far preferable to punishment."

"I don't know, but I doubt it. They couldn't live, if they hadn't a little of their own way. And, at any rate, I do not think it the best treatment towards children to cow them right down. I have seen such, in my time. Little, dejected-looking, spiritless creatures, afraid to speak above their breath."

"The happiest family I ever saw was the most orderly," I replied. "A child no more thought of disobeying a direction of the father or mother, than of jumping from a window."

"No doubt the parents were very happy in having a quiet house. But what of the children?"

"They were cheerful, and full of life. Not one of them showed fear or unpleasant restraint while with their parents; but only respect and affection."

"They must have been of a very different breed from mine; that's all I have to say," returned Mrs. Carver. "I'll defy any one to mould my children into such a shape. It can't be done."

I smiled incredulously, and then asked—

"Have you ever thought of the use of obedience?"

"Oh, certainly. It makes a very comfortable time for the mother, and everybody else about the house."

"No, but the use to the child himself?" I said.

"The use to the child? Why, no, I can't say that I have."

"That is the most important question, depend upon it, Mrs. Carver."

"Suppose you give us your views upon the subject," said the husband.

"With pleasure," I returned, "although my own ideas have not been as well digested as I could wish. For what purpose are children born into the world?"

"To grow up into men and women, and be happy, if they can," replied Mrs. Carver.

"Think again. Cannot you imagine some higher end?" I said.

"To go to heaven, and live there for ever," was added.

"That is coming nearer to the point, my dear friend," was my answer; "much nearer. Earth is designed to be a seminary of heaven. Every child is born with the capacity of becoming an angel. As parents, our duty is to do all in our power to further this great design; to develop this latent capacity. The state here is merely a preparatory one. That which begins at the time we leave our earthly existence is our true state, which will endure for ever. This premised, I will endeavour to show you the great use there is in exacting from children strict obedience. You can see that men and women ought to be obedient to the laws of their country?"

"Oh, yes, certainly."

"Think, now, what will be the best possible course for you to pursue, in order to so impress your children's minds with the duty of obedience to the law, that obedience will become, as it were, natural to them, when they arrive at a rational age?"

Both father and mother became thoughtful at this question. The remark of the father showed that light was breaking into his mind.

"If children," said he, "do not obey their parents, I fear that there will be very little hope of their obeying the law."

"It requires no very abstract thought to determine that," I answered. "Depend upon it, that a willingness to obey the laws of one's country is a fruit springing from seed scattered by a tenderer plant—obedience to parents. This plant takes root, grows, produces seed, and then dies. Its seed falls into the ground, becomes vitalized, springs forth, and yields a hardier plant when man becomes a rational, intelligent, and responsible being. But a still higher use is typified in this. There is to come another maturity, another withering of vegetation, another casting of seed, in the man that lives to right purpose."

I paused. My young friends were listening intently.

"Go on," said the husband.

"As I have remarked," I continued, "the child is born with the capacity of becoming an angel in heaven. But he cannot become an angel, unless, after reaching manhood, he lives in obedience to divine laws. It is not obedience to parents that takes to heaven. This is a compulsory state—a state of non-freedom. Nor is it obedience to civil law, which takes the place of parental obedience, that saves the soul, for this all can do, the wicked and the good; but it is obedience to a divine spiritual law, that elevates man into heaven. As obedience to parents gives birth to obedience to civil law, so does obedience to civil law, from a right ground, give birth to spiritual obedience—obedience to truth for the truth's sake, which elevates man into real intelligence and wisdom, which constitute an angel; for an angel is only such because he is spiritual in intelligence and wisdom from the Lord. You can see, now, the use of making children obedient; for obedience to parents forms a vessel in the mind, into which can flow obedience to civil law; and this, in turn, forms a vessel into which can flow obedience to the Lord. And, moreover, the respect, deference, and subordination in which a child is towards his father will be, mainly, the measure of his respect, deference, and subordination to the Lord. To the child, while he remains such, his father is the superior being up to whom he looks, and whose dictate he feels bound to obey. When he becomes a man, there is none above him but God. Men are his equals. No one has a right to require his service but God alone. Think, then, how important is the parental relation, and what vital consequences depend upon it!"

My words, or rather the reflections they awakened, threw a deep shade over the spirits of my friends. They both sat with their eyes upon the floor for some time, in silence. At length, with a sigh, Mr. Carver remarked,

"I am seriously afraid that we are not forming in the minds of our children, vessels for the reception of obedience either to civil or spiritual law."

"If Mrs. Elmwood's doctrine be true, I am sure we are not," was his wife's reply. "As to obedience, there is nothing of it about our children. I never saw any so perverse in this thing as they are. If they were engaged in the most interesting play, and I were to tell them to go on with it, I am sure they would stop. I have only to give a command, to inspire them with a spirit of disobedience."

"The picture is too true," the husband said, gloomily.

"You may depend upon it," I ventured to say, plainly, "that it is your own fault. If you had, from the first, required obedience, it would be remembered now, without a murmur. I never saw the child that I could not make regard my commands, if he knew I had the authority to require obedience. When a child once learns to regard all your words as spoken in earnest, he submits without a murmur."

"I am sure I speak in earnest," said Mrs. Carver.

"What I mean by 'in earnest,' is with the fixed resolution to be obeyed. A mere tone of voice is nothing. It is the way in which a child understands what you say. 'If you do that, I will skin you alive,' I heard a mother say to her child. She spoke earnestly enough. But the child didn't believe her, as was evidenced from the fact that he was engaged in doing the very thing she had forbidden him to do, not five minutes afterwards. If she had merely said to him—'You must not do that, my son,' and he had known from previous experience that he could not disobey without certain punishment, it would have been enough."

"But my mind revolts at punishment. There seems to me to be something brutal in beating children all the while."

"So there is, Mrs. Carver," I returned. "I am no more an advocate for beating children than you are. There are many ways to punish a child besides the rod. A child may be undressed and put to bed in a room by himself hours before night; or be kept from the table with the family; or punished by various privations of desired things."

"You saw how outrageously my children acted at the table to-night. How would you go about preventing a repetition of similar conduct?'

"By being rigidly obeyed in every just command."

"But that is too vague," returned Mrs. Carver. "Be more specific."

"I will try. Take that restless little Johnny of yours to begin with. To-morrow morning, I would be sure to have all three of the children with me in my chamber, or in the nursery, when the breakfast-bell rang. Then I would make them all three walk out to the breakfast-room, quietly:—you can easily do this, by taking Johnny's hand yourself, and causing Helen and Jane to walk behind you. Seat all the children yourself, with a grave face, and in a formal manner, and then take your own place. Your error is in permitting them to rush to the table before you get there. This little movement of yours will have its effect upon them, and cause them to look at you with a slight degree of expectation or wonder. No doubt, by the time you have commenced putting sugar and cream in the cups, Johnny will be calling out for something, and perhaps the other children also. But keep cool. Suffer nothing like impatience to arise. Think only of the good of your child, and how you shall best promote it. Ask, calmly, his father to help him to what he wants. This will be done. You hand him his cup of milk and water. It does not suit him, perhaps. He wants more sugar. You tell him that you have given him enough. Then he begins to cry. Ring the bell, and when a domestic appears, say, 'Johnny, you must stop crying, and drink your tea, or you will be taken from the table.' Of course, he will not stop crying. Then be sure to have him taken away, no matter how loudly he screams; and do not, by any means, let him appear at the table during the meal. The effect of this upon the other children will be good. You will have little trouble with them at that meal. At dinner-time, come with a fixed resolution to act with Johnny in a precisely similar manner. See that all again come quietly and in an orderly manner to the table. Perhaps the little fellow will try the matter over again. If he does, as you value his welfare, send him away; and continue doing it until he gives up. After that, your task will be comparatively an easy one, if you will let him see and feel, that you mean always just what you say. Persevere with him, and with all the rest, and you will have as orderly and obedient children as are to be found anywhere. You have good elements to work with."

"I see the truth of what you say, and feel its force," Mrs. Carver returned.

"Then there is but one course before you, and that is to do your duty. You cannot shrink from that without jeopardizing your own soul, and the souls of your children. Let the ground for the implantation of good seed in after-life be formed in parental obedience. Make your children know that your word is law. Lay your positive commands upon them as little as possible, but when you do so, be obeyed at all risks."

This and much more I said to my friend and her husband, especially urging him to give more thought and attention to the moral well-being of his children. When I went away, I was satisfied that my words had made a good impression.

A few weeks afterwards, I spent another afternoon and evening with my young friends. My surprise and pleasure were great at noticing a most remarkable change, for so short a time, in the children. Especially was this apparent at the tea-table. Johnny was a little restless, and seemed, as I thought, disposed to take some advantage of my presence. But his mother's eye frequently rested upon his with a steady, meaning look, and caused him to keep quiet. Towards the conclusion of the meal, he committed some impropriety, not necessary to mention—but of a kind that should always cause a child to be sent away. The bell was promptly rung, and the domestic who answered it directed to take Johnny away and put him to bed. "And now remember, Johnny, if you scream while Ellen is putting you to bed, you will not be allowed to sit at the table with us to-morrow morning," said Mrs. Carver, firmly.

Johnny was taken from the table sobbing, but he did not scream aloud. His mother looked after him earnestly. It was a hard trial for her, I could see.

"You are getting along bravely," said I, in an under tone of encouragement.

"Much better than I expected. But it is a very hard trial."

Nothing more was said on the subject during the time that we remained at the table. Helen and Jane had shown a little disposition to be unruly, but the prompt visitation made on their brother's fault completely settled them.

After tea, Mrs. Carver gave me a history of her efforts to bring about a state of order and obedience. I found that the trial had been a severe one indeed. But, from a clear sense of duty, she had persevered, and her efforts had been crowned with far more success than she could have dreamed of.

"Are your children less happy than before?"

I asked. "Has a closer discipline broken down their spirits?"

"Oh! no; not by any means. They are far happier than before. They do not quarrel as much as they did, and are not half so fretful."

"The result of order and judicious restraint," said I.

"No doubt of it. I could not have believed that a little firmness and decision on my part would have produced so great a change as has taken place. It strikes me with wonder. Not for the world would I relinquish strict discipline. It is indeed to my whole family a blessing."

I have frequently since visited my friends, socially and familiarly. She has not relaxed discipline. Her children are growing up polite, orderly, and obedient. The mother looks more cheerful, and the father takes a lively interest in his children.

THE PRODIGAL'S RETURN.

"YOU won't forget your mother, William?" Mrs. Enfield said, pushing aside the clustering locks from the fair brow of her boy, and imprinting thereon a fervent kiss.

"Forget you, dear mother! Oh, no! I cannot forget my kind, good mother. How could I ever cease to remember her and love her?"

"And yet, William," the mother added, with something sad in her tone, "it is no strange thing for a son, as he goes out into the world, and mingles in its excitements, to esteem lightly the deep affection and unchanging interest of a mother's heart. You are but twelve now, and you leave us to-morrow for college, never again, perhaps, to make one of the home-circle. New scenes, new companions, new pleasures will be yours; and, unless you guard your heart, your mother's image may grow dim therein. Then guard that heart, my boy, for your mother's sake."

Tears were in Mrs. Enfield's eyes, and her son wondered that she should feel thus and talk thus. He loved her tenderly, and could not imagine why a question of that love's continuance could stir in the heart of his mother.

"I can never forget you, mother, I can never cease to love you!" he replied, with tenderness and fervour. "I will write to you often, and think of you always. If others, as they grow up, forget their home, it cannot be so with me. How could I ever cease to love you, as I now do?"

"I will trust you, William. My heart tells me that I may trust you!" Mrs. Enfield said, in a changed tone, and again impressed her lips upon the high, white forehead of her boy.

On the next day, William Enfield left his home and his mother, and entered one of the collegiate institutes of the country, more than two hundred miles away from his homestead. A new world was, indeed, opened to him, but its wonders dimmed not by contrast the home affection. Almost every week he wrote to his father, or his mother, and his letters were full of earnest and true love of the dear friends from whom he had been separated. But he dreamed not of the deep and intense fervour of that affection which burned for him in the heart of his mother with an inextinguishable flame. Day and night she thought of him, and morning and evening prayed that no ill might harm her boy. The world she knew was full of evil, and the snare of the fowler laid in many places to catch the young and unwary. That evil thoughts and evil affections should ever rule her now innocent boy, were ideas that made her heart ache. Yet she could not conceal from herself the danger that must lurk in his path and hover over him continually.

"I often wish we had kept William at home," she said one day to her husband, a man of a strong and decided cast of mind. "We have many good schools in the city, and some of high standing. I cannot but think that it would have been much better to have paid as much regard to the keeping of his moral life unspotted, as to the providing for the high degree of mental attainments that we desired for our boy. If his affections are not wisely guided, they will mar and pervert all his intellectual attainments."

"Do not fear for him," the father replied. "I have observed his character closely, and am well convinced that it is the right course to throw him young upon the world, that he may feel its unkindness, its selfishness, its heartlessness, and learn to contend with them early. I fear less their effects upon him than the enervating influence of home to one of his gentle and affectionate nature. He is to be a man, and must be prepared to meet the world as a man, and take a man's place in it."

"You know much better than I do, no doubt," Mrs. Enfield replied, meekly; "still I cannot but have these thoughts and feelings."

"They are the weaknesses of a mother's heart;

the over-fond yearnings of an intense affection; and they are natural. Still, they must suffer violence."

"With all my anxiety for William, I must confess that one selfish feeling predominates over all the rest," Mrs. Enfield said, after a pause.

"And what is that?" asked the father.

"The anxious fear lest he should cease to love me with the tenderness that I know he now bears towards me."

"Do not give way to such thoughts. They are but active principles of unhappiness in your mind," Mr. Enfield said. "William were unworthy the name he bears, and unworthy the love of so devoted a mother, did he ever love you less than he loves you now. But this cannot be. Do not, then, give way to such vain thoughts and feelings. It is injustice to him, and injustice to yourself."

At the end of the first collegiate term, William came home, to spend three weeks with his parents and his dear little sister Florence, just completing her seventh year. He had improved much even in that short space of time. He was more manly and self-possessed; and there was about him something of the dignity of independent thought. The father saw all this with a pride that he could not conceal; the mother looked deeper, and scanned, with the penetrating insight of affection, the change that had passed upon his moral nature. That there was a change, the modulation of the first uttered word told her as plainly as if she had marked his every action for days; but its exact nature she could not tell. He did not seem to love her less; nay, she felt sure that his love was altogether unchanged.

The brief period of vacation quickly passed, and William again left his home, and with far less of reluctance than he had at first experienced. He had begun to entertain an affection for the new condition of life into which he had been thrown, and, as this affection increased, the excellence and attractiveness of home faded from his mind. During the next term, his letters, from having been weekly, fell off in frequency, and he deemed once a month often enough to write.

Mrs. Enfield noted this change with an instinctive fear. It indicated to her that home affections were being superseded by others, which might be good or evil.

Again William came back to spend a few weeks. He was now thirteen, and a fine, intelligent boy, improved in every way. Even the mother forgot her fears in her pride, as she pressed him to her heart.

And thus time wore on. Every six months, William came home and spent a few weeks with his parents, but never long enough for the mother to become familiar with and apprehend fully the changes which time and the democracy of a college life had wrought in her child. Mr. Enfield was satisfied with the rapid advancement which had been made in the various branches of education by William, and looked forward with an emotion of pride to the time when the name of his son should be distinguished and honoured in the world. He thought not of looking deeper, and, indeed, in the brief periods allowed for intercourse during the few weeks of vacation, there was too much pleasure in meeting to leave room for serious scrutiny into the principles of action which were, as a matter of course, beginning to be developed in the mind of William. Painful, indeed, were then the surprise and mortification which he experienced, when it came upon him, with the startling suddenness of a clap of thunder from a serene sky, that his boy had been expelled the institution, where he had been for six years, instead of bearing off, as he had proudly hoped, its highest honours.

A brief glance at William Enfield's college-life will explain the painful fact just alluded to. After the third year of his attendance at the literary institution where he was pursuing his studies, a fondness for social intercourse led him to become one of a club of young men whose love of fun and frolic was the annoyance of the whole faculty, as well as of the quiet inhabitants of the village in which the institution was located. He did not join them, at first, in any of their unlawful acts, but contented himself with making one of their number when these wild doings were the subjects of exulting discussion. Still, he sympathized with the reckless spirit of those in whose society he took pleasure, and hesitated to partake in their sports, as they called them, only because he feared the consequences. Thus, he consented to wrong. And let every reader lay this truth up in his heart, that, whenever he takes pleasure in seeing another do what is evil, it is a proof that he would himself do the same evil, if it came in his way, and there were no external restraints to prevent him. To delight in witnessing others commit wrong actions is an evidence that we would ourselves commit similar wrongs, were we not afraid of the loss of reputation, or something else that we value.

It was not many months, however, before William Enfield could not only join his companions in their wild sports, but enjoy them with as keen a relish as any. These consisted in annoying the other students in various ways; such as locking their room-doors and hiding the keys; or locking them in their rooms, so that they could not get out when the breakfast or supper-bell rang; destroying their books; disturbing their sleep; and a thousand other unkind acts, which no really noble-minded boy or young man will engage in, for they are acts committed at the expense of the comfort and happiness of others. Then they made it a standing rule of their club to let no professor in the institution, no matter how just and amiable his character might be, pass unmolested for a longer period than one month at a time; nor was any single law established by the faculty to remain unbroken for a longer period. Every week, too, the rules of the club said, some quiet inhabitant of the village must be disturbed. Sometimes a board would be placed over the top of a chimney, and the inmates of the house almost suffocated before the cause of the sudden smoking could be discovered. Bells were rung; signs taken down and changed; families roused in the middle of the night by hurried messages from pretended sick relations, or by fearful cries in the street. The ingenuity of some twenty young men, whose talents for this kind of work increased by exercise, was constantly on the alert for new sources of annoyance to the other students, the faculty, or the villagers. And so secretly were all these things conducted, that the effort to discover the perpetrators was in vain.

In meeting frequently to plot mischief, these young rebels were often at a loss for amusements, and, to make the time pass pleasantly, as they alleged, cards were usually introduced, and among other acquired evil habits, was added, finally, that of gambling—for the simple playing of cards for amusement was by far too spiritless an occupation for such wild young fellows. A stake had to be introduced; and the loser or winner, it was established, must yield, and take, or there would be no fun at all in the game. Of a keen and ready intellect, William Enfield soon became the leader of the club; for those of a less active mind naturally fell into a position of subordination. The love of power and influence added their incitements to the mind of the foolish young man, thus early ambitious of evil instead of good, and he was fast acquiring a position that was dangerous to any who might occupy it.

So great at last became the annoyance of this "Dare-Devil Club," as it was called, that a considerable reward was offered by the faculty for the detection and conviction of any one of the members in unlawful acts. The penalty was to be immediate expulsion from the institution. This being the case, another step was taken in evil, and that was, to swear each member, by a profane use of that holy book, the word of God, to the profoundest secrecy. And now, the rules of the club were so changed as to extend the regular periods of annoyance, and thus make the danger of detection less, for not one of them had any wish to be expelled. Gambling, in consequence, became a more frequent resort. In this, William Enfield grew more and more expert every day, and as he indulged in the delight of winning the money of his fellow-students, the generous impulses of his nature became more and more deadened, until he could take the last dollar from a poor young man who had weakly and wickedly risked the hard-earned pittance of a kind father—

sent to meet his expenses—and not feel one throb of human sympathy.

Thus, from small beginnings result important aggregates of evil. The first departure from the strict law of rectitude, though small, and, to the youth, seeming but an innocent departure, was like the first shooting up from the earth of a noxious weed, that looked as fair as the healthful plants springing around it. But, as in the one case, so in the other, a beginning had been made, and towards that beginning, as to a centre, tended, by a law of nature, the principles that were to nourish and invigorate. A germ of good is met by the affinities which like principles of good have for each other; and a germ of evil is met by the affinities of evil principles. Thus, both tend onward towards maturity by an immutable law. How great, then, the danger of giving life to the smallest thought of evil by bringing it down into action!

Let those who are just entering upon life, and are yet innocent, keep this thought ever before them. Let them beware of the first deviation. It never occurs without the quick perception of wrong, which is the best safeguard that youth can have, becoming less tender and acute. But to proceed.

William Enfield had attained the age of nearly eighteen years, and had, during that time, far surpassed any student in the institution. He spent at home the last vacation preceding his final removal from college, preparatory to entering upon some business or profession; and left with his mother's blessing upon him. His sister Florence, now grown up to a tall girl of thirteen, received her brother's parting kiss with the fond hope that soon he would return to be near her always. She dreamed not, that beneath the calm brow and polished exterior of her brother, were hid evil passions that were soon to work anguish of mind and sad estrangement. Mrs. Enfield's perceptions were all too sensitive not to discover that there was something about her son, manly, handsome, and generous as he seemed, that was not right. She was troubled, she knew not why; and often chid herself for entertaining vain fears. But no reasonings could quiet her vague and uncertain forebodings.

When William returned to college, he entered, from a brief interregnum, with a keener zest into his former reckless companionship.

"Old P——," he said, one evening, to the members of the club, alluding to the president of the institution, "has had a long respite. We must stir up his blood a little."

"We have exhausted every good trick," remarked one of the club. "Cannot you, Enfield, devise something notable, that shall make a nine-days' wonder to the whole college?"

"Yes, Enfield must do it." "He is the chap for it," went round the circle. And then a formal vote was taken that he should plan some scheme, transcending all that had yet been done, for its keen annoyance of the head of the Faculty.

"If I must, I must," he said. "My time is nearly up, and I ought to do something to make the 'Dare-Devil Club' venerate the name of their president."

On the next evening the club were assembled, but in a different room, for it was a law of their organization never to meet in the same room more than once a month. Enfield was busy in the preparation of some strange mixture, and all the rest were looking on with eager interest.

"What *is* it?" asked one.

"You shall soon see," William replied. "The old lady, Madame President, you know, is nervous, as they say. A little shock sometimes does wonders in these affections."

"Well?" inquired half a dozen of his companions, as Enfield paused.

"Wait a while, and you shall see."

And then all was curious interest in the preparations making by Enfield for the evening's frolic. He had procured a large celery-glass, upon the top of which he was arranging a small cup holding about a gill, so that by drawing upon a small cord it could be made to turn over and empty whatever it might contain into the large bell-shaped vessel below. This all ready, he fastened the apparatus to the end of a

.ong pole, and then poured a quantity of the oil of turpentine into the celery-glass.

"All ready now," he said, rising, "forward, march, for the president's quarters.

It was past eleven o'clock, and the night was exceedingly dark, when the party sallied forth, observing, as they went, a profound silence. The windows of the chamber in which the president of the institution slept were about fifteen feet from the ground, and fronted the broad college-lawn. Under these the party soon halted, when Enfield, with three or four to assist him, retired behind an angle of the building with a dark lantern, and proceeded to finish the arrangements.

"But what *are* you going to do?" asked one of the few who now attended him.

"You shall soon see," Enfield said, drawing a vial from his pocket. "This is nitric acid, of the highest power," he continued, as he proceeded to fill the small cup suspended on a pivot over the glass containing the oil of turpentine.

At once the truth flashed upon the minds of his companions, whose knowledge of chemistry made them familiar with the effect produced when these two substances are brought into contact with each other.

"I wouldn't do that," said a young man in a decided tone, straightening himself up, and looking Enfield steadily in the face.

"Why wouldn't you?" asked the latter.

"Because Mrs. P—— is in ill health, and in an exceedingly nervous condition. It might cost her her life."

"Nonsense!" exclaimed one or two; "she would be a hard subject to kill."

"But," remonstrated the first speaker, "it would be cruel to frighten any one in such a way. A strong man would be exceedingly alarmed, much more a weak woman, in ill health, with her whole nervous system out of order. Indeed, indeed, I would not do it."

"Dick Miller has grown wonderfully tender-hearted all at once," said one, sneeringly.

"I have a mother in ill health," he replied, in a tone of feeling. "I could not bear that any one should treat her with so much cruelty."

There was a brief pause after this remark, during which William Enfield thought of his own mother. Her image came up before him with a thrilling distinctness, as he had last seen her, drooping with infirmity, and starting at any sudden noise or unusual occurrence; and for a moment he wavered.

"We'll send Dick Miller home to his mamma," broke in one with a sneering laugh, and instantly the image of Enfield's mother faded from his mind, and he said, in a clear determined tone—

"All ready now."

There was no further remonstrance or opposition

and the party was soon under the window close to which slept the president and his invalid wife. The vessels containing the oil of turpentine and nitric acid were then elevated on the pole, and brought on a plane with the window; the pole on such an angle that the holder of it was at some distance from under the apparatus. When all was ready, Enfield carefully drew the cord, and the contents of the vessel containing the acid were poured upon the oil of turpentine. Instantly ensued a slight explosion, and then the whole place was lit up with a strong glare, while brilliant sparks with light explosions were emitted in all directions from the substances so suddenly ignited by coming in contact. A wild prolonged scream from within answered this mad exploit, and then the vessels were dashed to the ground and each of the party retired, precipitately and in silence, to his own room.

All that night, and for most of the ensuing day, the wife of President P. lay in nervous spasms, from which she finally recovered, with her system more shattered than ever. The whole institution was in a state of feverish excitement; and there was a united and determined effort to discover the actors in this daring and cruel outrage. And they were discovered; Enfield, among the rest, identified as the leader and publicly expelled the institution.

And now came the moment of reflection. William knew that his father would suffer a mortification of the profoundest kind at this result, and he knew also that he was stern and unrelenting to a fault. Instinctively he took the direction of home, in company with a young man from the South, who was leaving the institution under the same disgrace.

"Are you going home?" asked his friend and companion in evil deeds thus early entered into.

"I am afraid to go home, Tomkins; my father will never forgive me, and I cannot bear the distress of my too kind and good mother."

"Then what do you think of doing?"

"I do not know," was answered in a desponding tone.

"Come with me."

"Where are you going?"

"To seek my fortune. Like you, I cannot think of going home."

"How!"

"I can play a pretty good game, and so can you. There is enough to do in this line in the South and Southwest."

Thus sang the tempter. William was not altogether depraved, and, for a brief season, the struggle in his mind was powerful. But he had already consented to gamble at college, and it was more from the idea of becoming a professed gambler, that he shrank than from any instinctive virtuous horror of the vice He consented—wrote a brief but farewell letter to his father and mother and sisters, begging their forgiveness, but alleging that, since he had so disgraced himself and them, he would never see their faces again.

We will not attempt to picture the thrilling anguish that fell upon the heart of the mother as this letter followed the official announcement of the expulsion of her son, for such unfeeling and cruel conduct, from one of the oldest literary institutions in the country. We must draw a veil over it.

We cannot, in the limits to which we must confine this sketch, trace step by step the downward career of William Enfield. For a space of nearly five years, he continued a course of vicious conduct, and became known in the Southern country as a most heartless and abandoned gambler. So callous had he grown in regard to the feelings of his friends at home, that towards the close of that period, he frequently wrote to his father for money; thus keeping afresh and smarting, wounds that would not heal. No notice, however, was taken by the father; but the mother's heart was not steeled towards the son of her love. Secretly she would answer these letters, and enclose money; conjuring him, by all the love he bore her, to come home, and be to them all that he once had been. These were sometimes like arrows to his soul, but they wrought no change.

At the end of about five years after his expulsion from college, with shattered health, and a growing disgust for his profession, he went over to the island of Cuba, and there entered a corps of engineers. Fortunately, he was here thrown into contact with men of virtue and principle. Gradually his health became renovated, and, what was much better, the moral tone of his mind began to strengthen with something of that energy which is derived from good resolutions. Every day he began to think more and more of his mother. The good lessons which she had taught him in childhood would frequently come up before his mind, suddenly, and with a vividness that would startle and pain him by their contrast with the evil of his life.

One night, he was awakened by a dream, the effect of which could not be shaken off. He thought that he was at home; and that it seemed as though he had never been exiled from that home by evil actions. He sat by the side of his mother, as he had sat in former years, and listened to her voice with the same pleasure that he had listened to it in former times. But suddenly her face grew very pale, and she leaned back, faintly, in her chair. "She is dead!" exclaimed his father, bursting into the room, "and you are her murderer!" Instantly the idea of his dream changed, and he saw himself the prodigal of virtue; the blight upon the heart of her who had borne him, and nourished him, and loved him with a yearning tenderness that was unutterable. The shock awoke him. Sleep sealed not again his eyelids during the remaining dark watches of that night. All the next day he was thoughtful and serious, and, on the morning of the next, took passage in a ship bound for the United States.

It was about six weeks from the day when William Enfield left the island of Cuba, that Mr. and Mrs. Enfield, and Florence, now a beautiful young woman, were seated in their parlour. Mr. Enfield was reading, while the mother, now a drooping invalid, unable to sit up but a few hours at a time, sat in her easy-chair, her mind all absorbed in thoughts about her still dear though absent and wandering child. Every day she thought of him; nay, every hour; but now her mind was all absorbed in pondering upon his wayward life, and the mirror of her imagination pictured, with a distinctness that veiled every other object, the image of her child.

Suddenly the door was thrown open, and a young man of fine appearance, though with a sad, pale face, entered. The mother started, the father rose to his feet hastily, and Florence stood still, where she had been arranging some flowers, and looked with a strange wonder upon the sudden apparition.

"Mother! father! Behold your son! Can you, will you forgive me?" And he fell upon one knee, and covered his face with his hands, still at a distance from them.

Mr. Enfield drew himself up sternly, and turned partly away; but the poor mother, unable to rise, stretched out her hands, and murmured—

"William!—William!—oh, my boy! my boy!" while tears gushed from her eyes, and streamed upon the floor.

For a few moments, the young man remained thus, no one speaking, no one offering to touch his hand or raise him. He heard, indeed, the low, and to him sweet, forgiving murmurs of his mother's voice. But all else was to him still and stern.

"Dear father!" whispered Florence, coming to Mr. Enfield's side, and clasping his arm, "see! he is weeping. Tears come not from an unrepentant heart. Oh, father, forgive him!"

Slowly Mr. Enfield turned towards the young man still kneeling. One look sufficed to melt down his feelings. He saw the position; the tears falling like rain through his fingers; remembered his penitent words, and then nature gave way. With an impulse that he could not restrain, he sprang towards him, and lifting him up, embraced him, while his own tears mingled with those of his penitent son.

Who can tell the delight of that mother's heart, when she again entwined her arms around her boy, and did so with an assurance, which was as strong as a voice from heaven to her spirit, that her son was truly the returning prodigal!

And William Enfield did not again destroy by wrong doings the new hope thus suddenly kindled in the hearts of his parents and sister. From that hour he was all they could desire.

THE HAPPY NEW YEAR.

It is but rarely that fathers are entirely satisfied with the men chosen by their daughters for husbands; and the father who has but one daughter, is, in most cases, fated to peculiar trials in this particular. The suitor for her hand must have more than human perfection, if he pleases in every thing.

Mr. Freeland had three sons, and an only daughter. Effie was, of course, tenderly beloved by her father; the more so, as she was his youngest child, and had grown up a most lovely young woman—lovely in mind as well as person.

That Effie would, sooner or later, have a lover; and that this lover would be more to her than even her father, Mr. Freeland knew very well, or ought to have known. But, when such a thought intruded itself upon his mind, he thrust it aside with jealous displeasure. Still, for all this, young men could not help being attracted by the charming girl, nor help showing that they were so attracted. But of all the candidates for her favour, none pleased the fancy of Mr. Freeland, when thought of as the future husband of Effie—and such a thought would now and then arise.

One day, while Mr. Freeland was alone in his office, a young attorney, named Elliot, who had a few weeks before, been admitted to the bar, called in to see him. This young man was boyish in his appearance, considering his age, and had never attracted much notice from Mr. Freeland, although he had often seen him in the office of a counsellor with whom he had frequent business intercourse.

"Well, Edward," said Mr. Freeland, indifferently, and without rising, as the young man came in.

Elliot looked slightly embarrassed, and his voice was not marked by its usual steadiness, as he said, "I would like to speak a word with you, Mr. Freeland."

"Very well, take a chair—what can I do for you?"

The young man sat down, still exhibiting a want of self-possession, and some time elapsed before he spoke. Then he said, as with a sudden and forced effort, "Mr. Freeland, I am, and have been for some time, sincerely attached to your daughter, and I now ask for the privilege of addressing her."

Had a bombshell exploded in the room, or his house tumbled down over his head, the father of Effie could not have been more astounded than by this declaration.

"I wish to act honourably and above-board,"

Elliot was going on to remark, when Mr. Freeland, whose face instantly reddened, arose from his chair, and pointing to the door, said, in an angry and insulting tone, "Please to walk out of my house."

The young man did not pause for a second invitation of the kind. He possessed a nice sense of honour and had a proud spirit. The first brought him thus formally, to ask of the father the privilege of addressing his daughter, ere he had signified to her the sentiment that was in his heart; and the second caused him to shrink away from the touch of rudeness and insult. Young as he was, and even boyish in his appearance, there was a stratum of pure gold in his character, and his mind was one gifted with more than ordinary native ability. He felt that the germs of power were in him, and that sooner or later he would play his part on the world's arena. But Mr. Freeland saw only his unimposing exterior, and permitted a feeling of contempt to find a place in his mind. The presumption of asking for the hand of his daughter outraged him beyond all forbearance, and led him, as has been seen, to treat the young suitor with most unjustifiable rudeness, not to call it even by a harsher name.

Edward retreated with his mind in a perfect whirl, and left the father of Effie little less disturbed in feeling. Hiding himself in his office, he there tried to compose himself for reflection. Pride, anger, and even a feeling of revenge, were all aroused in his mind, and for a season he moved about his little room in a high state of excitement. He sat down and penned a note to Mr. Freeland, in which he reproved him for his conduct in terms that, while they were perfectly just, made him still more angry with the young presumptuous.

It so happened, that by some accident, this note dropped from the pocket of Mr. Freeland, and came into the hands of Effie, thus letting her into a secret of which she was before ignorant; for though Elliot loved her, he had not yet whispered the story in her ears. The letter was intelligible to her mind. It told of his affection and rude repulse.

The next time the young couple met in company, Elliot made it a point to avoid Effie as much as possible. But every time his eyes turned to where she was, he found her looking at him, and with an expression of tender interest on her face, that his heart did not fail to interpret aright. He correctly inferred that she had by some means learned the application he had made, and that she was by no means indifferent to the sentiment he had avowed on the occasion.

Elliot was far from being so unworthy the hand of Effie, as Mr. Freeland, deciding without reflection, had supposed. He had judged him from mere appearances, and condemned him without knowing what was in him.

Perceiving, after one or two meetings with Effie,

like the one just referred to, that so far from being indifferent to him, he occupied really the first place in her feelings, and adjudging her father as entitled, by his ungentlemanly conduct, to no further consideration or respect, Elliot yielded to the genuineness of the sentiment felt for the charming girl, and drew to her side whenever an opportunity offered, regardless whether Mr. Freeland happened to be present or not. The displeasure of Effie's father was great when he saw this, and he immediately sought, by disparaging remarks, to create in the mind of his daughter a prejudice against the presumptuous suitor. Effie heard him in silence, but with a manner that told him too plainly that his words made no impression. Then, unable to act calmly in the matter, he passionately forbade her, on pain of his strong displeasure, having any intercourse with the young man whatever.

This was folly, and Mr. Freeland ought to have known it. Such conduct only adds fuel to a flame like that enkindled in the young girl's bosom. A week did not elapse before the lovers were thrown into each other's society, and met as before. The father was present—maddened by such an entire disregard of his feelings and wishes, he took another step, marked by still greater folly than any he had yet taken in regard to the matter. He called at Elliot's office, on the next day, and threatened to cowhide him in the street if he even knew him to speak to his daughter. To this the young man replied, by ordering him peremptorily to leave his office, and in doing so, exhibited a fiery determination that, to some extent, changed the estimate which Mr. Freeland entertained of his character. A personal collision would, most likely, have taken place, had not an individual entered the office at the moment, when Mr. Freeland prudently retired.

On that very evening, young Elliot met Effie at a party, where her father and mother were present, and danced with her. Yet, for all this, Mr. Freeland did not attempt the personal violence he had threatened. It was well he did not, for the high-tempered, resolute young man, had armed himself, and, in the blindness of his anger, might have used his deadly weapon.

Thus, under most unhappy auspices, began the intimacy of Elliot and his future bride. Both were worthy of each other, and the former was in every way worthy to assume toward Mr. Freeland that relation he had sought to form in the most open and honourable manner. But a foregone conclusion in regard to the young man's character, which had its basis in a mere prejudice, closed the mind of Mr. Freeland to any thing like a calm investigation of his merits, and the indignant manner with which Elliot flung back the insult he had offered him the moment there was an opportunity of doing so, fixed his dislike of him into angry resentment.

Meantime, disregarding all opposition, the young couple met whenever opportunity offered. The very fact of opposition led the way to an early declaration of his sentiments on the part of Elliot, which were unhesitatingly responded to by Effie. A regular correspondence then commenced, and frequent meetings at the house of a mutual friend ensued. This went on for about a year; at the close of which period, Elliot removed to the city of New York, there to take part in the business of a well-established attorney, whose large practice required him to call in aid. He had met Elliot frequently, and seeing the ability that he possessed, made him highly advantageous offers, which were immediately accepted. About six months after his removal, Mr. Freeland received from him the following note:—

SIR,—My marriage with your daughter will take place on the 20th proximo. It will rest with you to say. whether the ceremony shall be performed at your house or not. Respectfully,

EDWARD ELLIOT.

Although fully aware that such an event would take place sooner or later, Mr. Freeland was almost maddened at what seemed the cool defiance of this note. Taking it in his hand, he went to his daughter, and assuming that it was sent as a gross insult, made to her a most passionate appeal on the strength of this assumption. But Effie was immovable

Could it be otherwise? She saw all that was excellent in her betrothed, and knew that in deference to her wishes and feelings, he had sent the letter to her father.

Opposition being hopeless, Mr. Freeland, for the sake of appearances, yielded to the wishes of every member of his family, all of whom saw with a clearer vision than he did, and consented that the marriage of his daughter should take place at home. Tearfully did Effie urge both her lover and father to become reconciled to each other, before the nuptial rites were solemnized. But neither was in a state to make overtures. Elliot felt that he had been grossly insulted without cause, and Mr. Freeland was not going to make any concessions to a "presumptuous, beardless boy." And so the rite was said, and the daughter passed away from the home of her father, whom she loved fondly, without his blessing on her married life.

Neither the husband nor the father of Effie, was disposed to yield a position when once taken, and this made their estrangement entire. They did not speak, nor look at each other on the occasion of the wedding; and when Elliot, on the eve of his return to New York, received from the arms of her father his weeping bride, he did so with an averted face.

Five years passed, and yet there was no reconciliation. In that time, in conjunction with his partner, Elliot had conducted three or four suits of great importance in the New York courts, to a successful issue, and in doing so, had attracted attention as a young lawyer of singular ability and great promise in his profession. He had proved, in every way, that Mr. Freeland had misjudged him, and in throwing him off with contempt, had committed one of the most serious errors of his life. A few times Effie had visited her father, for whom she had a most tender affection, but she loved her husband deeply and devotedly, and she knew how worthy he was of such love; and she could not feel like going often where his presence would be unwelcome.

But for this sad estrangement, Effie would have been one of the happiest of women. That, however, marred every pleasure, and threw across the sunshine of her life a perpetual shadow. Often she urged her husband to such a reconciliation; but on that subject, he always heard her with evidences of impatience, and she at length ceased to refer to it at all.

Ever since their children were old enough to enter into and enjoy a scene of social festivity, Mr. and Mrs. Freeland had given them a little entertainment on New Year's night. As they grew older, this entertainment took a higher character, and after the marriage of Effie's brothers, they constituted a sort of family reunion. Since Effie passed from under the paternal roof as the wife of Elliot, her place had been vacant at the annual reassembling. But, though absent, she was with the loved ones of her old home in spirit. Why he had always found Effie in tears on New Year's night, her husband could not tell. He did not know of these dear reunions, hallowed by the earliest and tenderest associations. The first time this occurred, they had a few friends to tea; missing Effie from the parlour longer than seemed proper under the circumstances, her husband sought her in her chamber, where he found her lying upon the bed weeping. Failing in the effort to rally her spirits, he was at length compelled to ask their company to excuse her for the evening, as she had become suddenly indisposed. On the next New Year's day, Effie's thoughts were again turned towards home. With a strong effort she kept up her spirits through the day, and received the complimentary calls of the season; but when evening came, she was unable longer to control her feelings, and again hid herself in her chamber to think of home and weep. It was the same on the third year, and also on the fourth. Her husband thought it very strange; though he inquired earnestly for the cause, Effie concealed it in her own bosom.

As New Year's day once more approached, Elliot thought he saw the spirit of his wife again begin to droop.

"What can it mean?" said he to himself, thoughtfully. While yet musing on the subject, accident threw in his way an open letter directed to Effie, and seeing that it was from her mother, he felt constrained to read it. It was as follows:—

"My Dear Effie:—In two weeks, New Year's night will be here again. We meet, as of old, but not with our old feelings. To me, these reunions have become inexpressibly sad—yet, for the sake of those who gather about us, then I put on a cheerful face. But I think only of you, my dear, dear absent one! And it is so with your father. After all have gone, we sit together and weep in silence. And must this be so again? Effie, my child! It seems as if I could not bear it. I am growing older, and my heart gets softer as the years press me down. And it is so with your father. I often hear him breathing your name in sleep. He was wrong towards Edward, and he knows it. But he is a proud man. I have heard him say that Edward was an ornament to his profession. Oh! if Edward would only yield a little! He should reflect that, for an only daughter, a father might well feel a jealous pride; and that, if it led him into error, it is not a sin past forgiveness. I am sure, if Edward would only make the first advance step, all would be reconciled. Ah, me! that so much unhappiness should spring from the error of a moment. We are not happy, and you cannot be. I have urged your father to write to Edward. He says nothing in reply. I sometimes hope he will do so. But, I know his spirit, and I fear he will break rather than bend.

Oh! if we could only have you with us on the coming New Year's night, how happy we should be. Your dear little Flora, you say, grows sweeter every day. Oh, how we do want to see her! When I read to your father what you said of her in your last letter, he burst into tears and left the room. If Edward will not accompany you, will you not come yourself, with dear, sweet Flora, and make us happy for once?"

The reading of this letter touched Mr. Elliot deeply, and turned his thoughts into a new channel. He now understood, fully, the reason why his young wife had been so much dispirited on every New Year's night since their marriage. A few days after reading the letter, he said to her—

"Effie, I have business in Philadelphia next week. How would you like to go on there with me, and spend a few days?"

"I should like it very much, Edward," said Effie, her face instantly brightening.

"Would you take Flora along?"

"Yes. Mother has not seen her since she was six months old."

"Very well. We will go on next Thursday morning. Friday is New Year's day, and you will thus escape the annoyance of receiving calls."

The sober face that Effie had worn for several days, was changed to one of brightness. Still, there yet remained a pressure upon her heart. She would see her father and mother, and others whom she tenderly loved, but she could not join in the annual family reunion, because, in doing so, she would have to be separated from her husband; and to that she would not consent. It was on her lips a dozen times, to urge Edward, once more, to seek to heal the breach that existed; but, ever as she came to the point, her heart failed her. Many times she thought that she would place her mother's letter in his hands; but a doubt of the result would cause her to hesitate.

At last, the Thursday of her departure came, and they started for Philadelphia, taking with them little Flora, who had nearly entered her fifth year. Effie had written to her mother that she was coming, and had given the letter to her husband to mail. From some cause, however, he had neglected doing so, or else the letter had miscarried, for, on the evening of the day on which their daughter left New York, Mr. and Mrs. Freeland sat alone, talking of her, the mother wondering why Effie had not written.

"I am almost sorry," remarked Mrs. Freeland, "that we set out to have the children at home to-morrow night, as usual. These used to be the happiest seasons; but they are so to me no longer. I lose more than half the joy experienced in seeing those who are present, for thinking of the one who is absent."

A deep sigh was the only answer made by Mr.

Freeland. He felt that he had been most to blame for the misery they had all endured for years. He had, in a moment of angry false judgment, flung from him, with biting insult, the lover of his child, and that lover, proud as himself, had indignantly resented the outrage, and up to this day there had been no reconciliation.

He sighed, and remained silent. It was hard, he thought, if he was to be punished through life with unforgiveness. And he thought, too, that if he would only make a single advance towards Edward, all might be at once and for ever reconciled. Yet he was not fully prepared for that. Edward had repelled insult with insult; and since that time had maintained a cold and repulsive exterior; and he did not see how, at his age, he could stoop to one so young.

Another deep sigh struggled up from his bosom, as his mind came to this old view of the case.

Just then, some one was admitted by the servant, and the sound of feet was heard in the hall. A moment more, and Effie entered, leading a beautiful little girl by the hand. Close behind her was Elliot, looking as calm, kind, and self-possessed, as if no angry feelings had ever found a place in his bosom. He could not have come at a more auspicious moment.

"Edward!" exclaimed old Mr. Freeland, rising quickly, and passing his daughter, that he might first offer the hand of reconciliation to her husband

"Edward! Edward!" His voice trembled—"Let us forget the unhappy past."

The young man grasped the extended hand.

"It is forgotten," said he.

"I wronged you, Edward."

"Have we not agreed to forget the past?" interrupted the young man, smiling.

At that moment, Effie threw herself, weeping tears of joy, upon the bosom of her father, murmuring—

"Oh! I am so happy!"

Little Flora was in the arms of her grandmother, and wondering what all this sudden excitement could mean, and why a lady she did not remember to have seen before, should hug her so wildly to her bosom, and half smother her with kisses.

The day that followed was, indeed, a happy New Year to all; and the reunion that then took place was the most joyful they had ever known.

So ended the strife of passion—the angry estrangement of years; the feeling, but little less than hatred, which had kept asunder those who possessed all the qualities requisite to a lasting friendship. A tornado destroys in a minute what it may take years to restore; and so it is with the tempest of passion. Let us be careful how we misjudge; and far more careful how we suffer that misjudgment to influence our actions

ORIGIN AND DESTINY.

Among those who aspired to the hand of Laura Woodville, was a young man named Percival, whose father, a poor day-labourer, had, by self-denial through many years, succeeded in giving him an education beyond what was usually acquired at that time by those in the lower walks of life. When sixteen years of age, an attorney of some eminence, who perceived in the lad more than ordinary ability, took him into his office, and raised him to the profession of law. At the time of which we write, Percival, who was twenty-five years old, had already obtained some reputation at the bar, having conducted, to a successful issue, several very important cases.

Mr. Woodville, to the hand of whose daughter, as has just been said, Percival aspired, was a merchant in rather reduced circumstances; but connected with certain old families more distinguished for aristocratic pride than virtues. This connection was the more valued in consequence of the loss of wealth through disasters in trade and the inability to keep up those external appearances which dazzle the multitude and extort a homage that is grateful to weak minds.

Laura, a beautiful and highly accomplished girl, was a favourite in all circles, and there were many among the wealthy and fashionable who, for her personal attractions alone, were ready to approach and offer the homage of a sincere affection. Among these was a young man named Allison, whose family had, in the eyes of Mr. Woodville, every thing to render a marriage connection desirable. But Laura never encouraged his advances in the least; for she felt for him a strong internal repulsion. He was wealthy, accomplished, attractive in person, and connected, both on his father's and mother's side, with some of the oldest, and, so called, "best families" in the State. These, however, were not, in her eyes, attractions sufficiently strong to induce her to overlook qualities of the heart. Already, in her contact with the world, had she been made to feel its hollowness and its selfish cruelty. For something more than mere fashionable blandishments had her heart begun to yearn. She felt that a true and virtuous friend was a treasure beyond all price.

While this state of mind was in progress, Laura met Henry Percival. A mutual regard was soon developed, which increased until it became a deep and sincere affection. In the mean time, Allison, confident from his position, became bolder in his advances, and, as a preliminary step, gave Mr. Woodville an intimation of his views. The old merchant heard him gladly, and yielded a full consent to the prosecution of his suit. But perceiving what was in the mind of the young man, Laura shrank from him, and met all his advances with a chilling reserve that was not for an instant to be misunderstood. In the mean time, Percival daily gained favour in her eyes, and was at length emboldened to declare what was in his heart. With ill-concealed pleasure, Laura referred the young man to her father. As to the issue of the reference, she had well-grounded fears.

The day that followed this declaration was one of anxious suspense to Laura. She was alone, late in the afternoon, when her father came into the room where she was sitting. She saw instantly what was in his mind; there was a cloud on his face, and she knew that he had repulsed her lover.

"Laura," said he, gravely, as he sat down by her side, "I was exceedingly surprised and pained to-day, to receive from a young upstart attorney, of whose family no one has ever heard, an offer for your hand, made, as was affirmed, with your consent. Surely this affirmation was not true?"

A deep crimson flushed the face of Laura, her eyes fell to the floor, and she exhibited signs of strong agitation.

"You may not be aware," continued Mr. Woodville,

"that Mr. Allison has also been to me with a similar application."

"Mr. Allison!" The eyes of Laura were raised quickly from the floor, and her manner exhibited the repugnance she felt. "I can never look upon Mr. Allison as more than a friend," said she, calmly.

"Laura! Has it indeed come to this?" said Mr. Woodville, really disturbed. "Will you disgrace yourself and family by a union with a vulgar upstart from the lower ranks, when an alliance so distinguished as this one is offered? Who is Percival? Where is he from? What is his origin?"

"I regard rather his destiny than his origin," replied the daughter; "for that concerns me far more nearly than the other. I shall have to tread the way my husband goes, not the way he has come. The past is past. In the future lies my happiness or misery."

"Are you beside yourself?" exclaimed the father, losing his self-command before the rational calmness of his child.

"No, father," replied Laura; "not beside myself. In the principles that govern Mr. Allison, I have no confidence; and it is a man's principles that determine the path he is to tread in life. On the other hand, I have the fullest confidence in those of Mr. Percival, and know where they will lead him. This is a matter in which I cannot look back to see from whence the person has come; every thing depends on a knowledge as to where he is going."

"Do you know," said Mr. Woodville, not giving the words of his child the smallest consideration, "that the father of this fellow, Percival, was a day-labourer in one of old Mr. Allison's manufacturing establishments? A mere day-labourer!"

"I have heard as much. Was he not an honest and honourable man?"

"Madness, girl!" ejaculated Mr. Woodville, at this question, still further losing his self-control. "Do you think that I am going to see my child, who has the blood of the P——'s, and R——'s, and W——'s in her veins, mingle it with the vile blood of a common labourer? You have been much in error if, for a moment, you have indulged the idle dream. I positively forbid all intercourse with this Percival. Do not disobey me, or the consequences to yourself will be of the saddest kind."

As her father ceased speaking, Laura arose, weeping, and left the room.

A deep calm succeeded to this sudden storm that had fallen from a summer sky. But it was a calm indicative of a heavier and more devastating storm. Laura communicated to Percival the fact of her painful interview with her father, and at the same time gave him to understand that no change in his views was to be expected, and that to seek to effect a change would only be to place himself in the way of repulse and insult. Both of these the young man had already received.

A few months later, and, fully avowing her purpose, Laura left the house of her parents and became the wife of Percival. A step like this is never taken without suffering. Sometimes it is wisely, but oftener unwisely taken; but never without pain. In this case, the pain on both sides was severe. Mr. Woodville loved his daughter tenderly, and she felt for her father a more than common attachment. But he was a proud and selfish man. The marriage of Laura not only disappointed and mortified him, but made him angry beyond all reason and self-control. In the bitterness of his feelings, he vowed never to look upon nor forgive her. It was all in vain, therefore, that his daughter sought a reconciliation; she met only a stern repulse.

Years went by, and it remained the same. Many times during that long period did Laura approach her old home; but only to be repulsed. At last, she was startled and afflicted by the sad news of her mother's death. In the sudden anguish of her feelings, she hurried to her father's house. As she stood with others who had gathered around, gazing upon the lifeless form of her dead parent, she became aware that the living one had entered the room, and, to all appearance, unconscious of her presence, was standing by her side. A tremor went through her frame. She felt faint and ready to drop to the floor.

In this season of deep affliction, might he not forgive the past? Hope sprung up within her. In the presence of the dead he could not throw her off. She laid her hand gently on his. He turned. Her tearful eyes were lifted in his face. A moment of thrilling suspense! Pride and anger conquered again. Without a sign of recognition, he turned away and left the chamber of death.

Bracing herself up with an intense struggle, Laura pressed her lips to the cold brow of her mother, and then silently retired.

During the time that intervened from his marriage up to this period, Mr. Percival had been gradually rising in the confidence, respect, and esteem of the community, and was acquiring wealth through means of a large practice at the bar. As a husband, he had proved most kind and affectionate. As a man, he was the very soul of honour. All who knew him held him in the highest regard. After the death of his wife, Mr. Woodville fell into a gloomy state of mind. His business, which had been declining for years, was becoming less and less profitable; and to increase his trouble, he found himself progressing toward embarrassment, if not bankruptcy. The man whom of all others he had wished to see the husband of his daughter, married a beautiful heiress, and was living in a style of great elegance. He met the brilliant bride occasionally, and always with an unpleasant feeling. One day, while walking with a gentleman, they passed Allison, when his companion said—

"If that man doesn't break his wife's heart within five years, I shall think she has few of woman's best and holiest feelings."

"Why do you say that?" asked Mr. Woodville, evincing much surprise.

"In the first place," replied the friend, "a man with bad principles is not the one to make a right-minded woman happy. And, in the second place, a man who regards neither virtue nor decency in his conduct is the one to make her life wretched."

"But is Allison such a man?"

"He is, to my certain knowledge. I knew him when a boy. We were schoolmates. He then gave me evidence of more than ordinary natural depravity; and from the training he has received, that depravity has been encouraged to grow. Since he became a man, I have had many opportunities of observing him closely, and I speak deliberately when I say that I hold him in exceedingly low estimation. I am personally cognisant of acts that stamp him as possessing neither honour nor, as I said before, decency; and a very long time will not, probably, elapse, before he will betray all this to the world. Men like him indulge in evil passions and selfish desires, until they lose even common prudence.'

"You astonish me," said Mr. Woodville. "I

cannot credit your words. He belongs to one of our best families."

"So called. But, judged by a true standard, I should say one of our worst families."

"Why do you say that?" asked Mr. Woodville, evincing still more surprise.

"The virtues of an individual," replied the gentleman, "make his standard of worth. The same is true of families. Decayed wood, covered with shining gold, is not so valuable as sound and polished oak. Nor is a family, raised by wealth or any external gilding into a high social position, if not possessed of virtue, half so worthy of confidence and esteem as one of less pretension but endowed with honourable principles. The father of Mr. Allison, it is well known, was a gentleman only in a Chesterfieldian sense. A more hollow-hearted man never existed. And the son is like the father; only more depraved."

Mr. Woodville was profoundly astonished. All this he might have known from personal observation, had not his eyes been so dazzled with the external brilliancy of the persons condemned, as to disqualify them for looking deeper, and perceiving the real character of what was beneath the brilliant gilding. He was astonished, though not entirely convinced. It did not seem possible that any one in the elevated position of Mr. Allison could be so base as was affirmed.

A few months later, and Mr. Woodville was surprised at the announcement that the wife of Allison had separated herself from him, and returned to her father's house. Various causes were assigned for this act, the most prominent of which was infidelity. Soon after, an application for a divorce was laid before the legislature, with such proofs of ill-treatment and shocking depravity of conduct, as procured an instant release from the marriage-contract.

By this time the proud, angry father was begining to see that he had, probably, committed an error. An emotion of thankfulness that his child was not the wife of Allison arose spontaneously in his breast; but he did not permit it to come into his deliberate thoughts, nor take the form of an uttered sentiment. Steadily the change in his outward circumstances progressed. He was growing old, and losing the ability to do business on an equality with the younger and more eager merchants around him, who were gradually drawing off his oldest and best customers. Disappointed, lonely, anxious, and depressed in spirits, the conviction that he had committed a great mistake was daily forcing itself more and more upon the mind of Mr. Woodville. When evening came, and he returned to his silent, almost deserted dwelling, his loneliness would deepen into sadness; and then, like an unbidden but not entirely unwelcome guest, the image of Laura would come before his imagination, and her low and tender voice would sound in his ears. But pride and resentment were still in his heart, and after gazing on the pensive, loving face of his child for a time, he would seek to expel the vision. She had degraded herself in marriage. Who or what was her husband? A low, vulgar fellow, raised a little above the common herd! Such, and only such, did he esteem him; and, whenever he thought of him, his resentment toward Laura came back in full force.

Thus it went on, until twelve years from the time of Laura's marriage had passed away; and in that long period the father had seen her face but once, and then it was in the presence of the dead. Frequently, in the first years of that time, had she sought a reconciliation; but, repulsed on each occasion, she had ceased to make approaches. As to her husband, so entirely did Mr. Woodville reject him, that he cast out of his mind his very likeness, and, not meeting him, ceased actually to remember his features, so that, if he had encountered him in the street, he would not have known him. He could, and had said, therefore, when asked about Percival, that he "didn't know him." Of his rising reputation and social standing he knew but little; for his very name being an offence, he rejected it on the first utterance, and pushed aside rather than looked at any information regarding him.

At last, the external affairs of Mr. Woodville became desperate. His business actually died out, so that the expense of conducting it being more than the proceeds, he closed up his mercantile history, and retired on a meagre property, scarcely sufficient to meet his wants. But scarcely had this change taken place, when a claim on the only piece of real estate which he held was made, on the allegation of a defective title. On consulting a lawyer, he was alarmed to find that the claim had a plausible basis, and that the chances were against him. When the case was brought up, Mr. Woodville appeared in court, and with trembling anxiety watched the progress of the trial. The claim was apparently a fair one, and yet not really just. On the side of the prosecution was a subtle, ingenious, and eloquent lawyer, in whose hands his own counsel was little more than a child, and he saw with despair that all the chances were against him. The loss of this remnant of property would leave him utterly destitute. After a vigorous argument on the one side, and a feeble rejoinder on the other, the case was about being submitted, when a new advocate appeared on the side of the defence. He was unknown to Mr. Woodville. On rising in court, there was a profound silence. He began by observing that he had something to say in the case ere it closed, and as he had studied it carefully and weighed with due deliberation all the evidence which had appeared, he was satisfied he could show cause why the prosecution should not obtain a favourable decision.

In surprise, Mr. Woodville bent forward to listen. The lawyer was tall in person, dignified in manner, and spoke with a peculiar musical intonation and eloquent flow of language, that marked him as possessing both talents and education of a high order. In a few minutes he was perfectly absorbed in his argument. It was clear and strong in every part, and tore into very tatters the subtle chain of reasoning presented by the opposing counsel. For an hour he occupied the attention of the court. On closing his speech, he immediately retired. The decision was in Mr. Woodville's favour.

"Who is that?" he asked, turning to a gentleman who sat beside him, as the strange advocate left the floor.

The man looked at him in surprise.

"Not know him?" said he.

Mr. Woodville shook his head.

"His name is Percival."

Mr. Woodville turned his face partly away to conceal the sudden flush that went over it. After the decision in his favour had been given, and he had returned home, wondering at what had just occurred, he sat musing alone, when there came a light tapping, as from the hand of a child, at his door. Opening it, he found a boy there, not over five or six years of age, with golden hair falling over his shoulders, and bright blue eyes raised to his own.

"Grandpa!" said the child, looking earnestly into his face.

For a moment the old man stood and trembled. Then stooping down, he took the child in his arms, and hugged him with a sudden emotion to his heart, while the long sealed fountain of his feelings gushed forth again, and tears came forth from beneath the lids that were tightly shut to repress them.

"Father!" The eyes were quickly unclosed. There was now another present.

"My child!" came trembling from his lips, and Laura flung herself upon his bosom.

How changed to the eyes of Mr. Woodville was all, after this. When he met Mr. Percival, he was even more surprised than in the court-room at his manly dignity of character, his refinement and enlarged intelligence. And when he went abroad, and perceived, what he had never before allowed himself to see, the high estimation in which he was held by all in the community, he was still further affected with wonder.

In less than a year after this reconciliation, Mr. Percival was chosen to a high office in the State; and within that time, Mr. Allison was detected in a criminal conspiracy to defraud, and left the commonwealth to escape punishment.

So much for origin and destiny. Laura was right; it concerns a maiden far more to know whither her lover is going than whence he came; for she has to journey with him in the former, and not the latter way.

WHAT'S IN A NAME?

A MOST important event had occurred in the family of Mr. Pillsbury; an event long looked for with strange and doubtful feelings. Mr. Pillsbury, in his station, hardly knew what to do with himself; and Mrs. Pillsbury was so happy that she did nothing but smile all the time. She would have laughed outright at least a dozen times an hour, so exceedingly joyful did she feel, had it not been for a certain grave-faced, matronly personage, whose business it was to see that she did not get over-excited about any thing, and thus endanger her health. But we are getting no nearer to what we are trying to say, than when we began. So we shall have to come bolt out with the truth, in plain, understandable English, and tell the reader that Mrs. Pillsbury had a baby. Being the first baby that had appeared in the family, of course it was the dearest little darling that ever blessed a mother's delighted eyes.

What a sensation did the little stranger's advent create! What new hopes and feelings were awakened! How the minds of the parents enlarged with higher views of their responsibility in life! They had never been so happy; had never regarded each other with so tender a love as now pervaded their bosoms. An hour, and, sometimes, two hours earlier than usual, would the father return from his store in the evening, and for no other reason than to gratify the desire he felt to see the baby. He was far more punctual at dinner-time than he had been, and rarely ever went out at night. Before the baby came, Mr. Pillsbury had acquired rather a bad habit of spending his evenings away from home.

The first few weeks that succeeded to the baby's appearance were paradisaical in their peace and joy; and there is no telling how long this delightful state would have remained, had not the question been daily asked, by new and old visitors—

"What's its name?" "Haven't you named the baby yet?" "How do you call the little dear?" And so on, in a hundred varied ways.

"Name it William," said one. "Call it Edward," suggested another. "Oh! Ferdinand is such a beauty of a name: call him Ferdinand," urged another. And so it went on, until almost every christian and unchristian name in the whole catalogue had been brought forward.

But, of all the names that had been offered or suggested to her own mind, only one was considered by the mother as worthy of her baby. As for your common, unmeaning Johns and Henrys and Peters, she could not tolerate them. Mr. Pillsbury had different views.

"Give the child a good plain name. One that he will never be ashamed of as a boy or man. William is an excellent name; so is Henry; so is Edward; and so is Alfred. In fact, there are dozens of names, any one of which will sound as musical as a flute in a week's time."

But Mrs. Pillsbury shook her head in a most positive way at all these suggestions. No vulgar Dicks, Toms, Bills, or Neds for her. On this subject she was, I am sorry to admit, positively rude, at times, to her husband. If she didn't say outright, she thought—"I reckon it's *my* baby; and I'll have *some* say in naming it." The "some" proved in the end, to be all the "say."

There was one name, it has been admitted, worthy, in the mind of Mrs. Pillsbury, to distinguish her baby from all other babies. Mrs. Pillsbury was a pious woman, and every Sabbath, when she could get to church, she sat under the teachings of the excellent and beloved parson, King Crabtree. In her eyes, earth had never seen such a man as the good Mr. Crabtree; and, as name is significant of quality, Crabtree always fell upon her ears with a peculiar music, and brought to her mind images of things good and beautiful. To every suggestion of a name by her husband, of course Mrs. Pillsbury shook her head.

"What then, *will* you have him called?" at last asked Mr. Pillsbury, in despair.

"King Crabtree," replied the young mother firmly.

"Oh, dear!" There was pain in the expression of Mr. Pillsbury's voice. "Why, Emeline! Are you really beside yourself?"

"Not by any means," said the lady, drawing her lips firmly together. "I speak the words of truth and soberness. I wish him named King Crabtree, after our dear, good pastor."

"Horrible! horrible! Crab—tree—King! Why not call him Catamount, or Snapping-turtle, at once, and be done with it? Oh, no, no, no! I'll never give in to that—never!"

Mrs. Pillsbury had but one answer to make to this—but one weapon with which to fight her battle. A plentiful shower of tears came gushing over her cheeks, and turning her face from her husband, she commenced grieving and sobbing most piteously. Poor Mr. Pillsbury felt that the odds were against him. He already saw his beautiful boy with the millstone, King Crabtree, hung about his neck, and his heart sank within him. As for the parson, he had never been one of Mr. Pillsbury's favourites. In fact, he had little faith in him. But, in the eyes of Mrs. Pillsbury, and the major part of the ladies of his congregation, he was little less than a saint. Already some half a dozen young urchins had been christened King Crabtree, and there was a fair prospect of a dozen more being blessed with the same beautiful name.

Well, the father stood out as long as a mortal could well endure the various influences brought to bear upon him. At last he withdrew his positive *refusal* to have the baby named after the good parson—he never would give his *consent*—and the christening took place.

It was a long time before Mr. Pillsbury could say "Crabtree," although he heard the word sounded in his ears as often as fifty times a day. The best he could do was to "King" the little fellow, and that went terribly against the grain. But the child grew hourly more beautiful and interesting to the father, and by the time he was three years old, he almost forgot the unmusical name he bore, and could say "Crabtree" with the rest, and feel no unpleasant jarring of his nerves.

As for young King Crabtree, he had no fault to find with any one on the subject of his name during the years of babyhood, nor for a certain period of time after the days of jacket-and-trousers came. To him, Crabtree was as good as any other name, and a little better, for it meant himself, and he entertained for himself, quite naturally, we must admit, a particularly good opinion. But, as his mind opened and he began to understand the meaning of words, and, moreover, began to come in contact with boys at school, he was made sensible that there was something wrong. One sharp-witted lad called him, in a deriding way, "Crab,"—another dignified him with the title of "Parson Crabtree," and a third cried after him, as he passed homeward from school, "Hallo there, Mr. Landcrab!" Grieved are we to record the fact, but it must be told—young King Crabtree Pillsbury had not fully attained the age of seven mature years, when he scandalized the name of the good parson after whom he had been called, by using the carnal weapons of fists and feet in kicking and cuffing a young chap a year older than himself, for calling him "Crab-apple."

"Oh, Crabtree! Crabtree!" exclaimed the grieved mother, when she learned the fact, "what will our good parson say, when he hears this of you? You, who bear his name! Oh! it is dreadful!"

"Served the young rascal right!" murmured Mr. Pillsbury, aside. "Glad he's got some spirit in him. Hope the parson *will* hear it."

As for Crabtree himself, the reproof of his mother did not make a very deep impression, as was plain from the fact that, while she talked, he kept jerking his head over his left shoulder in a threatening way, and saying—"He called me 'Crab-apple,' so he did! and I won't stand it! The boys are always calling me names, so they are."

"What do they call you?" asked the mother.

"Why they call me 'lobster,' and 'crab,' and 'Parson Crabtree,' and every thing."

"Just as I expected. Confound the name!" grumbled Mr. Pillsbury, in a low voice: not so low but that his words reached the ears of his wife, who cast upon him an offended look. As soon as they were alone, she tried to read him a little lecture, but he broke the ceremony short off by declaring that Crabtree was an awful name, and would curse their child through life.

"Beelzebub is nothing to it," he added by way of making his denunciation emphatic.

There was no way to meet this but by the old dernier method of tears. As soon as Mr. Pillsbury saw the approach of these, he made a hasty retreat.

Long before Crabtree attained his twelfth year, he was known as the most fiery young belligerent in the town. It took a boy who could bear to stand a good blow, or one far over the size of this pugnacious lad, to venture upon the experiment of saying "crab," "lobster," or "parson," within reach of his ears.

"I'm sorry to hear bad accounts of you, my lad," said Parson Crabtree to the boy, in the presence of his mother.

Crabtree hung his head and bit his finger-nails.

"I'm told that you have a fight with some of the boys at school almost every day. This is very wicked How comes it?"

"The boys won't let me alone," replied Crabtree, looking up.

"Won't let you alone?"

"No, sir."

"What do they do to you?"

"They call me Parson Crabtree."

"Call *you* Parson Crabtree!" exclaimed the minister, a little taken by surprise.

"Yes, sir."

"Well, they call me that, too; but I don't see any cause to fight about it," said the parson, recovering himself.

"But I'm *not* a parson! And then they call me 'king-crab,' and 'land-crab,' and 'lobster,' 'crab-apple,' and every thing. If they'd let me alone, I'd let them alone; but they won't."

The parson said no more on the subject. Something struck his mind at the moment, and he addressed himself to Crabtree's mother, on a matter touching the welfare of the church.

For the first time, a dim impression that an error had been committed stole into the mind of Mrs. Pillsbury. She saw that the name of her boy was, to some extent, at the bottom of his quarrelsome temper. "Quarrelsome" was the word that she, as well as others, applied to the boy's disposition to resent the many insults and indignities he almost daily suffered. Lads not half so amiable by nature, nor with half the good qualities he possessed, who were so fortunate as to be the only Charleses, or Henrys, or Williams, got on well enough. No one charged them with being quarrelsome. The fact was, they had little or no provocation. With half as much to provoke them as Crabtree suffered, they would have doubled their fists with the most hearty good-will.

Yes, the error was dimly seen. But, by the time King Crabtree reached his fifteenth year, it was seen far more clearly. For some time previously, a few "enemies" of Parson Crabtree, as they were called, had hinted at certain scandalous things, most disgraceful to the minister and the church. Once the parson had boldly demanded of his congregation that said allegations should be investigated; but his friends in the church said, that no one who knew him asked for such a thing; and, moreover, they prudently enough concluded, that the least said about a charge like the one preferred against the parson, the better. And so all remained quiet for a time.

But, the "enemies" of the parson continued to grow bolder, and to gain daily in numbers. Things of a scandalous and wicked nature were boldly alleged to have been done by the clerical gentleman; and hints of an intention to cite him before the civil courts were at length thrown out. The good people of his congregation could no longer shut their ears to what was passing. Common decency required them to sift the matter to the bottom; and so the leading and official men were called, the parson cited to appear, and witnesses, said to know of his delinquencies, called in and examined. Some pretty hard stories were told by some of the latter; but, as they were generally based upon what Mr. or Mrs. Such-and-such-a-one said, the eloquent parson, by virtue of his peculiar oral abilities, backed by tears at pleasure, succeeded in making it believed that he was a basely persecuted and deeply injured man. He was fully acquitted of the evils laid to his charge.

This was a great triumph to the parson's friends. Still, the tongue of scandal was not hushed. Fretted at this, threats of prosecution for defamation of character were thrown out; but these did not produce the silence expected. Two or three members of the congregation, who took the matter most seriously to heart, were actually about instituting proceedings against one of the busiest of their minister's defamers, when the whole town was electrified by the news that Parson Crabtree had been cited to appear before one of the civil courts, to answer for crimes of a most heinous character. What these crimes were, or at least a part of them, delicacy forbids us to state. But they were minutely detailed in evidence before the court, and spread, in newspaper reports, all over the country. The position of Parson Crabtree, not only as a preacher of the gospel, but as the author of one or two religious books, made him a conspicuous object to all. There was not a newspaper-reading man, woman, or child, in the whole country, who did not become familiar with his name and the offences charged against him. The trial lasted for weeks, during which time the public mind, every where, continued to be greatly excited. At last, the court summed up the evidence, and the case was left with a jury of twelve men, four of whom were members of the parson's own congregation. In ten minutes, a unanimous verdict of "guilty" on all the charges was found; though the wretched criminal, under the influence of a false humanity, was recommended to the mercy of the court. Upon this recommendation, however, the court did not see that it was right to act. The position, standing, and influence of the culprit, rather increased than lessened the guilt of his offences. He was, therefore, sentenced to pay a certain amount of damages, and to be imprisoned at hard labour for the term of three years.

At the age of sixteen, the son of Mr. Pillsbury was sent to college. He entered as K. C. Pillsbury.

"What do these initials represent?" asked the president, on receiving the lad, and making a minute of his name. There was a slight hesitation, and then the boy replied—

"King Crabtree."

"Indeed! Ah? I'm sorry you haven't a better name. I suppose you were called after that rascally parson who flourished in your town so many years?"

King said yes, though he was sorry for it.

"Of course, it's no fault of yours, my lad," returned the president, encouragingly. "And as long as you have to carry the name about you, let it be your business to redeem it from disgrace."

This was a much harder task than the president supposed, at the moment he made the suggestion. A name once disgraced, and in a public and scandalous manner, cannot be redeemed in a single generation; often not in ages. It was soon known among the students that the new-comer's name was King Crabtree. Some said he was the parson's nephew; and others declared that he was actually the parson's son. Certain little persecutions followed, that fretted the boy's temper, and made him so unhappy that in six months he went home, and stubbornly refused to return to college. His parents, who intended him for one of the learned professions, were greatly troubled at the perverseness of their son's temper. But neither threats, remonstrances, nor persuasions were of any avail. He remained firm to his declaration. Daily he was becoming more and more morbidly sensitive to the disgrace attached to his name; and rather than bear for a month longer what he had suffered at college, he would go before the mast as a common sailor. This state of his feelings he was bold to declare. It made not the slightest impression on him for his mother or father to say—

"Don't be so weak and foolish, King,"—even they had dropped the Crabtree;—"be more manly."

But young Crabtree knew where the shoe pinched; and felt the slightest pressure thereon as painful.

About this time, a good opening occurred in a shipping-house, in the town. A clerk had been sent out as a supercargo, thus leaving a vacancy in the establishment, which the partners were desirous of filling with a smart, intelligent lad. The situation was a most desirable one, and some friends of Mr. Pillsbury suggested to him that it was just the place for his boy, and said they would speak to Mr. Green, the principal member of the house, if he desired it. The father was much pleased at this prospect, and so was his son, when he heard of the place. Mr. Green was accordingly spoken to on the subject, and said that he would like to see the lad. So, King was sent to the store.

"You're the son of Mr. Pillsbury?" said the merchant, when the lad introduced himself.

"Yes, sir," was modestly replied.

"You're a fine-looking lad. And so you would like to be a merchant?"

"Yes, sir."

"Well—let me see—what is your name?"

The colour mounted to the boy's face, as he half stammered out—

"King Crabtree Pillsbury."

"King Crabtree. Hum—m—m. Rather an unfortunate name!"

The boy remained silent. Mr. Green sat and thought for some moments. Then he said—

"Very well, my lad. I will think about you. There are half-a-dozen applicants for the place, and we will not decide about it for a week to come."

The boy departed with a weight upon his feelings. He was satisfied that *he* would not get the place.

"I've seen Mr. Pillsbury's son," said Mr. Green, on meeting, shortly afterward, one of the individuals who had interested himself in the boy's favour.

"Have you?"

"Yes."

"How do you like him?"

"Fine, smart-looking boy; but he has a dreadful bad name."

"Bad name! I never heard of it. Who says so?"

"Himself. Do you want a worse name than King Crabtree?"

"Oh!"

"It may be prejudice; and, probably is; but I couldn't have any one about me with that name. Besides, I understand the boy's mother is distantly related to the old rascally parson after whom she called her child."

"I never heard that."

"I reckon it will be found true. Be this, however, as it may, I can't take the lad. I never could like him or trust him with that name, and it's no use to try the experiment. His parents had better have drowned him at the christening."

Mr. Pillsbury never guessed the reason why Mr. Green did not take his son; but King Crabtree understood it fully. For a year the unhappy boy loitered away his time, and then, almost in despair, accepted a place as mail-packer, in a printing-office, at a dollar a week. But he did not stay long in this situation. Some light remark about his name caused him to assault a small lad in the office, and this caused his dismission. Disgusted and disheartened with every thing, the poor lad next set his heart upon going to sea. This was opposed until opposition wore itself out. Then he was permitted to go on board a vessel trading to South America. On the first voyage he behaved himself so well, that the captain took him for his clerk, in which capacity he sailed three times to Rio and back. During the last voyage home, one of the men took occasion, several times, to be rude to Crabtree. Repeating this rudeness in a more aggravated form than usual, one day, the young man caught up a handspike, and, in the heat of the moment, knocked the sailor down. The blow was heavier than Crabtree intended to give, and the result more disastrous than he expected. One of the sailor's arms was broken, and he was severely bruised by his fall over a piece of wood that lay on the deck.

As soon as the vessel arrived in port, the sailor made complaint against Crabtree, who was arrested and placed on trial. The prosecutor made out a very clear case, and the young man was found guilty of the assault charged. The court ordered him to pay five hundred dollars damages, and to suffer an imprisonment of sixty days.

"Were this your first offence, King Crabtree Pillsbury," said the judge, in passing sentence, "your age, and the provocation alleged to have been received, would have inclined the court to visit your conduct with a lighter penalty. But though young in years, you come before this court as an old offender. In the hope that you may be led to change your evil courses, I give you sixty days imprisonment as a time for sober reflection."

Utterly confounded by such a declaration on the part of the judge, the unhappy young man was taken from the court-room and conveyed to prison. The captain with whom he had sailed, and who was much attached to him, was present during the trial, and at its conclusion. He was no less confounded than Pillsbury, at the strange assumption of the judge. As soon as the court adjourned, he called upon the judge, and said to him—

"You appear to be labouring under some error

in regard to the young man you committed to prison?"

"What young man?" inquired the judge. "The one arraigned on the charge of beating a sailor?"

"Yes."

"In what respect?"

"You spoke of him as an old offender."

"And so he is. Already he has been before this court twice, for outrages on the rights of others."

"King Crabtree Pillsbury!"

"Yes."

"Depend upon it, you are in error, Judge."

"Oh, no! Do you think I could ever forget that name, rendered infamous by a certain parson who is still, I trust, in the penitentiary?"

"Are you certain that the offender of whom you speak was named Pillsbury?"

The judge thought a few moments.

"Not absolutely certain," he replied. "But surely there cannot be found another man on the face of the earth with such a Christian name?"

"It is barely possible, Judge. Of one thing I am very sure, my clerk has not been before this court, nor any other in the United States, within the time you mention."

"You are positive of that?"

"Positive."

"The docket of cases tried will show," said the judge.

Accordingly there was an examination made, when it turned out that the previous culprit was named King Crabtree Parker. He was from the same town with Pillsbury, and had been named in compliment to the good Parson Crabtree. His name had doubtless proved his ruin.

This discovery altered the case entirely. The unhappy young man was brought before the court, and the sentence commuted to a fine of one hundred dollars.

"And now, young man," said the judge, in dismissing him, "take my advice and petition the legislature to change your name; for, depend upon it, while you bear the one you now have, no good fortune can ever find you in this world. It is as bad as the mark upon the forehead of Cain."

This piece of advice was acted upon by Pillsbury immediately. The legislature being in session, he sent up a petition, and in less than four weeks he was plain John Pillsbury. From that time he felt like a new man, and when he wrote his name, he did so without the sense of disgrace that had for years haunted him like a blasting spectre. He becamo more cheerful, and companionable, and more confident as he looked into the future. In a year or two, he became mate of the vessel, and, in a few years afterwards, on the captain's retiring, was elevated to his place. About this time he married. On the birth of his first child, its young mother had a fancy to name the boy after an uncle for whom she had a warm affection, and proposed to call him Lloyd Erskine.

"No, no," said the father most positively, "let it be Tom, Dick, or Harry, just as you please. Any plain, common name is good enough, and will carry him safely through life. But I wouldn't call a child of mine after the angel Gabriel."

"Why not?" innocently inquired the wife.

"Simply because, if the angel Gabriel were to fall and disgrace his name, my boy would have to bear a part of the stigma. No—no. Never name a child after anybody; for all are human, and therefore liable to fall into evil. Arnold was once thought to be an honourable man; and, during this period of his life, some relative or friend may have called a child after him. If so, how deeply disgraced must that second-hand bearer of the name, Benedict Arnold, have felt through his whole life. No—no. Let it be plain John, William, or Edward, as you fancy; but nothing more."

And so the child was called John Pillsbury. We will simply remark, in conclusion, that, unlike his father, he was never ashamed of his name.

SEEING ABOUT IT.

I ONCE spent a few days in the family of a much esteemed friend, who had an interesting boy, between seven and eight years of age. One morning as the father was about leaving for his store, little Edgar came running after him, crying—

"Father! father! won't you buy me some paints and a paint-brush?"

"I'll see about it," the father quietly replied.

"Oh! father is going to buy me a box of paints," exclaimed Edgar, dancing back into the house, almost as happy, in anticipation, as if the box were actually in his hands.

"What are you going to do with your paints?" I asked of the little fellow, drawing him to my side.

"I'm going to paint all the pictures in my Parley's Every Day Book, and make them look so beautiful!" said he—"I wish it wasn't so long until dinner-time. But I'll wait."

"Yes, you must wait patiently. We cannot always have what we want in a moment."

"Father could send them home by John; I wish

I had asked him to do so. But I'll wait." And the little boy strove to be as patient as possible.

As often as every half-hour, at least, during the morning, Edgar came to me to talk about the box of paints his father was going to bring home.

"I wish it was dinner-time," he would sometimes say, or—"Isn't dinner-time a long while coming?"

All Edgar's usual modes of passing the hours happily, were neglected. He could think of nothing but his paint-box.

"It's one o'clock!" he cried, bursting into my room, where I sat reading, as the clock struck the hour he had named. "Father comes home at two. A'n't you glad I'm going to get my paint-box soon?"

"Yes, very glad, Edgar."

"So am I. I wonder how large a box he will buy? Henry Thomas has one so big, (measuring nearly twelve inches in length with his hands,) and ever-so-many brushes. He can paint elegantly. You ought to see the bunch of flowers he painted; they looked just like real ones."

"Can you paint a flower yet?"

"Oh, no. I haven't learned. But I am going to learn. I mean to ask father to send me to a drawing-school."

Four or five times during the next hour, Edgar came into my room to talk about his box of paints. For more than a quarter of an hour before the usual time for his father to return, he was at the window, and there remained, patiently, on the look-out for him. At length I heard him crying out—"Father is coming! father is coming!"—and running wildly down-stairs.

The little fellow had talked to me so much about his paint-box, that I felt almost as much interest as he did, and could not help leaving my room and going down to see and enjoy his pleasure, on receiving it.

"Where is my paint-box? Give me my paint-box, father!" cried Edgar, eagerly seizing hold of my friend, as he came up the steps.

"What box, child?" returned the father, coldly. "I don't know any thing about your paint-box."

"The paint-box you promised me you would buy. Where is it, father? In your pocket?"

"I didn't promise to buy you a paint-box."

"Oh, yes, you did, father!" The tears were springing to the child's eyes. "Don't you know I asked you this morning to get me one?"

"I believe you did, Edgar; but did I say I would buy it for you?"

"You said you would see about it, father."

"That is one thing, and promising to buy the box another. I haven't had time to see about it, Edgar."

This was said with an air of indifference that to me was inconceivable. The disappointed child shrank away, and went quietly up-stairs to his mother, into whose lap he laid his face, sobbing most bitterly.

"What is the matter, my dear?" asked his mother.

The child made no answer.

"Edgar, what ails you, my son?"

But the boy's heart was too full. He could not speak.

"Why don't you say what is the matter?"

The mother's voice had changed from its first expression of tenderness. Still there was no answer.

"Don't come crying to me, unless you can tell what ails you." And Edgar was pushed away.

The child felt that injustice had been done to him, and the repulse of his mother made him angry. His low, distressed cry changed to one of passion.

"Edgar, what *are* you crying about? I never saw such a boy! You are always crying about something!"

This had no favourable effect. The tones in which it was spoken were fretful, and these excited rather than soothed the child. He went away from his mother's side, and leaned against the wall, still continuing to cry, but with more bitterness.

"Edgar, stop crying!"

The mother spoke with authority, and stamped her foot, to give emphasis to what she said. But her words had no effect

"Look here, Edgar! If you don't stop, instantly,

you shall be shut up in the closet, and kept there until after dinner."

The poor child's disappointment had been so great, that he felt indifferent about every thing. If his mother had expressed sympathy and spoken kindly, it would have soothed and comforted him. But her words, and the tones in which they were uttered, aroused angry feelings, that made him stubborn. The threat of punishment had no effect; he still cried on.

"A'n't you going to stop?" This was the last angry appeal; and it might as well not have been made. It had no effect whatever.

Being now out of all patience, Edgar's mother seized him by the arm, and, thrusting him into a dark closet, shut the door. His crying instantly ceased. His anger was changed into grief. He had been wronged, and he felt it keenly. Laying his little head upon a pillow that was on the floor of the closet, he sobbed himself to sleep, and was found there when the door was opened about an hour afterwards.

"Where is Edgar?" asked my friend, looking towards his vacant chair at the dinner-table, after we were all seated.

"He has been a naughty boy, and cannot come to the table to-day," replied the mother, smiling, as she glanced towards me.

"What has he been doing?" asked my friend.

"He came up to me, crying, a little while ago, and would neither tell me what ailed him, nor stop his noise. I persuaded and threatened, but all to no purpose; and had, at last, to shut him up in the closet. He is a very self-willed boy. When he once gets set out, there is no doing any thing with him."

My friend said nothing. What he thought, I do not know: but I have very good reasons for believing that he did not for a moment imagine that he, and he alone, was to blame in the matter. When he told Edgar, in reply to his request for a box of paints, that he would see about it, he did so by way of getting off from the child's importunity. From that moment he thought no more about it. Not so with the child. He fully believed that his father had promised to buy him what he so much desired, and, confiding in this promise, he expected to get the box of paints upon his return home, at dinner-time. But he was sadly disappointed, and was too young to bear the disappointment.

So little had Edgar's father thought of what his child asked of him, and so little notice did he take of the effect produced by his failure to get the paints, that it did not occur to him that Edgar had been crying from the disappointment. The mother was, of course, entirely ignorant of the cause of her son's unhappiness. It is true, he had talked to her about the paint-box he was to get when his father came home to dinner: but she had so many matters of interest to which her daily attention was called, that she never thought about any of them longer than ten minutes at a time. The child's crying she attributed to some trifling crossing of his temper, and she did not feel at all disposed to humour him.

I saw all this, and it grieved me deeply. But my position was such that I could say nothing. About two hours after I had left the dinner-table, as I was about going out for a walk, I found Edgar sitting on the front door-steps. He was alone, and was looking at some children playing in the street. He did not show any disposition to join them. As I passed him, he looked up at me with a sober face. I did not speak to him, for I did not know what to say. Once or twice, I turned back to look at him—his eyes were following me.

"Shall I buy him a box of paints?" I asked myself. "Will it be right?"

For some time, I argued these questions, and finally determined that I would risk gratifying the child. His father, I felt quite sure, had given the matter so little thought, and was so entirely ignorant of the effect produced by his failure to buy the paint-box, that he would not look upon my act as an officious one, meant to rebuke him.

I came back sooner than I had intended, with the paint-box in my possession. Edgar still sat where I had left him. His mother came to the door just as I placed my foot upon the step to enter. She greeted me pleasantly, and then said—

"Edgar, why don't you go out and play with the children? There's William Ellis, and Mary Miller, and Thomas Gray, who all love to have you play with them. Go, my son."

"I don't want to play," replied Edgar, looking up into his mother's face. "I would rather sit here."

"Sit there, then. You are a strange child, sometimes."

There was petulance rather than tenderness in the mother's voice. The boy sighed, and remained sitting where he was.

"It's a very hard matter to get along with children," remarked my friend's wife. "You never know how to take them. One moment they are on the mountain top, and the next in the valley. Yesterday, it was next to impossible for me to keep Edgar away from those children, and now he cares nothing about them. It seems as if all their moods and tempers were ever in direct opposition to your wishes or feelings. Yesterday, I did not want him to go into the street, and then nothing else would suit him. To-day, I would rather he would amuse himself with the children; but he chooses to sit moping at the door. It requires a great deal of patience to get along with children; much more than I possess."

I did not assent to the last part of the sentence

uttered, although, from all I had seen, I was very well satisfied of its truth.

"I have no doubt," I made answer, "that it is one of the most difficult things in the world to understand the dispositions and feelings of children, and so to act as not to do violence to what is good in them. Their varied moods and tempers are not always mere impulses; they depend upon what we would consider, if we knew all, adequate causes. Subjected, as they are, entirely to others—possessing no abstract freedom of their own—they must be constantly meeting with checks and disappointments. We know how little able we are to encounter such things without disturbance, although our reason is matured, and we can understand causes, and although much experience in life has tended to sober our feelings and give us some support in a rational philosophy. Reflecting thus, we ought not to be surprised at any thing we see in children; but should rather seek to understand the reason why they are at any time disturbed."

"But suppose, as was the case with me to-day, you are not able to draw from the child what it is that disturbs him,—how are you to act?"

"I am not able to answer that question," I replied, smiling. "Circumstances always alter cases."

"It is very easy to theorize—one of the easiest things in the world. But it is quite another thing to practise."

To this remark, I had nothing to say I tacitly admitted its truth. At the same time I could not help feeling that the practice of some people might be better than it was, by a great deal.

"Come up-stairs and see me, Edgar," said I to the boy, after I had changed the subject of conversation with his mother, and chatted with her a little while longer.

The child arose quickly, and walked by my side up-stairs and into the chamber I occupied. Although I did not mean that it should be so, yet I saw, from Edgar's manner, that my voice had betrayed the secret that I had something for him. I had no opportunity, therefore, for surprising him

"I have got a little present for you, Edgar," said I, drawing forth a small package enclosed in paper.

"What is it? a paint-box?" eagerly asked the little fellow, his face brightening.

"Yes, a paint-box. How do you like it?"

I had by this time taken off the envelope and displayed the box. I really thought the sight of it would set the child wild with delight. He seized it in his hands and fairly hugged it. Then, drawing off the lid, he counted over each paint, and handled and tried the brushes.

"Let me go and show it to mother," said he, and away he ran, crying to his mother that I had given him a box of paints.

"Artless, innocent childhood!" I could not

help saying—"how brief is thy remembrance of wrong!"

His mother had punished him because he had cried from the severity of his disappointment in not getting his expected box of paints; but this was all forgotten now.

After the box was shown to his mother, Edgar went into the dining-room to paint, and we saw and heard no more of him until tea-time. When his father came home, Edgar was as eager to show his prize to him as he had been to his mother.

The incidents of the day made me thoughtful. I had always entertained for my friend a very high opinion; and had especially esteemed him for his goodness of heart and benevolence. But the circumstance I have just related caused doubting questions to arise. Was it possible for a man of true benevolence to act towards his confiding child with such culpable indifference? I could not reconcile my previous opinion with the fact that had just transpired. They were at variance with each other.

The more I thought about the matter, the more I felt disturbed.

"Can it be possible?" I at length asked myself, "that my friend is naturally a selfish, bad-hearted man, who takes upon himself, in common society, semblances of virtue?"

"No—no—this cannot be," was my mental answer. "His worst fault must be thoughtlessness."

On the next day, I happened in at my friend's store. Whilst I sat reading a newspaper, and he was busy at his desk, a little girl, rather poorly clad, came in, and said something to him in a low, earnest tone. My friend hesitated, and the child spoke more earnestly. He then asked two or three questions, to which he received answers.

"Very well, I will see about it," he said with a smile.

The little girl seemed satisfied, and went away.

"Your little visitor was quite importunate," I remarked.

"Yes," he replied. "Her father used to work for me. He is an honest, industrious man, but has been sick for some time. He is getting better, however, and now wants me to speak to one of my neighbours about a situation in his store. I told her that if her father would send her, it would do just as well. But she said he wished me to go particularly, for he knew, if I spoke for it, I could get it."

"And so you promised to see about it?" said I, letting my voice rest, with some emphasis, upon the last words of the sentence.

"Yes—I could do no less," he replied, not observing that I had used his own words.

I felt strongly inclined to call my friend's attention to the fact of his having spoke in the same way to Edgar, but could not see my way exactly clear to do so, just then.

Two days afterwards, while I was again sitting in my friend's store, the same little girl came in. Before she had time to speak, my friend said—

"I declare! I have entirely forgotten you! But wait a minute, and I will go and see about it at once."

The child looked disappointed, but sat down quietly. My friend put on his hat and went out. In a little while he came in, and said to her—

"Tell your father that Mr. P—— says that he would have given him the situation with pleasure, if he had applied earlier, but that it was now filled."

The little girl looked into my friend's face for some time, with what seemed to me a sad expression, and then went slowly away.

"Really, I must blame myself for not having gone at once to see about the situation for this poor man. If I had gone yesterday, I might have secured it for him."

"It's a pity, certainly," I ventured to remark.

"It is, indeed. I really feel bad about it. But, the fact is, he ought to have sent direct to Mr. P——, and not to have asked me to speak to him."

"No doubt, he believed you would have more influence, and thus make his application more certain."

"Yes. But the result has shown differently."

"It would not have shown differently if you had seen Mr. P—— immediately."

"No. But I didn't; and there I was to blame. It can't be helped now, however. I am sorry, and that is as much as I can say."

We talked some time on the subject, I improving an opportunity that offered to call his attention to the sad disappointment his thoughtless promise to see about a box of paints for Edgar had occasioned the little boy. He was surprised and astonished at what I said; and seemed deeply grieved at the pain his child had suffered and the wrong that had been done to him. So little had he thought about what he had said to Edgar in reply to his request, that it had by this time retired so far from his memory that it was recalled with considerable difficulty.

We were yet conversing, when a man entered the store, and came slowly back to the little room in which we were sitting. He walked with a feeble, tottering step.

"Why, John, is this you? I am glad to see you out. How are you getting?" said my friend, the colour rising to his face as he spoke.

The man did not smile in return, but knit his brow, compressed his lips, and looked up sternly.

"I am really sorry, John," said my friend, speaking with much apparent confusion, "that I couldn't get that place for you. Mr. P—— said that he would have taken you with pleasure, if the application had not come too late."

An expression of impatience, mingled with something like contempt, flitted over the man's pale face. He was evidently struggling hard with himself to keep from speaking out too plainly what was in his mind. At length he said, in a subdued but earnest tone—

"Mr. ——, it may be only right for me to let you know, that, in neglecting to see about the situation for me, as you promised you would do, you have put it out of my power to get bread for my family. They have only had potatoes to eat for many days. No one can earn any thing but myself, and I have been sick for some weeks and unable to work. If you had told my little girl that you could not apply to Mr. P—— for me, I would have hobbled out myself. But you promised to see about it, and I rested satisfied that it would be done. Perhaps I was wrong in presuming to trouble you; but I always considered you a kind-hearted man, and believed it would give you pleasure to do me a good turn."

The brows of my friend contracted in anger. Although the man's manner was not insolent, yet the fact of his calling to take him to task, chafed his feelings. He was about making some harsh reply, when the man, feeling, perhaps, that he had, in the excitement produced by the intelligence brought back by his little girl, been led to act improperly, and yet, feeling unwilling to apologize for what had already transpired, turned away, and walked from the store as fast as his feeble steps would carry him.

My friend looked at me, and I looked at him. It was some time before any thing was said.

"I shall have to correct this fault of mine," he at length remarked, with a long inspiration after uttering the sentence. "I am too much in the habit of saying I will see about a thing, without really thinking that the words amount to a promise. John's manner has irritated me; but I suppose I must make every allowance for one in his circumstances. He must have a situation. I will get him one somewhere, immediately, if I have to furnish the wages and let his labour go for nothing. But he must not know that I have any thing to do in it."

Before two hours had passed, a storekeeper in the neighbourhood sent for John, and engaged him as a porter. He inquired very kindly of him as to how long he had been sick, and what were his circumstances, and then offered him a month's wages in advance. The agency of my friend in this, John more than suspected, for he came before night and apologized for what he had said in the morning.

Spite of all my reasoning on the subject, I could not think so highly of my friend as I did before I had the privilege of spending a short time in his family and observing him in his every-day relations. The amiability of temper and urbanity of manner which he always displayed whenever I saw him, made me consider him one of the best of men I had ever met. But now he stood on the common plane, with faults such as were possessed by common men. I hold up his peculiar failing as a mirror into which others who are like him may look, and see something of their own character, by reflection.

THE IRON WILL.

"FANNY, I've but one word more to say on the subject. If you marry that fellow, I'll have nothing to do with you. I've said it; and you may be assured that I'll adhere to my determination."

Thus spoke, with a frowning brow and a stern voice, the father of Fanny Crawford, while the maiden sat with eyes bent upon the floor.

"He's a worthless, good-for-nothing fellow," resumed the father; "and if you marry him, you wed a life of misery. Don't come back to me—for I will disown you the day you take his name. I've said it, and my decision is unalterable."

Still Fanny made no answer, but sat like a statue.

"Lay to heart what I have said, and make your election, girl." And with these words, Mr. Crawford retired from the presence of his daughter.

On that evening, Fanny Crawford left her father's

house, and was secretly married to a young man named Logan, whom, spite of all his faults, she tenderly loved.

When this fact became known to Mr. Crawford, he angrily repeated his threat of utterly disowning his child; and he meant what he said—for he was a man of stern purpose and unbending will. When, trusting to the love she believed him to bear for her, Fanny ventured home, she was rudely repulsed, and told that she no longer had a father. These cruel words fell upon her heart, and ever after rested there, an oppressive weight.

Logan was a young mechanic, with a good trade and the ability to earn a comfortable living. But Mr. Crawford's objection to him was well-founded, and it would have been much better for Fanny if she had permitted it to influence her; for the young man was idle in his habits, and Mr. Crawford too clearly saw that idleness would lead to dissipation. The father had hoped that his threat to disown his child would have deterred her from taking the step he so strongly disapproved. He had, in fact, made this threat as a last effort to save her from a union that would, inevitably, lead to unhappiness; but having made it, his stubborn and offended pride caused him to adhere with stern inflexibility to his word.

When Fanny went from under her father's roof, the old man was left alone; the mother of his only child had been many years dead. For her father's sake, as well as for her own, did Fanny wish to return. She loved her parent with a most earnest affection, and thought of him as sitting gloomy and companionless in that home so long made light and cheerful by her voice and smile. Hours and hours would she lie awake at night, thinking of her father, and weeping for the estrangement of his heart from her. Still there was in her bosom an everliving hope that he would relent; and to this she clung, though he passed her in the street without looking at her, and steadily denied her admission, when, in the hope of some change in his stern purpose, she would go to his house and seek to gain an entrance.

As the father had predicted, Logan added, in the course of a year or two, dissipation to idle habits, and neglect of his wife to both. They had gone to housekeeping in a small way, when first married, and had lived comfortably enough for some time; but Logan did not like work, and made every excuse he could find to take a holiday or be absent from the shop. The effect of this was an insufficient income. Debt came, with its mortifying and harassing accompaniments, and furniture had to be sold to pay those who were not disposed to wait. With two little children, Fanny was removed by her husband into a cheap boarding-house, after their things were taken and sold. The company into which she was here thrown was far from being agreeable; but this would have been no source of unhappiness in itself. Cheerfully would she have breathed the uncongenial atmosphere, if there had been nothing in the conduct of her husband to awaken feelings of anxiety. But, alas! there was much to create unhappiness here; idle days were more frequent, and the consequences of idle days more and more serious. From his work, he would come home sober and cheerful; but after spending a day in idle company, or in the woods gunning, a sport of which he was fond, he would meet his wife with a sullen, dissatisfied aspect, and, too often, in a state little above intoxication.

"I'm afraid thy son-in-law is not doing very well, friend Crawford," said a plain-spoken Quaker to the father of Mrs. Logan, after the young man's habits began to show themselves too plainly in his appearance.

Mr. Crawford knit his brows, and drew his lips closely together.

"Has thee seen young Logan lately?"

"I don't know the young man," replied Mr. Crawford, with an impatient motion of his head.

"Don't know thy own son-in-law—the husband of thy daughter?"

"I have no son-in-law—no daughter!" said Crawford, with stern emphasis.

"Frances was the daughter of thy wedded wife, friend Crawford."

"But I have disowned her. I forewarned her of the consequences if she married that young man. I told her that I would cast her off for ever, and I have done it."

"But, friend Crawford, thee has done wrong."

"I've said it, and I'll stick to it."

"But thee has done wrong, friend Crawford," repeated the Quaker.

"Right or wrong, it is done, and I will not recall the act. I gave her fair warning; but she took her own course, and now she must abide the consequences. When I say a thing, I mean it. I never eat my words."

"Friend Crawford," said the Quaker, in a steady voice, and with his calm eyes fixed upon the face of the man he addressed, "thee was wrong to say what thee did; thee had no right to cast off thy child. I saw her to-day, passing slowly along the street; her dress was thin and faded, but not so thin and faded as her pale young face. Ah! if thee could have seen the sadness of that countenance. Friend Crawford, she is thy child still; thee cannot disown her."

"I never change," replied the resolute father.

"She is the child of thy beloved wife, now in heaven, friend Crawford."

"Good-morning!" And Crawford turned and walked away.

"Rash words are bad enough," said the Quaker

to himself; "but how much worse is it to abide by rash words after there has been time for reflection and repentance."

Crawford was troubled by what the Quaker said, but more troubled by what he saw a few minutes afterwards, as he walked along the street, in the person of his daughter's husband. He met the young man, supported by two others, so much intoxicated that he could not stand alone. And in this state he was going home to his wife—to Fanny.

The father clenched his hands, set his teeth firmly together, muttered an imprecation upon the head of Logan, and quickened his pace homeward. Try as he would, he could not shut out from his mind the pale, faded countenance of his child, as described by the Quaker, nor help feeling an inward shudder at the thought of what she must suffer on meeting her husband in such a state.

"She has only herself to blame," he said, as he struggled with his feelings. "I forewarned her; I gave her to understand clearly what she had to expect; my word is passed. I have said it, and that ends the matter; I am no childish trifler. What I say, I mean."

Logan had been from home all day, and, what was worse, had not been, as his wife was well aware, at the shop for a week. The woman with whom they were boarding came into her room during the afternoon, and, after some hesitation and embarrassment, said—

"I am sorry to tell you, Mrs. Logan, that I shall want you to give up your room after this week. You know I have had no money from you for nearly a month, and, from the way your husband goes on, I see little prospect of being paid any thing more. If I was able, for your sake, I would not say a word; but I am not, Mrs. Logan, and therefore must, in justice to myself and family, require you to get another boarding-house."

Mrs. Logan answered only with tears. The woman tried to soften what she had said, and then went away.

Not long after this, Logan came stumbling up the stairs, and, opening the door of his room, staggered in and threw himself heavily upon the bed. Fanny looked at him a few moments, and then crouching down, and, covering her face with her hands, wept long and bitterly. She felt crushed and powerless. Cast off by her father, wronged by her husband, destitute and about to be thrust from the poor home into which she had shrunk, faint and weary, it seemed as if hope were gone for ever. While she suffered thus, Logan lay in a drunken sleep. Arousing herself at last, she removed his boots and coat, drew a pillow under his head, and threw a coverlet over him. She then sat down and wept again. The tea-bell rang, but she did not go to the table. Half an hour afterwards, the landlady came to the door and kindly inquired if she would not have some food sent up to her room.

"Only a little bread and milk for Henry," was replied.

"Let me send you a cup of tea," urged the woman.

"No, thank you. I don't wish any thing to-night."

The woman went away, feeling troubled. From her heart she pitied the suffering young creature, and it had cost her a painful struggle to do what she had done; but the pressing nature of her own circumstances required her to be rigidly just. Notwithstanding Mrs. Logan had declined having any thing, she sent her a cup of tea and something to eat; but they remained untasted.

On the next morning, Logan was sober, and his wife informed him of the notice which their landlady had given. He was angry, and used harsh language towards the woman. Fanny defended her, and had the harsh language transferred to her own head.

The young man appeared as usual at the breakfast table, but Fanny had no appetite for food, and did not go down. After breakfast, Logan went to the shop, intending to go to work, but found his place supplied by another journeyman, and himself thrown out of employment, with but a single dollar in his pocket, a month's boarding due, and his family in need of almost every comfort. From the shop he went to a tavern, took a glass of liquor, and sat down to look over the newspapers and think what he should do. There he met an idle journeyman, who, like himself, had lost his situation. A fellow feeling made them communicative and confidential.

"If I was only a single man," said Logan, "I wouldn't care. I could easily shift for myself."

"Wife and children! Yes, there's the rub," returned the companion. "A journeyman mechanic is a fool to get married."

"Then you and I are both fools," said Logan.

"No doubt of it. I came to that conclusion, in regard to myself, long and long ago. Sick wife, hungry children, and four or five backs to cover; no wonder a poor man's nose is ever on the grindstone. For my part, I am sick of it. When I was a single man, I could go where I pleased, and do what I pleased; and I always had money in my pocket. Now I am tied down to one place, and grumbled at eternally; and if you were to shake me from here to the Navy Yard, you wouldn't get a sixpence out of me. The fact is, I'm sick of it."

"So am I; but what is to be done? I don't believe I can get work in town."

"I know you can't; but there is plenty of work

and good wages to be had in Charleston or New Orleans."

Logan did not reply, but looked intently into his companion's face.

"I'm sure my wife would be a great deal better off if I were to clear out and leave her. She has plenty of friends, and they'll not see her want."

Logan still looked at his fellow journeyman.

"And your wife would be taken back under her father's roof, where there is enough and to spare. Of course she would be happier than she is now."

"No doubt of that. The old rascal has treated her shabbily enough. But, I am well satisfied that, if I were out of the way he would gladly receive her back again."

"Of this there can be no question. So, it is clear that, with our insufficient incomes, our presence is a curse rather than a blessing to our families."

Logan really admitted this to be true. His companion then drew a newspaper towards him, and after running his eyes over it for a few moments, read :

"This day, at twelve o'clock, the copper-fastened brig Emily, for Charleston. For freight or passage, apply on board."

"There's a chance for us," he said, as he finished reading the advertisement. "Suppose we go down and see if they won't let us work our passage out."

Logan sat thoughtful a moment, and then said, as he arose to his feet—

"Agreed. It'll be the best thing for us, as well as for our families."

When the Emily sailed, at twelve o'clock, the two men were on board.

Days came and passed, until the heart of Mrs. Logan grew sick with anxiety, fear, and suspense. No word was received from her absent husband. She went to his old employer, and learned that he had been discharged; but she could find no one who had heard of him since that time. Left thus alone, with two little children, and no apparent means of support, Mrs. Logan, when she became at length clearly satisfied that he for whom she had given up every thing had heartlessly abandoned her, felt as if there was no hope for her in the world.

"Go to your father, by all means," urged the woman with whom she was still boarding. "Now that your husband has gone, he will receive you."

"I cannot," was Fanny's reply.

"But what will you do?" asked the woman.

"Work for my children," she replied, arousing herself, and speaking with some resolution. "I have hands to work, and I am willing to work."

"Much better go home to your father," said the woman.

"That is impossible. He has disowned me—has ceased to love me or care for me. I cannot go to him again; for I could not bear, as I am now, another harsh repulse. No—no—I will work with my own hands. God will help me to provide for my children."

In this spirit, the almost heart-broken young woman, for whom the boarding-house keeper felt more than a common interest—an interest that would not let her thrust her out from the only place she could call her home—sought for work, and was fortunate enough to obtain sewing from two or three families, and was thus enabled to pay a light board for herself and children. But incessant toil with her needle, continued late at night and resumed early in the morning, gradually undermined her health, which had become delicate, and weariness and pain were the constant companions of her labour.

Sometimes, in carrying her work home, the forsaken wife would have to pass the old home of her girlhood, and twice she saw her father at the window. But, either she was so changed that he did not know his child, or he would not bend from his stern resolution to disown her. On these two occasions she was unable, on returning, to resume her work. Her fingers could not hold nor guide the needle; nor could she, from the blinding tears that filled her eyes, have seen to sew, even if her hands had lost the tremour that ran through every nerve of her body.

A year had rolled wearily by since Logan went off, and still no word had come from the absent husband. Labour beyond her bodily strength, and trouble and grief that were too severe for her spirit to bear, had done sad work upon the forsaken wife and disowned child. She was but a shadow of her former self.

Mr. Crawford had been very shy of the old Quaker who had spoken so plainly to him; but his words made some impression, though no one would have supposed so, as there was no change in his conduct towards his daughter. He had forewarned her of the consequences if she acted in opposition to his wishes. He had told her that he would disown her for ever. She had taken her own way, and painful as it was to him, he had to keep his word—his word that had ever been inviolate. He might forgive her; he might pity her; but she must remain a stranger. Such a direct and flagrant act of disobedience to his wishes was not to be forgotten nor forgiven. Thus, in stubborn pride, did his hard heart confirm itself in its cold and cruel estrangement. Was he happy? No! Did he forget his child? No. He thought of her and dreamed of her, day after day, and night after night. But—he had said it, and he would stick to it! His pride was unbending as iron.

Of the fact that the husband of Fanny had gone off and left her with two children to provide for with the labour of her hands, he had been made fully aware, but it did not bend him from his stern purpose.

"She is nothing to me," was his impatient reply to the one who informed him of the fact. This was all that could be seen. But his heart trembled at the intelligence. Nevertheless, he stood coldly aloof, month after month, and even repulsed, angrily, the kind landlady with whom Fanny boarded, who had attempted, all unknown to the daughter, to awaken sympathy for her in her father's heart.

One day, the old Friend, whose plain words had not pleased Mr. Crawford, met that gentleman near his own door. The Quaker was leading a little boy by the hand. Mr. Crawford bowed, and evidently wished to pass on; but the Quaker paused, and said—

"I should like to have a few words with thee, friend Crawford."

"Well, say on."

"Thee is known as a benevolent man, friend Crawford. Thee never refuses, it is said, to do a deed of charity."

"I always give something when I am sure the object is deserving."

"So I am aware. Do you see this little boy?"

Mr. Crawford glanced down at the child the Quaker held by the hand. As he did so, the child lifted to him a gentle face, with mild, earnest, loving eyes.

"It is a sweet little fellow," said Mr. Crawford, reaching his hand to the child. He spoke with some feeling, for there was a look about the boy that went to his heart.

"He is, indeed, a sweet child—and the image of his poor, sick, almost heart-broken mother, for whom I am trying to awaken an interest. She has two children, and this one is the oldest. Her husband is dead, or what may be as bad, perhaps worse, as far as she is concerned, dead to her; and she does not seem to have a relative in the world; at least, none who thinks about or cares for her. In trying to provide for her children, she has overtasked her delicate frame, and made herself sick. Unless something is done for her, a worse thing must follow. She must go to the almshouse, and be separated from her children. Look into the sweet, innocent face of this dear child, and let your heart say whether he ought to be taken from his mother. If she have a woman's feelings, must she not love this child tenderly; and can any one supply to him his mother's place?"

"I will do something for her, certainly," said Mr. Crawford.

"I wish thee would go with me to see her."

"There is no use in that. My seeing her can do no good. Get all you can for her, and then come to me. I will help in the good work cheerfully," replied Mr. Crawford.

"That is thy dwelling, I believe," said the Quaker, looking round at a house adjoining the one before which they stood.

"Yes, that is my house," returned Mr. Crawford.

"Will thee take this little boy in with thee and keep him for a few minutes, while I go to see a friend some squares off?"

"Oh, certainly. Come with me, dear?" And Mr. Crawford held out his hand to the child, who took it without hesitation.

"I will see thee in a little while," said the Quaker, as he turned away.

The boy, who was plainly, but very neatly dressed, was about four years old. He had a more than usually attractive face; and an earnest look out of his mild eyes, that made every one who saw him his friend.

"What is your name, my dear?" asked Mr. Crawford, as he sat down in his parlour, and took the little fellow upon his knee.

"Henry," replied the child. He spoke with distinctness; and, as he spoke, there was a sweet expression of the lips and eyes, that was particularly winning.

"It is Henry, is it?"

"Yes, sir."

"What else besides Henry?"

The boy did not reply, for he had fixed his eyes upon a picture that hung over the mantle, and was looking at it intently. The eyes of Mr. Crawford followed those of the child, that rested, he found, on the portrait of his daughter.

"What else, besides Henry?" he repeated.

"Henry Logan," replied the child, looking for a moment into the face of Mr. Crawford, and then turning to gaze at the picture on the wall. Every nerve quivered in the frame of that man of iron will. The falling of a bolt from a sunny sky could not have startled and surprised him more. He saw in the face of the child, the moment he looked at him, something strangely familiar and attractive. What it was, he did not, until this instant, comprehend. But it was no longer a mystery.

"Do you know who I am?" he asked, in a subdued voice, after he had recovered, to some extent, his feelings.

The child looked again into his face, but longer and more earnestly. Then, without answering, he turned and looked at the portrait on the wall.

"Do you know who I am, dear?" repeated Mr. Crawford.

"No, sir," replied the child; and then again turned to gaze upon the picture.

"Who is that?" and Mr. Crawford pointed to the object that so fixed the little boy's attention.

"My mother." And as he said these words, he laid his head down upon the bosom of his unknown relative, and shrank close to him, as if half afraid because of the mystery that, in his infantile mind, hung around the picture on the wall.

Moved by an impulse that he could not restrain,

Mr. Crawford drew his arms around the child and hugged him to his bosom. Pride gave way; the iron will was bent; the sternly uttered vow was forgotten. There is power for good in the presence of a little child. Its sphere of innocence subdues and renders impotent the evil spirits that rule in the hearts of selfish men. It was so in this case. Mr. Crawford might have withstood the moving appeal of even his daughter's presence, changed by grief, labour, and suffering as she was. But his anger, upon which he had suffered the sun to go down, fled before her artless, confiding, innocent child. He thought not of Fanny as the wilful woman, acting from the dictate of her own passions or feelings; but as a little child, lying upon his bosom—as a little child, singing and dancing around him—as a little child, with, to him, the face of a cherub, and the sainted mother of that innocent one by her side.

When the Friend came for the little boy, Mr. Crawford said to him, in a low voice—made low to hide his emotion—

"I will keep the child."

"From it's mother?"

"No. Bring the mother, and the other child. I have room for them all."

A sunny smile passed over the benevolent countenance of the Friend, as he hastily left the room.

Mrs. Logan, worn down by exhausting labour, had at last been forced to give up. When she did give up, every long-strained nerve of mind and body instantly relaxed; and she became almost as weak and helpless as an infant. While in this state, she was accidentally discovered by the kind-hearted old Friend, who, without her being aware of what he was going to do, made his successful attack upon her father's feelings. He trusted to nature and a good cause, and did not trust in vain.

"Come, Mrs. Logan," said the kind woman, with whom Fanny was still boarding, an hour or so after little Harry had been dressed up to take a walk—where, the mother did not know or think—"the good Friend who was here this morning, says you must ride out. He has brought a carriage for you. It will do you good, I know. He is very kind. Come, get yourself ready."

Mrs. Logan was lying upon her bed.

"I do not feel able to get up," she replied. "I do not wish to ride out."

"Oh, yes, you must go. The pure, fresh air and the change will do you more good than medicine. Come, Mrs. Logan. I will dress little Julia for you. She needs the change as much you do."

"Where is Henry?" asked the mother.

"He has not returned yet. But come! The carriage is waiting at the door."

"Won't you go with me?"

"I would with pleasure—but I cannot leave home I have so much to do."

After a good deal of persuasion, Fanny at length made the effort to get herself ready to go out. She was so weak, that she tottered about the floor like one intoxicated. But the woman with whom she lived, assisted and encouraged her, until she was at length ready to go. Then the Quaker came up to her room, and, with the tenderness and care of a father, supported her down stairs, and when she had taken her place in the vehicle, entered with her youngest child in his arms, and sat by her side, speaking to her, as he did so, kind and encouraging words.

The carriage was driven slowly, for a few squares, and then stopped. Scarcely had the motion ceased, when the door was suddenly opened, and Mr. Crawford stood before his daughter.

"My poor child!" he said, in a tender, broken voice, as Fanny, overcome by his unexpected appearance, sank forward into his arms.

When the suffering young creature opened her eyes again, she was upon her own bed, in her own room, in her old home. Her father sat by her side, and held one of her hands tightly. There were tears in his eyes, and he tried to speak; but, though his lips moved, there came from them no articulate sound.

"Do you forgive me, father? Do you love me, father?" said Fanny, in a tremulous whisper, half rising from her pillow, and looking eagerly, almost agonizingly, into her father's face.

"I have nothing to forgive," murmured the father, as he drew his daughter towards him, so that her head could lie against his bosom.

"But do you love me, father? Do you love me as of old?" said the daughter.

He bent down and kissed her; and now the tears fell from his eyes and lay warm and glistening upon her face.

"As of old," he murmured, laying his cheek down upon that of his child, and clasping her more tightly in his arms. The long pent-up waters of affection were rushing over his soul and obliterating the marks of pride, anger, and the iron will that sustained them in their cruel dominion. He was no longer a strong man, stern and rigid in his purpose; but a child, with a loving and tender heart.

There was light again in his dwelling; not the bright light of other times; for now the rays were mellowed. But it was light. And there was music again; not so joyful; but it was music, and its spell over his heart was deeper, and its influence more elevating.

The man with the iron will and stern purpose was subdued, and the power that subdued him was the presence of a little child.

HAVEN'T TIME.

"THAT boy needs more attention," said Mr Green, referring to his oldest son, a lad whose way. ward temper and proclivity to vice demanded a steady, consistent, wise, and ever-present exercise of parental watchfulness and authority.

"You may well say that," returned the mother of the boy; for to her the remark had been made. "He is getting entirely beyond me."

"If I only had the time to look after him!" Mr. Green sighed as he uttered these words.

"I think you ought to take more time for a purpose like this," said Mrs. Green.

"More time!" Mr. Green spoke with marked impatience. "What time have I to attend to him, Margaret? Am I not entirely absorbed in business? Even now I should be at the store, and am only kept away by your late breakfast."

Just then the breakfast bell rang, and Mr. and Mrs. Green, accompanied by their children, repaired to the dining-room. John, the boy about whom the parents had been talking, was among the number

As they took their places at the table, he exhibited certain disorderly movements, and a disposition to annoy his younger brothers and sisters. But these were checked, instantly, by his father, of whom John stood in some fear.

Before the children were more than half done, Mr. Green laid his knife and fork side by side on his plate, pushed his chair back, and was in the act of rising, when his wife said—

"Don't go yet. Just wait until John is through with his breakfast. He acts dreadfully the moment your back is turned."

Mr. Green turned a quick, lowering glance upon the boy, (whose eyes shrank beneath his angry gaze,) saying, as he did so—

"I haven't time to stay a moment longer. I ought to have been at my business an hour ago. But see here, my lad,"—addressing himself to John —"there has been enough of this work. Not a day passes that I am not worried with complaints about you. Now, mark me! I shall inquire, particularly, as to your conduct when I come home at dinner-time: and, if you have given your mother any trouble, or acted in any way improperly, will take you severely to account. It's outrageous that the whole family should be kept in constant trouble by you. Now, be on your guard!"

A moment or two, Mr. Green stood frowning upon the boy, and then retired.

Scarcely had the sound of the closing street-door, which marked the fact of Mr. Green's departure, ceased to echo through the house, ere John began to act as was his custom when his father was out of the way. His mother's remonstrances were of no avail; and, when she finally compelled him to leave the table, he obeyed with a most provoking and insolent manner.

All this would have been prevented, if Mr. Green had taken from business just ten minutes, and conscientiously devoted that time to the government of his wayward boy and the protection of the family from his annoyances.

On arriving at his store, Mr. Green found two or three customers therein, and but a single clerk in attendance. He had felt some doubts as to the correctness of his conduct in leaving home so abruptly, under the circumstances; but the presence of these customers satisfied him that he had done right. Business, in his mind, was paramount to every thing else; and his highest duty to his family he felt to be discharged, when he was devoting himself most assiduously to the work of procuring for them the means of external comfort, ease, and luxury. Worldly well-doing was a cardinal virtue in his eyes.

Mr. Green was the gainer, perhaps, of half a dollar, in the way of profit on sales, by being at his store ten minutes earlier than would have been the case had he remained with his family until the completion of their morning meal. What was lost to his boy by the opportunity thus afforded for an indulgence in a perverse and disobedient temper, it is hard to say. Something was, undoubtedly, lost—something, the valuation of which, in dollars and cents, it would be difficult to make.

Mrs. Green did not complain of John's conduct, to his father, at dinner-time. She was so often forced to complain, that she avoided the task whenever she felt justified in doing so; and that was, perhaps, far too often. Mr. Green asked no questions; for he knew, by experience, to what results such questions would lead—and he was in no mood for unpleasant intelligence. So John escaped, as he had escaped hundreds of times before, and felt encouraged to indulge his bad propensities at will, to his own injury and the annoyance of all around him.

If Mr. Green had no time in the morning or through the day to attend to his children, the evening, one might think, would afford opportunity for conference with them, a supervision of their studies, and an earnest inquiry into their conduct and moral and intellectual progress. But such was not the case. Mr. Green was too much wearied with the occupation of the day to bear the annoyance of the children; or, his thoughts were too busy with business matters, or schemes of profit, to attend to the thousand-and-one questions they were ready to pour in upon him from all sides; or, he had a political club to attend, an engagement with some merchant for the discussion of a matter connected with trade, or felt obliged to be present at the meeting of some society of which he was a member. So, he either left home immediately after tea, or the children were sent to bed in order that he might have a quiet evening for rest, business reflection, or the enjoyment of a new book.

Mr. Green had so much to do and so much to think about, that he had no time to attend to his children; and this neglect was daily leaving upon them ineffaceable impressions, that would, inevitably, mar the beauty of their after-lives. Particularly was this the case with John. Better off in the world was Mr. Green becoming every day—better off as it regarded money; but, poorer in another sense; poorer in respect to home affections and home treasures. His children were not growing up to love him intensely, to confide in him implicitly, and to respect him as their father and friend. He had no time to attend to them, and rather pushed them from than drew them towards him, with the strong chords of affection. To his wife he left their government; and she was not equal to the task.

"I don't believe," said Mrs. Green, one day, "that John is learning much at the school where he goes. I think you ought to see after him a little. He never studies a lesson at home."

"Mr. Elden has the reputation of being one of

our best teachers. His school stands high," replied Mr. Green.

"That may all be," said Mrs. Green. "Still, I really think you ought to know, for yourself, how John is getting along. Of one thing I am certain, he does not improve in good manners nor good temper, in the least. And he is never in the house between school-hours, except to get his meals. I wish you would require him to be at the store during the afternoons. School is dismissed at three o'clock, and he ranges the streets with other boys, and goes where he pleases from that time until night."

"That's very bad,"—Mr. Green spoke in a concerned voice,—"very bad. And it must be broken up. But, as to having him at the store, that is out of the question. He would be into every thing, and keep me in hot water all the while. He'd like to come well enough, I do not doubt; but I can't have him there."

"Couldn't you set him to doing something?"

"I might. But I haven't time to attend to him, Margaret. Business is business, and cannot be interrupted."

Mrs. Green sighed, and then remarked—

"I wish you would call on Mr. Elden, and have a talk with him about John."

"I will, if you think it best."

"Do so, by all means. And besides, I would give more time to John in the evenings. If, for instance, you devoted an evening to him once a week, it would enable you to understand how he is progressing, and give you a control over him not now possessed."

"You are right in this, no doubt, Margaret."

But reform went not beyond this acknowledgment. Mr. Green could never find time to see John's teacher, nor feel himself sufficiently at leisure, or in the right mood of mind, to devote to the boy even a single evening.

And thus it went on from day to day, from month to month, and from year to year, until, finally, John was sent home from school by Mr. Elden with a note to his father, in which idleness, disorderly conduct, and vicious habits were charged upon him in the broadest terms.

The unhappy Mr. Green called immediately upon the teacher, who gave him a more particular account of his son's bad conduct, and concluded by saying that he was unwilling to receive him back into his classes.

Strange as it may seem, it was four months before Mr. Green "found time" to see about another school, and to get John entered therein; during which long period, the boy had full liberty to go pretty much where he pleased, and to associate with whom he pleased. It is hardly to be supposed that he grew any better for this license.

By the time John was seventeen years of age, Mr. Green's business had become greatly enlarged and his mind was still more absorbed therein. With him, gain was the primary thing; and, as a consequence, his family held a secondary place in his thoughts. If money were needed, he was ever ready to supply the demand; that done, he felt that his duty to them was, mainly, discharged. To the mother of his children, he left the work of their wise direction in the paths of life, their government and education—but she was inadequate to the task imposed.

From the second school at which John was entered, he was dismissed within three months, for bad conduct. He was then sent to school in a distant city, where, removed from all parental restraint and admonition, he made viler associates than any he had hitherto known, and took, thus, a lower step in vice. He was just seventeen, when a letter from the principal of this school conveyed to Mr. Green such unhappy intelligence of his son, that he immediately resolved, as a last resort, to send him to sea, before the mast—and this was done, spite of all the mother's tearful remonstrances, and the boy's threats that he would escape from the vessel on the very first opportunity.

And yet, for all this sad result of parental neglect, Mr. Green devoted no more time nor care to his children. Business absorbed the whole man. He was a merchant, body and soul. His responsibilities were not felt as extending beyond his store and his counting-room, further than to provide for the worldly well-being of his family. Is it any cause of wonder that, with his views and practice, it should not turn out well with his children; or, at least, with some of them?

At the end of a year, John came home from sea, a rough, tobacco-chewing, cigar-smoking, dram-drinking, overgrown boy of eighteen, with all his sensual desires and animal passions more active than when he went away, while his intellectual faculties and moral feelings were in a worse condition than at his separation from home. Grief at the change oppressed the hearts of his parents; but their grief was unavailing. Various efforts were made to get him into some business, but he remained only a short time in any of the places where his father had him introduced. Finally, he was sent to sea again. But he never returned to his friends. In a drunken street-brawl, that occurred while he was on shore at Valparaiso, he was stabbed by a Spaniard, and died shortly afterwards.

On the very day this tragic event took place, Mr. Green was rejoicing over a successful speculation from which he had come out the gainer by five thousand dollars. In the pleasure this circumstance occasioned, all thoughts of the absent one, ruined by his neglect, were swallowed up.

Several months elapsed. Mr. Green had returned home, well satisfied with his day's business. In his pocket was the afternoon paper, which, after the younger children were in bed, and the older ones out of his way, he sat down to read. To the telegraphic column his eyes turned. There had been an arrival in Boston from the Pacific, and almost the first sentence he read was the intelligence of his son's death. The paper dropped from his hands, while he uttered an expression of surprise and grief that caused the cheeks of his wife, who was in the room, to turn deadly pale. She had not power to ask the cause of her husband's sudden exclamation; but her heart, that ever yearned towards her absent boy, instinctively divined the truth.

"John is dead," said Mr. Green, at length speaking in a tremulous voice.

There was, from the mother, no wild burst of anguish. The boy had been dying, to her, daily, for years; and she had suffered, for him, worse than the pangs of death. Burying her face in her hands, she wept silently, yet hopelessly.

"If we were only blameless of the poor child's death," said Mrs. Green, lifting her tearful eyes, after the lapse of nearly ten minutes, and speaking in a sad, self-rebuking tone of voice.

When those with whom we are in close relationship die, how quickly is that page in memory's book turned on which lies the record of unkindness or neglect! Already had this page been turned for Mr. Green, and conscience was sweeping therefrom the dust, that wellnigh obscured the handwriting. He trembled, inwardly, as he read the condemning sentences that charged him with the guilt of his own son's ruin.

"If we were only blameless of the poor child's death!"

How these words of the grieving mother smote upon his heart! He did not respond to them. How could he do so at that moment?

"Where is Edward?" he inquired, at length.

"I don't know," sobbed the mother. "He is out somewhere almost every evening. Oh! I wish you would look to him a little more closely. He is past my control."

"I must do so," returned Mr. Green, speaking from a strong conviction of the necessity of doing as his wife suggested,—"If I only had a little more time"—

He checked himself. It was the old excuse—the rock upon which all his best hopes for his first-born had been fearfully wrecked. His lips closed, his head was bowed, and, in the bitterness of unavailing sorrow, he mused on the past, while every moment the conviction of wrong towards his child, now irreparable, grew stronger and stronger.

After that, Mr. Green made an effort to exercise more control over his children; but he had left the reins loose so long, that his tighter grasp produced restiveness and rebellion. He persevered, however, and, though Edward followed too closely the footsteps of John, yet the younger children were brought under salutary restraints. The old excuse—want of time—was frequently used by Mr. Green, to justify neglect of parental duties; but a recurrence of his thoughts to the sad ruin of his oldest boy had, in most cases, the right effect—and, in the end, he ceased to give utterance to the words—"I haven't time." However, frequently he fell into neglect from believing that business demanded his undivided attention.

POWER OF KINDNESS.

"Tom! here!" said a father to his boy, speaking in tones of authority.

The lad was at play. He looked towards his father, but did not leave his companions.

"Do you hear me, sir?" spoke the father, more sternly than at first.

With an unhappy face and reluctant step, the boy left his play and approached his parent.

"Why do you creep along at a snail's pace?" said the father, angrily. "Come quickly, I want you; when I speak, I like to be obeyed instantly.

Here, take this note to Mr. Smith, and see that you don't go to sleep by the way. Now run as fast as you can go."

The boy took the note; there was a cloud upon his brow. He moved onward, but at a slow pace.

"You, Tom! is that doing as I ordered? Is that going quickly?" called the father, when he saw the boy creeping away. "If you are not back in half an hour, I will punish you."

But the words had little effect. The boy's feelings were hurt by the unkindness of the parent; he experienced a sense of injustice, a consciousness that wrong had been done him. By nature, he was like his father, proud and stubborn; and these qualities of his mind were aroused, and he indulged in them, fearless of consequences.

"I never saw such a boy," said the father, speaking to a friend who had observed the occurrence. "My words scarcely made an impression on him."

"Kind words often prove most powerful," said the friend. The father looked surprised.

"Kind words," continued the friend, "are like the gentle rain and the refreshing dews; but harsh words bend and break like the angry tempest. The first develop and strengthen good affections, while the others sweep over the heart in devastation, and mar and deform all they touch. Try him with kind words; they will prove a hundred-fold more powerful."

The latter seemed hurt by the reproof, but it left him thoughtful. An hour passed away ere his boy returned. At times, during his absence, he was angry at the delay; but the words of remonstrance were in his ears, and he resolved to obey them.

At last, the lad came slowly in with a cloudy countenance, and reported the result of his errand. Having stayed far beyond his time, he looked for punishment, and was prepared to receive it with an angry defiance.

To his surprise, after delivering the message he had brought, his father, instead of angry reproof and punishment, said kindly—"Very well, my son, you can go out to play again."

The boy went out, but was not happy. He had disobeyed and disobliged his father, and the thought of this troubled him. Harsh words had not clouded his mind, nor aroused a spirit of reckless anger. Instead of joining his companions, he went and sat down by himself, grieving over his act of disobedience. While he thus sat, he heard his name called.

"Thomas, my son," said his father, kindly.

The boy sprang to his feet, and was soon beside his parent.

"Did you call, father?"

"I did, my son. Will you take this package to Mr. Long for me?"

There was no hesitation in the boy's manner; he looked pleased at the thought of doing his father a service, and reached out his hand for the package. On receiving it, he bounded away with a light step.

"There *is* power in kindness," said the father, as he sat musing, after the lad's departure. And even while he sat musing over the incident, the boy came back with a cheerful, happy face, and said—"Can I do any thing else for you, father?"

Yes, there is the power of kindness. The tempest of passion can only subdue, constrain, and break; but in love and gentleness ,there is the power of the summer rain, the dew, and the sunshine

PLAYING MOTHER.

"It's just as you raise them," said Mr. Warner, in his dogmatic way. "I don't believe in a boy's taking to a hammer and a girl to a doll from an instinct of nature. Girls are different, because they are educated differently; there is no other law in the matter."

"My experience," said a lady, who made one of a little company numbering about half a dozen, and she spoke in a quiet way, "leads me to a different conclusion. Each sex has a use in society peculiarly its own; and from the earliest childhood, impulses pointing thitherward may be seen. Gentle, tender, and loving are the uses of woman, and for these she is fitted by nature. Hardier, rougher, bolder is man, because he is designed for a different sphere of life. The boy takes the hammer, the whip, or any other plaything that is noisy, or calls for the exercise of strength and action; while the girl as naturally busies herself with her doll, or her cups and saucers."

"Simply," replied Mr. Warner, "because you

provide a hammer and whip for the one, and a doll for the other."

"No," returned the lady, "the cause lies deeper than this. It is radical. How is it with your own little Anna? She is here to-day."

"She never had a doll in her life; I will not permit such a thing to come into my house. I wish to develop the strength, not the weakness of her character." And, as Mr. Warner spoke, he threw a glance upon his wife, which said, plainly enough—"This wouldn't be so, if you had your way."

"Oh!" remarked the lady, "then you are trying to warp her character to suit your own theory. You are not willing to let it develop naturally, and, as I would say, healthfully."

"I wish to give it a strong and healthy development."

"Then it must grow from inward elements. If you warp it, as you are certainly doing, you will weaken and deform, instead of producing beauty, health, and strength."

"So you think," said Mr. Warner, a little rudely. Opinionated men are very often rude to ladies.

"Yes, I think so," replied the lady, not seeming to notice the ntleman's manner.

"Where is your dear little girl?" asked one of the company, a little while after, addressing Mrs Warner.

"She's playing about the garden. I saw her from the window a few minutes ago."

"It would be a pleasant experiment," said the lady with whom the child's father had held the controversy, "just to take a look after Anna, and see what she is doing. I'll warrant that the girl's instincts are predominant in her acts. You'll not find her dragging up the flowers, nor throwing stones at the birds, nor even digging in the dirt."

"You'll probably find her racing about with the boys," said the father.

"We'll see; come!" and the lady started for the door. The company followed her out. Anna was not in the garden among the flowers, nor romping with the boys.

"Anna!" called the mother. They listened, and her sweet, young voice was heard faintly answering. Guided by the sound, she was soon discovered by those in search of her.

"What is she doing?" asked Mr. Warner, whc did not at first see her distinctly.

"Playing mother," replied the lady with whom he had held the controversy; and she spoke in a tone of triumph.

"Nonsense," said Mr. Warner.

"See for yourself."

"The little witch!" exclaimed the father, affected with pleasure, in spite of himself, by what he saw.

Anna had found a cap belonging to the lady at

whose house they were visiting, and, with this drawn upon her head, was nursing a rabbit with the earnest fondness of a mother.

The ladies caught the happy child in their arms, and almost devoured her with kisses, while Mr. Warner escaped back into the house to re-arrange his forces for a new battle on his favourite hobby.

THE END.

www.ingramcontent.com/pod-product-compliance
Lightning Source LLC
LaVergne TN
LVHW020209110826
845151LV00003B/657